PRAISE FOR HA S

"These mesmerizing stories of disconn the surreal illogic of dreams—it's as im is to understand, in retrospect, how circumstance succeeded circumstance to finally deliver the reader into a moment as indelible as it is unexpected. Janet Hong's translation glitters like a blade."

—Susan Choi

"*Flowers of Mold* shows Ha Seong-nan to be a master of the strange story. Here, things almost happen, and the weight of their almost happening hangs over the narrative like a threat. Or they do happen, and then characters go on almost like they haven't, much to the reader's dismay. Or a story builds up and then, where most authors would pursue things to the last fraying thread of their narrative, Ha elegantly severs the rest of the story and delicately ties it off. And as you read more of these stories, they begin to chime within one another, creating a sense of deja-vu. In any case, one is left feeling unsettled, as if something is not right with the world—or, rather (and this latter option becomes increasingly convincing), as if something is not right with *you*."

—Brian Evenson

"Brilliantly crafted with precision and compassion, Ha Seong-nan's heartbreaking collection dives into the depths of human vulnerability, where hopes and dreams are created and lost, where ordinary life gains mythological status. A truly gifted writer."

—Nazanine Hozar, author of *Aria*

"I'm raving about this book. . . . It is brilliant, modern, and surprising."

—Charles Montgomery

"Ha Seong-nan's stories are familiar, domestic, and utterly terrifying. Like the best of A. M. Homes, Samantha Schweblin, or Brian Evenson, her elegantly terse style lures you in and never fails to shock. She writes the kind of stories I admire most. Ones you carry around with you long after reading."

—Brian Wood, author of *Joytime Killbox*

"Wrapped up in fantasy or dreams, these men, women, and children are often confused over what is and isn't real, the reader seeing before they do how their anxious yearning will go unfulfilled."

—Laura Adamczyk, *The A.V. Club*

"Be forewarned: it might make you reconsider your interest in your neighbors, because it could lead to obsession and madness—or something odder and less reassuring than a tidy end, of which there are few in this wonderfully unsettling book of 10 masterful short stories."

—John Yau, *Hyperallergic*

"Joining a growing cohort of notable Korean imports, Ha's dazzling, vaguely intertwined collection of 10 stories is poised for Western acclaim."

—*Booklist*, starred review

"This impressive collection reveals Ha's close attention to the eccentricities of life, and is sure to earn her a legion of new admirers."

—*Publishers Weekly*, starred review

"If you're looking for a book that will make you gasp out loud, you've found it."

—*Kirkus Reviews*

"Ha's ability to find startling traits in seemingly unremarkable characters makes each story a small treasure."

—Cindy Pauldine, *Shelf Awareness*

"Her characters are trying their best to get by, and I found them deeply sympathetic, but they often face obstacles they just do not know how to confront. The stories are beautiful, inventive, gorgeously-written, and often heart-wrenching."

—Rebecca Hussey, *Book Riot*

"Like *The Vegetarian*—another surreal and haunting text by a Korean woman—*Flowers of Mold* unsettles and unnerves, effortlessly. . . .

Flowers of Mold offers readers an alternative perspective on city life, relationships, and ambition; and while it may be dark and unrelenting, it is also hauntingly lyrical."

—Rachel Cordasco, *World Literature Today*

"As horror and art continue to steal and mix with each other, I'm sure we'll find more—on both sides of the aisle—that continue to push the envelope. *Flowers of Mold* pushes that envelope with its impressive style and stifling isolation, creating something that's as strange as it is incisive."

—Carson Winter, *Signal Horizon*

"In these stories, readers will find tales of alienation and unruly behavior that will likely jar them as much as any narrative of sinister creatures and haunted spaces."

—Tobias Carroll, Words Without Borders

"These aren't bedtime stories. Indeed, reading them before bed might not be a good idea at all."

—Peter Gordon, *Asian Review of Books*

"Here is, undoubtedly, one of the best translated short story collections of 2019."

—Will Harris, *Books and Bao*

"In Ha Seong-nan's gripping and courageous *Flowers of Mold*, the author triple-underlines those distasteful aspects of our lives that we'd rather ignore: the putridity of leaky trash; the greasy, lingering smell of fried chicken; children's crackers crushed underfoot; the solid clunk of an alarm clock to the jaw. . . . Ha is a master of the short story and hooks the reader without revealing or resolving too much too cleanly."

—Samantha Kirby, *Arkansas International*

STORIES

FLOWERS OF MOLD

HA SEONG-NAN

TRANSLATED FROM THE KOREAN
BY JANET HONG

OPEN LETTER
LITERARY TRANSLATIONS FROM THE UNIVERSITY OF ROCHESTER

Copyright © 1999 Ha Seong-nan
Originally published in Korea by Changbi Publishers, Inc.
All rights reserved
English translation copyright © 2019 by Janet Hong
English edition is published by arrangement with Changi Publishers, Inc.

First edition, 2019
All rights reserved

Library of Congress Cataloging-in-Publication Data: Available.
ISBN-13: 978-1-940953-96-0 / ISBN-10: 1-940953-96-0

Flowers of Mold is published under the support of the
Literature Translation Institute of Korea (LTI Korea).

This project is supported in part by an award from the National Endowment for the Arts
and the New York State Council on the Arts with the support of Governor
Andrew M. Cuomo and the New York State Legislature.

Printed on acid-free paper in the United States of America.

Text set in Caslon, a family of serif typefaces based on the designs
of William Caslon (1692–1766).

Design by N. J. Furl

Open Letter is the University of Rochester's nonprofit, literary translation press:
Dewey Hall 1-219, Box 278968, Rochester, NY 14627

www.openletterbooks.org

Contents

FLOWERS OF MOLD

Waxen
Wings

Your watch stopped at 3:14. The second hand fell off when the glass cover shattered. Within minutes you were unconscious. During what seemed like a nap that went on a little longer than usual, the seasons changed in the front lawn, right below your hospital room window.

When you could walk on your own you pushed the IV stand out onto the lawn and sat in the sun. Sometimes you glanced at your watch as if waiting for someone. It was always 3:14. From the lawn you had a clear view down to the main entrance. The gate was always crowded with ambulances and visitors bearing gifts. But the girl who looked about nervously while picking her way through the bustle caught your eye. She walked not on the sidewalk but up the middle of the road, with a large backpack and a shoe bag. Ambulances with their patients and taxis with their passengers passed through her and sped away. Each time, the girl went fuzzy like an image on a television set with poor reception. From where you sat, you waited for that little girl. Leaping through a hole in time, a ten-year-old you came mirage-like to visit the you who was now twenty-seven.

•

You, ten years old, are cutting across the school field. You're alone again, unable to tag along with the others. They had burst outside, crashing into you in their rush while you were still in your indoor shoes. They're probably hanging around the snack stand, the comic-book shop, or the stationery store in front of the school right now. You're shorter than the other girls your age by almost a foot. When you're standing next to them your small size becomes even more obvious. You look maybe six or seven at the most. The kids in your class call you Birdie. Your backpack straps dig into your shoulders and the shoe bag drags on the dirt, leaving a lazy, winding trail.

The abandoned field looks all the more vast today. You've never cut across it before. You prefer walking along its fringes, in the shadow of the school building. Already you feel it's too much; never again will you cut across another field, hotel lobby, or lounge. You had taken the shortcut in your haste to catch up with the others, but your steps lag. You finally make it to the school gate, but lack the courage to step out and talk to them. You walk toward the playground where rainbow-colored tires protrude from the ground. The swing is swaying gently, as if someone has just been on it. You sit on the wooden seat without taking off your backpack. As you trail your toes in the dirt, the swing starts to move. You cast off your bags, and kick your feet in the air. Back and forth you go, like seaweed rolling on the waves. Soon your seat goes up as high as the metal crossbeam from where the chains hang, and your body becomes parallel to the ground. You're covered with sweat and your mouth is pasty.

One day, after pumping yourself up as high as the beam, you let go of the chains. Freed from the swing, your body soars—only for the briefest moment—but you feel as though you're flying. If not for the law of gravity you would have risen into the air, past the leaves of the sycamores flanking the field, and disappeared beyond the five-story school building. But like Newton's apple, your small, light body is pulled to earth, and you land deftly on the sand. Soon enough you learn your hang time—the time you're able to remain airborne—is a little longer than the other children's. The other kids on the swings try to copy you and jump in midair. But no sooner have they jumped than they tumble onto the sand. By now, you can even pick a spot to alight on while you're pumping your legs. Where you've landed there are prints, as neat and clearly etched as a bird's.

While others move on to the adventure playground and seesaw, you stay on the swings, thinking of different ways to make a bigger jump, to hover longer in the air. But in the end, you curl up in midair and do a somersault. In a flash, all the kids abandon their games and gather around you.

"Hey, that's easy! I can do that, too."

A jealous classmate tries to copy you and jumps from the swings. But she lands headfirst and begins to howl through her sand-filled mouth. Her nose is bleeding and her face is scratched up. Your homeroom teacher comes running.

"This is very dangerous! Who started this?"

All at once, every gaze is directed at you, but now the eyes are cold. After this incident, you never see anyone jump from the swings, at least not on the school playground. You don't go near the swings again.

"Teacher, I want to fly, but the ground keeps pulling me down."

You sit facing your teacher in the empty classroom after everyone has gone home. For the first time she looks at you very closely.

What a small child, she thinks. She recalls the woolen dress she recently bought; it had accidentally shrunk in the wash. Every feature is smaller on this child, just like the shrunken dress. Suddenly, an uneasy thought flashes across her mind. This child who wants to fly, what if she decides to take flight from a rooftop? The teacher shakes her head as if to dislodge this disturbing thought, but in her mind you keep falling from the school roof. The teacher looks into your small eyes and speaks, emphasizing each word.

"I want you to listen very carefully. Only birds can fly. It's impossible for people to fly. You're just able to stay in the air a little longer, that's all. Can you tell your mother to come see me?"

Your mother comes home from work at seven o'clock every night, and if she misses even a single day, she'll lose three days' pay. For lack of anything better, your teacher makes you write "People cannot fly" over and over again on the chalkboard. Because you're so small, your writing reaches only halfway up the board. The teacher stands behind you and thinks, *So that's why they call you Birdie.*

•

When you enter middle school you push aside thoughts of flying; you're too old to play on the swings, and you're no longer naïve enough to confess your desire to fly. You learn more about this gravity that keeps pulling you down.

Back then it was the trend among students to write famous quotes on the covers of their notebooks. But instead of writing something like "Even if I knew that tomorrow the world would go to pieces, I would still plant my apple tree," you write, "The force of gravity between two objects is directly proportional to the product of their masses and inversely proportional to the square of the distance between them."

You believe if people could escape the confines of gravity, they could fly like birds. However, you find even the task of simplifying the law of gravity difficult. You're still smaller than the other girls. The average height of a middle school girl then was five foot two, but you're a mere four foot nine.

One day, the P.E. teacher tells you to go to the gym just as you're about to walk into your classroom.

The small indoor gym feels like the inside of a fridge. You shiver from the cold. A voice rings out from the dark.

"So you're the girl the P.E. teacher mentioned? Come over here."

You hesitate because of the thick exercise mats on the floor.

"It's okay, just walk across with your shoes on, but it'll be the last time."

You keep stumbling on the padded mats. A young woman with short hair is sitting on a vault. In her hand is a long stick that touches the ground. Although it's March and still cold outside, her legs exposed below her short skirt are bare. On her small dangling feet are kid-size indoor shoes.

"Shall we have a look?"

She hops down. Up close she's much smaller than you had guessed.

From now on as soon as you're dismissed from school, you run straight to the gym. There, no one calls you Birdie. Everyone is small like you. You finally feel at peace. You put the vault into position for the older students and clean the gym after practice. On sunny days you drag all the mats outside to air them out. Since your school sits on top of a hill, you can see them spread out in front of the gym, even from the bus stop at the bottom of the hill. The glare from the light hitting the mats turns the gym into a snow-capped peak. Practice starts with front and back rolls, then the splits. When you sit with your legs spread apart, straining to do the splits, the coach instructs the older students to sit on your shoulders. If you cry out, the coach jabs you in the stomach with her stick. The tender flesh around your groin turns black and blue. You wear the same leotard as the other gymnasts, but you're so scrawny the leotard keeps riding up to reveal the cheeks of your small bottom. You get home later and later. Now, it's your mother who waits up for you. She buys you a wristwatch, but your wrist is so small you have to punch a new hole in the strap. Summer comes and you practice your vaults. You don't take off the watch, even though the sweat that collects under the leather band makes your skin swell, leaving a pale strip around your wrist. While you perform your endless tumbles, autumn changes to winter, and winter changes to spring.

Your first period still hasn't come. You've noticed every month that the girl sitting next to you in class sneaks a hand into her bag, whisks out a mysterious object, hides it in the folds of her clothes, and then slips away to the bathroom. Neither do you show the usual signs of sexual maturity. You have no habits common to middle school girls, like pulling down a bra that keeps riding up, and there are no photos of golden-haired boys, singers, and movie stars in your bag. On your way to the gym after school, you see the other girls flock to the TV station to watch a broadcast on the large screen outside. They've never even heard of the people you follow, like Nadia Comăneci and Nellie Kim. Because of practices and meets, there are many days when your desk is empty. For this reason, you gain the envy of others.

In eighth grade, you start watching a girl named Yunhui—a tenth grader and already the Seoul representative at the national games, where she won gold in the balance beam. When Yunhui does a demonstration on the beam, you study her every move. You can tell she's special, just from the way she mounts the beam. Instead of placing the springboard at the end like the other gymnasts, she positions it alongside the beam. She does her approach run, jumps, and then lands doing the splits, on a surface only four inches wide. Even though you're still learning the basics, you sometimes go up on the beam when no one is around. Every time you take a step, you have to flap your arms like a bird to keep your balance. Like Yunhui, you grow out your hair and pull it back into a knot at the crown of your head. You need a dozen bobby pins to anchor the willful strands. With your hair pulled back so severely, your eyebrows and the corners of your eyes yank up, making you look always angry.

Your event is the uneven bars. When you soar between the 8- and 5-foot bars, your small size and long hang time become very clear. But when you try to keep yourself straight during the handstand, your arms keep shaking. Full turn after cast handstand, swing to low bar, then transfer to high bar. But your hands slip and you fall to the mat. Every time this happens, the coach's long stick jabs your stomach. As further punishment, you have to do an hour-long handstand in the middle of the gym. If you fall over or break your form, you have to start all over again. Blood pumps down into your face, and your arms start to wobble uncontrollably. Bare legs—some pale, others reddish or sallow—pass by, and an occasional sarcastic remark is tossed your way. A pair of pale slender legs stops before you. The calves and thighs visible above the legwarmers are covered with dark purple bruises. You raise your blood-gorged face. It's Yunhui. Because it's Yunhui, your face turns even redder.

"With handstands, try to forget you're holding up your body and pretend it's the ground instead you're holding up. It works for me. Your landing earlier was really impressive by the way."

You don't see Yunhui at the gym anymore. She was selected for the Asian Games and so she's moved to the athletes' village. Every night, you write her a letter. You lose interest in going to the gym. For being late, you have to do leapfrogs and handstands or hang from the bar. You see a photo of Yunhui in the sports section, in a feature on athletes to watch in the Asian Games. You're confident, of course, but so is your coach, that Yunhui will receive a medal. But when the news arrives, it's not about medals. Yunhui has had an accident. She took a bad fall in practice, damaged her spinal cord, and became paralyzed from the neck down.

Yunhui doesn't come back to school. Now, you no longer struggle to keep your body straight when doing a handstand on the bar. After a full turn on the high bar, you can pull off two and a half flips before you land. You recall how you used to go on the swing as a ten-year-old. Once again, the desire to fly takes hold and the familiar battle against gravity begins. In ninth grade, you become the star athlete of your school. By now, you have your own peculiar way of walking—body straight, chin and heels raised high.

Once you skip practice and visit Yunhui, who had remained in the hospital after the accident. It's lunchtime when you arrive. A middle-aged woman, who appears to be her mother, tries to feed her, but she clamps her mouth shut. After attempting to pry Yunhui's mouth open with the spoon, the woman smacks her daughter on the head. Yunhui falls across the bed and her face is buried in the pillow, but she cannot get up. The mother starts to weep; she pulls her daughter up and places a pillow behind her back. The girl who is leaning pathetically against the bedframe is not the Yunhui you knew. She is plump and white. Even her wrists peeping out from the cuffs of her hospital gown are covered with fat folds, like silkworms. Her hair, which used to be pulled back in a neat knot, is cut so short it leaves her ears exposed.

You go home without entering the ward. That day, you cut your hair short. Because you skipped practice and cut your hair, your coach yells at you while jabbing your stomach with her stick. You have to clean the gym, a lowly job reserved for seventh graders, and you stay behind, practicing well into the night to make up for missing practice. You keep falling off the uneven bars and run toward the springboard, only to stop and repeat the approach run. Once on the vault, before you can take a step, you tumble to the mat. All of a sudden, there are sharp pains in your stomach as if your coach is jabbing you with her stick. It's your first period.

In high school the routine is the same. You still go to the gym, you still train under the coach with the bare legs. When there's a tournament coming up, you don't go to class. Swing, support, release. While you repeat these steps, the bruises on your body multiply. Countless times a day you squeeze the rosin bag with your callused hands. Even though you chalk just your hands, there are white handprints on your leotard, legs, and arms as if someone slapped you. Menthol sports rubs are now your perfume. Your face is angular and your torso has taken on the shape of an inverted triangle.

You unfasten your watch. When you put the pin through the next hole in the strap, an ominous feeling comes over you. You're at the Seoul tryouts for the National Games to perform your uneven bars routine. There, your premonition becomes a reality. You could have done the routine with your eyes closed. Swing from low bar to high bar, grip, then cast to handstand, hold, release and catch bar three times in a row, somersault and catch bar again—the routine was as familiar to you as breathing. But instead of catching the bar again, you clutch at air and fall helplessly to the mat. To finish your performance, you take hold of the bar again. In the hope of making up for your deductions, you become too ambitious, and attempt a triple somersault instead of a two-and-a-half for your dismount. You've been practicing the triple salto on your own, but making it barely two times out of ten. You release the bar and flip three times in the air. Instead of landing on both feet, you plant your rear end on the mat. You receive a 7.8 out of a perfect 10. A student from another school becomes the Seoul representative.

At school, you sit at the very front of the classroom. You copy down the math problems from the chalkboard, but because of your frequent absences you can't understand any of the questions. Just then, the student behind you pokes you in the back with a pencil.

"Hey, you mind lowering your head a little? I can't see the board."

In half a year you've grown nearly five inches.

You're now the tallest on your team. Before you can manage two flips for your dismount, you land on your bottom. Your rear end, somehow having filled out, hits the mat with a dull thud, like a ripe persimmon bursting as it plops to the ground. The other gymnasts laugh. Once again people start to call you Birdie, but this time, it's for a different reason. Every day you stay late to practice on your own, but even hanging from a bar becomes difficult because of the weight you've put on. The girl from your childhood, the one who fell face first from the swings, comes to mind. You keep falling off and each time, you chalk up, spit into your hands, then leap up to the bars again. You even run out of saliva to spit into your hands. The gymnastics equipment is spread out around you. You find yourself thinking more and more about falling off than climbing on.

●

The coach calls out to you as you're about to remove your shoes.

"Don't bother, I just need to see you for a minute."

You realize at some point you've started to tower over her. You recall the first day you met her. Since then, she has gotten married and become the mother of two, but she hasn't changed a bit. She's barelegged as always and dressed in a short skirt. She taps the springboard with her stick.

"What in the world are you eating? Did somebody come up with a magic growth pill? Who would have guessed you'd shoot up like a bean sprout overnight?"

Her voice echoes in the gym. She's the one who's angry. You stand in front of her with your head hanging down, as if you've actually eaten something you shouldn't have.

"I've seen cases where people had to quit because of an injury to their Achilles tendon or spinal cord, but never something like this. Maybe it's better this way. After all, a gymnast's career is so short."

As you shove open the gym door, the coach calls out to you one last time. "Study hard, all right?"

Walking down the hill, you consider your options. Your palms smelled of rosin and spit no matter how often you scrubbed them with soap, and you felt more comfortable with the uneven bars, vault, and balance beam than with math, English, and Korean. You and your coach had believed you were done growing. Never, in your wildest dreams, had you imagined you would be tall one day.

You return to your eleventh-grade classroom. It's almost midnight when you get home after the review sessions. You take out your old textbook from tenth grade, but it's scarcely any easier. You occasionally go to the gym to practice. When you make a mistake, the coach no longer comes running. You don't even get in trouble. Sometimes you walk up to the gym door, but end up circling the building, unable to go inside. The orange glow coming through the window seems inviting. You stand outside, listening to the sounds of practice: the thump of bodies hitting the mats, the gymnasts' spirited cries, and the coach's fierce voice. Then you head home.

Dressed in a tracksuit with your gym bag in hand, you stand in front of Changgyeong Palace. To this day, you still don't understand why you went there. You probably remembered the zoo from childhood, but it's been moved to a new location. While you wait for the palace doors to open, you eat a corndog and some fish cake soup.

At the break of dawn you're the lone visitor. A few times, you walk slowly past Changgyeong, then across the bridge toward Changdeok Palace and back. You're joined by a crowd of Japanese tourists, who chat nearby in their language like the whine of mosquitoes. You sit on a bench in front of an old hut, an area most people don't seek. A flock of pigeons swoops down and pecks at the ground. You buy a bag of popcorn at the concession. A swarm chases after every handful of popcorn you throw. One is missing a left toe and another has a sty in its eye. There's also one standing motionless in the same spot, blinking very slowly, while the other pigeons surge greedily. You watch this pigeon. The PA system announces it's closing time. You grab your bag and are about to get up when the pigeon you've been watching collapses. For the first time in your life, you witness the moment life escapes from a living thing. All the visitors leave, but you continue to stand there, even after the concession clerks have gone home. The sun starts to set, and everything quickly grows dark. All the pigeons have flown off except for the one by your feet. Rigor mortis has set in. You open your bag to find something to dig with, but find only your leotard, a roll-on muscle relaxant, a notebook, and some pens. You start to dig with your pen, but it breaks. You use your fingers instead and dig a small hole. Blood forms under your dirt-filled fingernails. You shroud the pigeon in your leotard, lay it to rest in the hole, cover it up with dirt, and pat it down with your foot. Two security guards walk toward you. Before they see you, you scramble up onto the old hut behind the bench. The guards' flashlights move away. Sitting on the tiled roof, you gaze out into the woods, toward the lake and the bridge, but all you see are different shades of darkness. You peer at shadows to guess where the zoo used to be. From the top of the roof, you watch the sun come up. You climb down and walk toward the main entrance, but it's closed. For you, climbing over the Changgyeong Palace wall is a piece of cake.

You miss a day of school, but nobody notices, since it's more common for you to be absent. You no longer go to the gym. Around this time you hear Yunhui has entered a seminary. By the time you're off the gymnastics team for good, you've grown even more. You're now five foot five.

•

Your old watch stops often now.

"Excuse me, Miss, do you have the time?"

You're on your way back from the bank, where you'd gone to make a deposit before closing time. You help with the accounts at an apartment manager's office. Six years older and a graduate of a trade high school, the bookkeeper you work for always dawdles and finishes her work only when the bank is about to close, making you run every day. The way back takes twice as long.

"Miss, what's the time, please?"

The scooter blocking your path—you realize you've seen it before. You peer at your watch. "It's two thirty."

Confused, the man looks up at your face.

"That's strange. It was around two thirty when I was having lunch. Are you sure it's two thirty?"

There's a belligerent quality to his eyes. The second hand on your watch isn't moving. You hold your wrist up to your ear, but don't hear anything. When did it stop? You realize you haven't looked at your watch for a long time.

"It's okay, thanks anyway. Hey, do you take the number 62 bus?"

You're confused by his question.

"I see you waiting at the bus stop, same time every day. You know a water strider? The insect with long skinny legs that stands on water? You remind me of one, the way you stand at the bus stop. There's a watch repair shop on the main street, and a store next door with a big sign that says Movie Town. I work there. It's right across the street from the bus stop. I guess I'll see you around."

With that, he starts to putter off on the scooter. But then he yells, "It's actually five to five right now. And my name is Kang Hyeokjun!"

While the watch repairman puts a new battery in your watch, you look out the window. Across the four-lane street is your bus stop.

"Wow, it's been a while since I've seen one of these. I used to wear the same brand myself when I was a kid. They don't make them anymore. They've come up with these ones instead."

The man slides open the glass display and takes out a couple of watches from a bed of cotton. He sets them down on the glass.

"Take a look. The same manufacturer makes them. I'd say the design and quality are just as good as imports. I'm not asking you to buy one, all I'm saying is take a look. And what's wrong with owning more than one watch? This here with the leather strap is a great casual option, and this gold one is an excellent choice if you want a fancier look."

You hold one up to your ear in order to hear the second hand, but the shop is full of ticking noises. On the back wall are clocks of every kind, from wall clocks to alarm clocks with cartoon character designs. The hour and minute hands all point to the same time. You pick one out and use it to set your watch.

You stop by a bookstore and buy a full-color insect picture book. Within its pages is a photo of a water strider, darting over the water with long slender legs as taut as guitar strings. If a raindrop should hit it or the current turn rough all of a sudden, it looks as if it would get swallowed up. But as vulnerable as it appears, it also has a kind of charm. Why must it walk on water? There's more than enough land in the world for its legs to stand safely on. A water strider uses surface tension and the long hairs on its legs to walk on water. You picture it gliding across a pond.

The front window of Movie Town is plastered with posters advertising video release dates for the latest movies. While you wait for your bus you keep glancing at the store. The man's job is to deliver and then pick up the videos people order on the phone. Sometimes his scooter would be parked out front on the tree-lined sidewalk. At age twenty-three, you watch him as you once watched Yunhui. The #62 comes and goes without you on it.

"You just missed your bus! What are you doing?"

You didn't notice the scooter drawing up behind you.

"Did you hear me? Your bus just left. It's already the second one you've missed."

Instead of getting on the third #62, you sit across from him at a café called Jardin. You didn't realize it when he was sitting on the scooter, but the man is much shorter than you. A girl in a green apron sets down two cups of coffee.

"Wow, you're taller than I thought. Five foot six?" he says.

You grew a little more after you graduated from high school. You've never actually measured yourself, but when you talk to the men at work, you're at eye level with all of them. You're no longer a small high-school girl who picks out clothes from the juniors section.

He smiles awkwardly while adding sugar to his coffee.

"You like short guys?"

You saw many male gymnasts at various tournaments. They, too, were short compared to the other male students. You were used to short men. He tells you he was once a child star who played the lead in a children's show.

"Believe it or not, some people still recognize me. It's really embarrassing when they ask for an autograph."

He goes on to list a few actors he worked with who have risen to stardom. The names are familiar. He didn't grow after the age of fifteen. He's still waiting for the chance to make his big screen debut, and in the meantime, working at the video store wasn't a bad idea—he might as well hone his acting skills and watch movies for free. He has memorized every famous movie line and could even talk with a cigarette dangling from his mouth like Humphrey Bogart.

"The person who's supposed to grow stops growing and the person who isn't supposed to grow ends up this tall? 'Life isn't always what one likes, is it?' Have you seen *Roman Holiday*? It's from that movie."

So like all couples, the two of you sometimes go for a beer or catch a midnight flick. He tries to recite the right movie line at the right time and place, but he makes you laugh instead by toasting you with the famous line from *Casablanca*—"Here's looking at you, kid"—when you clink beer glasses together. He also makes you laugh when he says, "Nor art, nor nature ever created a lovelier thing than you" as he is leaving after walking you home. When he kisses you for the first time, it's "Don't kiss me. If you kiss me, I won't be able to leave."

He isn't where the two of you agreed to meet. You wait for his scooter in front of the video store. But when it arrives, it's a stranger who's riding it.

"Didn't Hyeokjun come in today?"

The man says he doesn't recognize the name and tells you to go ask inside. The owner, who's checking in some videos, recognizes you.

"He doesn't work here as of today. What do you expect with guys who work at a place like this? They migrate like birds, flying around from place to place. He asked me to give you this."

He hands you an envelope. There's a single sentence written in the center of a blank page: "I'd rather lose you than destroy you," and below in tiny print, "Maria in *Maria's Lovers*."

"What's it say? He didn't tell you some nonsense about how he used to be an actor, did he? Told you his name was Hyeokjun? I bet you that's fake, too. Probably has over ten names he goes by. Hyeokjun—yeah, right!"

You decide not to believe the owner. You cross the street and stand at the bus stop. The #62 goes by. You don't even know his name. Everything he did and said to you for the last six months—he could have taken it from some movie. Although he borrowed a line to say goodbye, you think the words "I'd rather lose you than destroy you" are true. A movie you once saw crosses your mind. In it, Audrey Hepburn says to Cary Grant, "Oh, I love you, Adam, Alex, Peter, Brian . . . whatever your name is." As you walk down the street you mumble to yourself, "Oh, I love you, Hyeokjun, Kyeongshik, Eunho, Changmin, Minsu . . . whatever your name is."

Your trowel doesn't work very well—the ground is too hard. And you can't quite remember the exact location either. Since the hole you dug wasn't deep, you should be able to feel it if you poke the ground with the trowel. The pigeon should have rotted away without a trace, but your leotard, made of a cheap nylon weave, won't decompose even after you die. Perhaps a heavy downpour swept away the top layer of earth, leaving the leotard in plain view, and the custodian tossed it out. All day until sunset, you poke and prod at spots that look right, but nothing turns up. You end up digging dozens of holes in front of the old hut you climbed that night. In the end, you start to think perhaps you had it all wrong and buried it somewhere entirely different, maybe Changdeok Palace and not Changgyeong Palace. That day, you'd walked back and forth between the two palaces at least five times. You're not even sure which wall you jumped—the one near the Donhwa Gate or the one near the Honghwa Gate. To your inexperienced eye, all the traditional buildings look the same.

•

Twenty-six years old, you soar through the sky. You, who stayed airborne for only a moment when you jumped from the swings, can now stay in the air for as long as you want. You belong to the hang gliding club called Icarus Wings. From high up, the houses and trees below look like they're stuck together. Once you've completed your test flights on ground and the bunny hills, you're able to hang glide from higher places. Once a month you attend the club meetings. The president of the club warned beginners not to be too ambitious. In hang gliding, there is something called the *glide ratio to target*, the ratio of the distance glided to the distance fallen. Although you haven't quite mastered it, you're able to stay aloft longer than the other beginners. In order to turn, you twist yourself to the left and to the right. You navigate the glider by moving the bar, which changes the direction of the sail. When you land, your gymnastics training is obvious. While others waddle unsteadily with their rear ends sticking out like ducks and then are dragged by the glider, you pull off a flawless landing.

You go up a mountain with expert pilots. Your hang glider, transported to the end of the road by car, must be carried to the summit. Under your waterproof parka, your clothes are soaked with sweat. At the top, you assemble the glider, attach the sail, and put on your helmet. You're fully aware of what to do in case of an emergency. Those who are more experienced go first. They sail slowly down the mountain in wide, gentle arcs. Since the current can change at any time, depending on the temperature and topography, you pay close attention to the person who goes before you. Below the cliff is a dense growth of pines with an occasional crag jutting out. You must sail over this area and land in a flat field. You take a running start and jump. You find yourself buoyed upward. It's as exhilarating as sticking your head out the window of a racing car. The sweat you worked up from the climb dries. Far below you can see the path you took, snaking its way to the peak. As you begin to pass the pine grove you see the landing area. Your companions who have already landed are waving at you. But the moment you try to square yourself to land, your sail begins to rattle violently. Suddenly the wind hitting your face changes direction. You push the control bar to the left, but a gust of wind from below sends your glider shooting up. In the blink of an eye, you're far from the field. You move the bar this way and that, but the sail doesn't obey. Another gust of wind hits you, this time from your right. Your glider starts to nosedive. You struggle to stay in the air a little longer, but it's no use. You're sucked into the

pines. A wide crag looms up, you let go of the bar, and cover your
face with your hands.

·

There is a flower basket on top of the bedside locker. "We wish you
a full and speedy recovery." It looks like you've had a visit from the
club; the words *Icarus Wings Hang Gliding Club* are written on the
pink ribbon trailing from the basket. The roses are withering into a
blackish red. Your mother tells you what one of the members said:
if not for the sail, your injury could have been much worse. But you
know it's your long hang time that spared you.

"People are meant to have both feet planted on solid ground."

Every time you wake, your mother says these words over and over
again. You get moved from the ICU to a general ward. Because of the
chitchat of visitors and the coin-operated TV, the room is always noisy.
After the scars heal and a stint in rehabilitation, you're discharged.

The president of the hang gliding club calls occasionally to see
how you're doing. You assure him you'll never make a mistake like
that again. After your crash, two other women dropped out of the
club. The next scheduled flight is in Jeolla Province. You recall the
sensation of soaring through the air. An aerial view of the narrow trail
you followed to the top rises before you.

"It might be a little difficult at this time, but next time you go,
please let me know."

You hang up with a chuckle. But you never hear from him again.

·

On nights you couldn't fall asleep, you went out onto the glassed-in
balcony and looked out. But too often you failed to catch the outside
view, and more and more you found yourself gazing at your own

reflection. You told yourself the sleepless nights would stop once you started exercising again. Illuminated by the security light, the playground sand shone like a glacier field. The shadows cast by the swings grew and shrank as they undulated on the sand. It was then you saw her—the girl on the swing. You recognized this girl. It was you, ten years old. You threw on a sweater and opened the door. It had been a long time since you took in some fresh air. Walking to the swings was as difficult as cutting across the school field as a child. But the girl was gone. You sat on the swing and gripped the metal chains. You backed up two paces and lifted your feet. The swing began to move slowly. The playground safety-rule board loomed up, and then grew distant. You felt dizzy. The chains started to squeak. It took much longer than before to propel yourself up. The moment your swing went as high as the beam, without thinking you let go of the chains and jumped. Your body hung in midair. You curled up in a ball, clutching your legs and drawing your chin into your chest. But there wasn't enough time for even one somersault. Like a gunnysack, you flopped onto the sand. As you hit the ground, you heard your right leg crack and out it popped from under your skirt, glancing off the seesaw and dropping to the sand.

"My leg!"

As you tried to stand to fetch your prosthetic limb, you noticed your watch. Even in the dim security light, you could read the two hands—3:14.

When you had woken up in the ICU, you had looked at the curled-up petals on the wilting rose wreath and the white bed sheet. Unlike the bulge in the sheet where your left leg was, the area covering what should have been your right leg had been flat and smooth.

You managed to rise on one leg and moved toward the seesaw. Your shadow was stretched out on the sand. You looked at the shadow cast by the stump and the empty space below it. In that shadow, half of you could now hang in midair forever.

Nightmare

The alarm didn't go off this morning. She lay curled up like a millipede and heard the old grandfather clock strike six times in the downstairs living room. It was always five minutes slow. She woke from habit and the early light, not the few digital tones of "Animal Farm" that her alarm clock normally played on loop until she turned it off. Her fingers crept up to her bedside, but she couldn't find the metal chill of the clock.

She lowered her hands and wrapped her arms around her knees. She whispered to herself, "Go on, sleep a bit more." She was given an alarm clock much earlier than other children her age. Her parents were always busy. They stopped waking her as soon as she turned nine. It wasn't that they neglected her. The orchard was simply too big for two people to manage. Except for the small front yard, the rest of their land was a pear orchard. Every day they pulled weeds, but tougher weeds grew back in their place. So it was the alarm clock that woke her. The clock didn't grumble like her exhausted mother. All it required was a new battery once a year.

She pulled the sheet over her face, but the sunlight bore through it and penetrated her eyelids. Each time she inhaled, the sheet clung to her nose. She smelled Tide, Ivory soap, and saliva, but together they smelled of the wind—the wind right before rain came, as it blew between the orchard trees.

The man's clothes and hair had smelled the same.

Her small room was as clean and tidy as a hospital room. The books she had hurled in self-defense were back on the shelf, and the buttons, wrenched from her pajama top, were firmly in place. But the stench of something rotting lingered in the air. She frequently had vivid dreams where she could fly. Rough hands pushed her off a cliff and footsteps pursued her into a dead-end street. She found herself in a car speeding at 150 kilometers per hour where the brakes didn't work, and she felt a man's hot breath on her ear. These bad dreams made her shoot up in height.

But this morning, her alarm clock hadn't gone off. Her bladder began to ache. As she climbed out of bed, she felt something sharp underfoot and her body pitched to the side. It was the alarm clock, hidden by the edge of the bedspread. It had stopped at 2:35 A.M. When it had hit the floor, the battery had tumbled out and was nowhere to be found. On the rim of the clock was a dried bloodstain the size of a pumpkin seed. This was no dream.

She had dashed down the stairs in the middle of the night. Though she weighed next to nothing, her steps rang out on the hollow wooden steps. The master bedroom door opened and a woman's face emerged, glancing about. Shortly afterward, the living-room lights switched on. The woman stuck her hand under her pajamas and scratched loudly. Then her sleepy and wrinkled eyes widened. Her daughter's pajama top was open, the buttons torn off, exposing her breasts. Her pale nipples were erect, and there was a towel stuffed in her mouth. The woman knew immediately what had happened. Her husband, who had followed her downstairs, ran up to their daughter's room and rushed back down once more. The front door swung open, slamming against the wall. He ran past the yard and cut through the orchard, his footsteps growing distant. The patter of dog paws followed close behind.

Some thirty workers were sleeping in the barrack. Not wanting to wake them, her father crept past the building. When her mother forced a spoonful of nerve tonic into her mouth, the girl choked and coughed it back up. Far away, the dogs barked fiercely. It could mean only one thing: the two shepherd dogs had scented a stranger. The tonic made the girl drowsy.

It was very late when her father returned. "No one fled through the pear trees. It was just the workers' clothes, hanging on the line. Plus, your bedroom window was locked."

"That's right," her mother said, as if putting a lid on the matter. "The window was locked from the inside."

The girl fell asleep on the living room sofa. When she opened her eyes again that morning, she was lying in her own bed, as if nothing had happened.

•

She limped to the bathroom. Her tailbone was sore. She sat on the toilet, emptying her bladder for a long time. She turned on the taps and washed her face. Water splashed and soaked the front of her shirt. The mirror steamed up. She ran her palm over it and gazed at her reflection. The longer she stared, the stranger her features appeared, like a Picasso painting. "So you think you can get away with it?"

Like any other morning, she smelled rice cooking. She heard bowls clattering and the knife clacking on the cutting board. The front door opened and her father walked in with the morning paper. He smiled brightly at her, who stood in the middle of the stairs. He passed her a section of the paper and they sat down at the table. She realized something was the matter only after she read the date on the paper. An entire day had vanished while she slept. In one corner was a short news report about an unidentified man who had lost his life after being hit by a car. It wasn't a story that would attract much attention. Hit-and-run accidents were common. But the site of the accident was right off the highway, an hour's distance away. In the middle of the night, she had heard the rumble of the tractor in low gear as it left the orchard. It had returned only before sunrise.

Her father had on his reading glasses and was reading aloud the weather report. The food was no different from any other breakfast: marinated soy bean sprouts, grilled mackerel, and radish broth. Even the way her mother seasoned the sprouts with an excessive amount of spice and salt was the same. The meal was much too ordinary to come on the heels of a distressing night. Any other mother would have taken to her bed. Then it would have been the girl sitting by her mother's side, holding her hand, murmuring, "I'm okay, so don't worry."

Her father complained about the food, saying too much salt might as well be poison. It was a familiar scene out of some tedious family drama. Her parents were like a pair of middle-aged actors well acquainted with their roles.

"What's wrong? No appetite?" he said worriedly to his daughter, who sat poking at her food. He snapped at his wife, "See? Who'd want to eat this garbage?"

The girl gazed at his smooth, round forehead. "Father, you don't have to keep smiling like that. I know what happened."

Stunned, he put down his spoon and chopsticks and gazed at her face. "Did you have a bad dream?"

"You saw him, too, didn't you? The one in white who ran off through the trees?"

"I don't know what you saw, but it must have been the workers' clothes on the line. Or maybe the men wandering around drunk. You've done nothing but sleep since you fell down the ladder two days ago. You had a bad dream."

"But someone came into my room."

Her father picked up his spoon once more. "Nonsense. As long as I'm here, this house is safe. You just had a nightmare. Let's not talk about this anymore."

The girl shut her mouth, as if swallowing a ball of rice. Her parents worried about her future. They bristled at the phone calls that had started coming for her as she grew older. They hoped she would become the wife of a promising young man, give birth to healthy children, and lead a life of ease and comfort in an apartment in the city, playing the piano, instead of pulling weeds. There were things impossible to share between parent and child. Forced to play the piano she hated, a pit formed inside her. Time passed and this pit grew a little deeper and a little wider. Her parents told visiting relatives and friends that she was a quiet girl of few words.

All through elementary school, she had bought her notebooks and pencils from The Smile Shop. The streets around the school were lined with stationery stores, but the children tended to gather at The Smile Shop after school, because it gave away things like coloring books, mini readers, and candy. The windowless store was always dim. It was long and narrow like a corridor, and at the back of the store was a room where the owner cooked and slept. A heavy smoker, the pale man coughed frequently. He sometimes pulled the girls who had come to buy notebooks onto his lap, and rubbed their cheeks or stroked their thighs. His palm was cold and moist. If they whined, he gave them another piece of candy. One day a girl in sixth grade went missing. She was found gagged in his back room with a doll, her hands tied to the door handle. He had used the doll to lure her.

"Did you go to that store, too?"

The parents had pressed the girl for an answer, but she shook her head. "No, no, I've never been there. I go to Smarties Supplies."

Dust settled and cobwebs covered the bric-a-brac tossed into her pit.

The father had returned home very late. She had heard his tractor in her sleep. He would have pursued the man in white until the very end. He knew the six-acre orchard like the back of his hand, and so would have known to wait for the man on a certain corner. The man, unfamiliar with the land, would surely have circled the same spot, and the father would have brought the pickaxe down upon his back. He would have loaded the man into the back of the tractor and headed for the highway, which most certainly would have been deserted at that hour. He blasted the radio, in case the man should wake and raise a ruckus, but there was no chance of that. A car that had come out for a late-night drive ran right over the man's body.

•

"Hey boss, a lot of the blossoms fell already. What should we do?"

"Today's supposed to be nice. That's what the weather report said." Her father shook the newspaper in the foreman's face.

The foreman blinked his cloudy eyes. "You can read all that with no reading glasses? Don't tell me you still trust that weather news! Did you forget when it hailed last summer? How it tore all the blossoms apart? My knee here is the weather base. It never lies and it's mighty sore right now."

The girl was used to seeing the two squabble with each other. The other workers started showing up at the house. Pear blossoms open for only ten days, and hand pollination had to be completed during this time. Blossoms had fallen on the workers' heads. It had been a rainy, windy night. Not a single blossom was intact; only three or four petals dangled on each one.

Brushing the blossoms off their heads, the men stepped into the living room. The girl helped her mother take the rice and side dishes to the living room where a low table was set up. The men smelled of the wind. They yawned, stretching wide their mouths. The smell of liquor lingered on their foul breaths. These men headed to the town's bars after work and stumbled back to the barrack after midnight. Some returned right before dawn, their clothes badly rumpled. Their dark skin was like recycled paper, weathered by the sun and stained from booze and cigarettes. Their eyes were always bloodshot, and their hair reeked of charred meat and cheap perfume—smells that had seeped into their pores.

Every spring and fall, buses came from all over the country, carrying men from faraway places. Bars and restaurants sprang up around the terminal, and drink stalls took over vacant lots. The piano institute where she taught was also located in town. She opened its doors around noon. She got off the bus and walked past the bars that stayed closed until 2 P.M. She sometimes stepped in vomit, and the stench of urine in the back alleys was overpowering. Women with disheveled hair and faces bare of makeup streamed out onto the street in flip-flops. At their side they carried plastic basins filled with shampoo, soap, and small cartons of milk for facials. The men came in the spring during pollination, and returned again late summer in time for the harvest, staying until early fall. Often, those waiting for their bus at the depot barely had enough for the fare home.

That night the dogs hadn't barked. Their ears were usually so keen they started wagging their tails as soon as they heard her father's tractor in the distance. The workers who had returned from town would have been passed out drunk in the barrack. Let loose, the dogs circled the house all night. The man wouldn't have been able to avoid them. Yet, he had climbed the drainpipe that led to the second floor and snuck into the girl's room. There was no time for her to scream. He covered her mouth with a hot hand, and hauled her up from behind. The back of her head pressed against his collarbone. His heart, as if being throttled, hammered against her spine. He wavered for an instant, and she managed to break free, hurling whatever her hand grasped. He punched her in the stomach. Her mouth popped open in pain, and he quickly stuffed a towel inside. The pear blossoms turned the world outside the window a silvery white, but all she could see was the outline of his face. He was tall and strong, and she could not budge from under him. His firm thigh shoved her legs apart. Once, when she was in middle school, a stack of pear cartons had fallen on her. Just like now, she'd been stuck until the workers had moved them off her. But the man weighed more than five of those 15-kilogram cartons. She swung her arms, groping for anything that might be used as a weapon. Her hand found the alarm clock. She heaved it at his face. The only thing she could attest to from that night was his weight.

"Hey, College Boy," a worker said, jutting his chin at someone across the table. "Go get some water."

A tall young man with slightly stooped shoulders rose to his feet. He went into the kitchen and carried out a 12-liter kettle with two hands, his wrists shaking under the weight. He poured water into the man's empty bowl and straightened his back. He seemed the youngest of all the workers. There was a Band-Aid on his pale angled jaw. All of a sudden, he glanced toward the stair landing where she sat watching, and ended up pouring water onto the crotch of the worker, who jumped to his feet, swiping away the water. The men burst into laughter. Embarrassed, the young man laughed, too. He went back to his seat and resumed eating, his back to her. The man next to him guffawed and thumped his shoulder from time to time. The young man quickly emptied his bowl and was the first to head outside. The foreman whispered to her father, "Hard worker. Says he's taking a break from some fancy college in Seoul. His hands are a bit slow, but he doesn't cause trouble."

From her house, which sat atop a low hill, she watched him walk past the tree shadows toward the barrack. He stared at the ground the entire time, with one hand stuck in the back pocket of his jeans. She couldn't see the back of his head because of his slumping, hunched shoulders, then lost sight of him altogether midway across the farm. She looked toward the barrack, but he didn't appear. In fact, he could be hiding in the shadows somewhere, spying on her standing at the second-floor window. Her gaze followed the pear blossoms that had blown all the way to the main road. They no longer looked beautiful. They were like laundry suds floating in a creek.

She tugged at each button of her pajama top. The buttons had flown off when the man had yanked her shirt open. While she slept, her mother would have sewn them back on. She tugged at the second button sewn firmly in place. This one, however, had always been loose. But of course her mother wouldn't have known. The girl's room was no longer a safe place. Sunlight wasn't the only thing that came in through the window.

It rained. More blossoms fell. The weather report had predicted a clear day. Looking out at the downpour, the foreman said, "What did I say? You still trust weather news? After all this rain, only the toughest blossoms will be left. You can bet those will be the ones to produce big juicy pears."

Her father and the foreman played baduk all morning. Carrying an umbrella, she walked past the barrack. The rain had turned the cement building a dark gray. The door was ajar. She had always avoided this area when leaving the orchard. There was an outdoor pump beside the barrack, and the men sometimes stripped down and washed themselves, even when the days were cool. The men were lounging on the floor with their hands behind their heads, or watching an American broadcast, with their backs against the wall. The sportscaster gave the play-by-play in an animated voice. Big men were wrestling each other in a ring. Most of the workers had put their money on the wrestler wearing the black mask. But regardless of who won the bet, all would be going into town that evening.

The young man lay on his stomach on the damp floor, flipping lazily through a magazine. He looked up at the screen whenever the men shouted, but his gaze soon returned to the glossy pages.

One of the workers, his attention on the screen, jabbed his foot into the young man's ribs. On his arm was a faded tattoo of several Chinese characters that gang members tended to get. He was graying at the temples.

"Hey, College Boy, what the hell are they yakking about?"

When the young man simply laughed, the man with the tattoo smacked him in the head. "Damn it, you did college, but you don't even know?"

"College, my ass!" said another worker, nibbling on a squid tentacle. "If he's a college student, then call me professor!"

The young man glanced outside while rubbing his head, and saw the girl watching. His dark, bushy eyebrows flinched like caterpillars. The Band-Aid on his chin was gone, revealing a gash. She hurried past the barrack. She decided to wait until he was alone.

•

She looked out at the rain, her chair facing the window of her piano institute. The droplets rolling down the glass made the bus terminal appear further away. People holding colorful umbrellas hurried past. Occasionally she saw those without umbrellas, completely soaked.

Already wet, they didn't run. Her young student, legs dangling from the bench, struck the piano with her fists. The windowpanes trembled.

"Teacher," the child said, coming to stand next to her. "Tell me if you know the answer, okay? When it's raining a lot, do you think someone who's walking will get more wet, or someone who's running?"

"Hmm, someone who's walking probably?"

The little girl giggled. "Wrong! The one who's running! Because when you run, the rain hits you from the top *and* the front!"

A blue truck stopped in front of the institute. The words NEW SPROUTS ORCHARD were written across the side. Those in the back hopped off. The man in the driver's seat rolled down his window and gazed at the institute. It was College Boy. He saw her and smiled. After parking the truck in the lot beside the terminal, he slowly tagged along after the rest of the men to Mokpo Tavern. The beaded curtains continued to sway even after he had stepped inside.

"Teacher, did you hear what I said?"

The child poked her side with a pencil and stared up at her.

"Oh, that's why," she said belatedly. "That's why people with no umbrellas don't run."

Shouts and music drifted out from inside the brightly lit bars. The smell of hot grease wafted out. Two women were fighting in the middle of the street, cursing and pulling each other's hair. They tumbled on the ground in a heap. Though they wore heavy makeup, they looked nineteen or twenty at most.

"So you think you can snatch my customer from right under my nose?" spat the girl sitting on top.

"Your customer?" the one underneath cried, clutching the other's hair. "Did you write your name on his forehead?"

People gathered. No one tried to break up the fight. From time to time, men stumbled out of the bars with their arms around bar girls, and then disappeared into dark alleys.

•

A ladder was propped against every tree. The workers were hand-pollinating the trees by transferring pollen from the stamen to the pistil. All she could see were their legs and dirty shoes.

"What a beautiful day! Even this flower gets to hook up with another flower, but how about me? Doomed to be single, that's me."

Curses spewed from the next tree. "Griping about that same shit again? Just shut up and work!"

The foreman made his rounds, barking orders. "If you've got enough energy to yap away, you've got enough energy to work! At this pace, you'll never get through half the blossoms before they drop off. You can forget about today's wages then! You won't even get a meal!"

"Aye-aye, sir!" a voice answered breezily.

With all the workers up in the trees, it wasn't easy to find the young man. Those who noticed her whistled. She ambled home. She had a view of the entire six-acre farm from the front yard. Sometimes she saw a man climb down from one tree, move the ladder to another tree, and then climb up again. The heat shimmered. She felt dizzy.

"You looking for me?" he said, as if they were on a first-name basis.

She knew who it was even before she turned around. He stood a few steps away, his gaze flicking over her body. He had just come from the kitchen and was carrying a pail of rice wine the men liked to have with their lunch. Venus, one of the shepherd dogs, stood next to him, licking his shoes.

"I know you've been watching me," he smirked.

"We need to talk."

She led the way. She heard the wine slosh in the pail behind her. Venus followed at his heels. Apollo was licking his empty bowl. She kicked at the ground, but Venus backed away and then drew near once more. She threw a rock in the dog's direction and stepped into the shed beside the barrack. It was the only place that would give them some privacy at this hour. On one side were yellow plastic crates stacked high to the ceiling. Pesticide containers labeled Derris and Hexaconazole sat on top of a shelf, and plastic buckets in the corner were filled with gardening tools, like rusted shears, hoes, and pick-axes. He put down his pail and lit a cigarette.

"So what'd you need to talk about? Can't you see I'm busy?" He gestured at the pail. "Those guys can't work if they don't have any booze in their system."

"That cut on your chin, how'd you get it?" she snapped.

Instead of answering, he sucked hard on his cigarette and drew his lips together as he blew out. Smoke rings rose from his mouth.

"Should I jog your memory? It was you, wasn't it? The rat that snuck into my room!"

He let out a long whistle. "You don't look like the type, but I guess I was wrong. You're saying someone came into your room? And that someone was me?" He ground out the half-smoked cigarette under his shoe and laughed. "Don't flatter yourself. There's more than enough girls in town."

"Where did you get that scar then? It's from the alarm clock I threw at you. That's the evidence," she mumbled quickly.

"Oh, this? I cut myself shaving. It's something men do. I'm sure you've noticed this place is crawling with men."

He drew closer and gripped her shoulders. He dug his fingers into her flesh, pressing hard, as if he were playing the piano. "It was all a dream. Virgins have dreams like that, don't they? I guess you could call it a kind of test run."

He went to the corner and rummaged through the buckets, finally holding up a pair of shears. He opened her hand and placed them in her palm.

"Next time, just stab him in the face. If it's not a dream, as you say, you'll leave him with a huge scar."

He picked up the pail. Just as he was about to step outside, he looked back. "I won't tell anyone about your dream, but here's some advice. Don't hang around the barrack anymore. They're simple men. They'll think you have a thing for them. You know how easy it is to climb to the second floor? Next time, it won't be a dream. Don't say I didn't warn you."

As soon as he went outside, Venus began to bark. She heard him kick the dog. She looked down at her hand. In it were pruning shears with long, sharp tips. She hid them inside the folds of her clothes.

•

The pear blossoms faded and the men left. From the window of the piano institute, she watched the buses pull out of the terminal. Some bar owners waited at the terminal to collect all outstanding tabs. The town became deserted, like an abandoned amusement park. Bar girls perched on wooden platforms out on the street and played flower cards together. "Let's see, bird, rain, and cherry blossoms. Why don't we take a stroll with lover-boy here on this moonlit night?"

These girls who had been squabbling over customers only the day before now sat huddled together, giggling like children. Despite their young faces, they had the raspy voices of old women. They squatted on the street, smoking. Even the drink stalls in the vacant lots cleared out, and a few days later, the girls left, one by one. The town turned quiet once more.

As always, the alarm clock woke her every day at six, and she pulled weeds all morning, wearing a visor and towel on her head. The weeds grew thick in no time, their roots tough from sucking up the nutrients meant for the pear trees. She headed to town in the afternoon and opened the doors to her piano institute, giving lessons to fifteen children until 5 P.M. She hated the piano, which sounded like noise to her.

The barrack floor was littered with the things the men had left behind. Because her father had scrimped on labor costs and applied the cement himself, the floor sloped unevenly. She found two empty soju bottles that had rolled down to the right wall, and a curled-up magazine, which the young man had been reading. It was a porn magazine featuring foreign girls, with obscene comments scrawled on every page. She sat cross-legged without removing her shoes. Her body tilted to the right. She felt dizzy. Next to the pile of grimy blankets and pillows was a pack of flower cards. She brought one knee up as she'd seen the bar girls do and spread the cards before her. She picked up a few, but didn't know how to play. She muttered, imitating what she'd heard them say, "Let's see, bird, rain, and cherry blossoms. Why don't we take a stroll with lover-boy here on this moonlit night?"

On the weekends, she took her father's car and went to Seoul. There, no one paid her any attention. She sat by the window of a café, smoking cigarettes and boldly making eye contact with those who walked by on the street. She wore crimson lipstick, and went with her friends across the Han River to the latest nightclubs. She drank and danced with the men who spoke to her. They all smelled of the wind. She spent the night in the car and returned home once she had sobered. Her alarm clock stopping ringing at six in the morning, but she didn't replace the battery. She didn't open the piano institute doors until after 2 P.M. Children grew tired of waiting by the locked doors and headed home. The monsoon rain started. Many days, she forgot to take an umbrella. She walked to the bus stop in the rain. Her hair and underclothes got soaked. People ran by, covering their heads with books or their hands. It was a small town. Rumors spread about the daughter of New Sprouts Farm, who roamed in the rain like a madwoman. There were fewer and fewer students. She went to the empty institute and gazed out at the street all day.

At the terminal new faces climbed off the bus. They went into a nearby store and asked about any farm work while buying cigarettes. Her father heated up the empty barrack. The wallpaper and linoleum floor had mildewed during the monsoon. He brought the power out to the orchard and strung light bulbs between the pear trees so that the men could work at night.

The men returned. It was a bumper year for pears. She heard her father say to the foreman that the price of pears was going to drop. The foreman acted as if he knew it all, saying it worked out to be the same, selling fewer pears at a high price or selling more pears at a low price. Cardboard cases with the words PREMIUM SINGO PEARS filled the house. On the days she didn't have to go to the institute, she folded cases. Workers filled the barrack once more. The drink stalls returned to the vacant lots, and girls with young faces stepped off the buses. They went back and forth between the bars and the public bath with plastic basins at their sides, and at four in the afternoon, dolled themselves up with the bar doors wide open. Her mother brought out the industrial-size rice cooker, and the smell of boiling rice filled the house once more. Dirty running shoes and military boots crowded the entrance. She glanced at the men eating breakfast and found College Boy sitting at the table.

He had grown leaner. His cheekbones protruded, and his hair now came down to his shoulders. He had taken the last bus into town. There were no cars heading to the orchard at that hour, so he'd walked.

The workers were up in the trees again. They climbed the ladders, picked the fruit, and put it in baskets. Sweet, juicy pears dangled from over a thousand trees. Branches sometimes snapped, unable to withstand the weight of the fruit. Because the pears were so big, each basket couldn't hold more than ten. When the baskets filled up, the workers climbed down to dump the fruit into plastic crates that were scattered on the ground. The foreman pushed his way through the trees, yelling at the men.

"Gentle! You've got to handle them gently! If I find any bruises or scratches, you can forget about getting paid!"

The workers snickered and wisecracked from the trees.

"I said, gentle! Like you're touching a virgin's ass!"

Though they were careful, the pears still suffered bruises, scratches, and cuts, for they injured one another with their only weapon—the stem. The treetops were full of rotting pears, because the magpies had already scooped out the flesh, and insects went for the sweetest fruit. The townspeople came to buy the damaged pears. They would sit in front of the bus terminal or in the corner of the market and sell them at giveaway prices. The ones no one wanted smelled terrible as they rotted. Soon they teemed with maggots.

On the way home, she could see the light bulbs even from far away, bobbing like fish-luring lights. The workers whistled at her whenever she walked by. The whistles no longer bothered her. She didn't run or hurry anymore. At the break of dawn, trucks loaded with cartons of pears left for Seoul, and late at night, trucks carrying workers returned to the orchard. Even after the shadows had staggered into the barrack, she could hear swearing and strains of pop songs until early morning.

It was past 2 A.M. when he slipped into her room on the second floor. He landed soundlessly on her balcony like a cat and tried her window. It was unlocked. He crept toward the girl where she lay in bed. Her eyes snapped open. When he raised the towel, she shook her head at him. He wavered, taking a step backward. She said softly, "When you've been rained on already, there's no need to run."

A weight equal to five 15-kilo cartons climbed on top of her. He smelled of liquor and the wind. He pressed his lips against hers. Her hand crawled up his back and suddenly traced an arc in the dark. He toppled to the floor. Then she smashed his head with a shovel she had hidden under her bed. He was motionless. Out in the orchard far away, a pear thudded to the ground. Plunged into the man's back were the shears he had given her, the handles protruding like the key of a wind-up toy. It seemed he would start lurching about like a robot if the key were turned. She dragged him by his feet toward the stairs. His head knocked against each step, all the way to the bottom. She was sweating. Her thighs chafed each time they rubbed against her damp pajamas. The house was silent.

She brought the wheelbarrow from the yard. Venus and Apollo were eating scraps of ham. They grew tense at her shadow, but went back to devouring their food as soon as they realized it was her. Now she knew why Venus had followed the man around. He moaned as she loaded him into the wheelbarrow. She hit him again with the shovel. The moaning stopped. She tossed it in the wheelbarrow as well. She pushed him through the orchard, keeping away from the barrack. His head and legs stuck out of the wheelbarrow, jerking every time the wheel hit a rock. If she happened to hear a noise, she stopped and stared into the darkness. But it was just the wind knocking fruit down from the trees. Rotten pears burst under her feet. She had forgotten to put on shoes. The wheelbarrow was difficult to push. Each time it lurched in a different direction, she swore like the workers. It was dark, but she knew the orchard like the back of her hand. The pear trees ended and she came to the hillside. The trees in this area had already been picked. Nobody would be wandering about here.

Digging a hole was difficult work. All she managed to do was scatter the soil a bit. She pushed the wheelbarrow up to the hole and tipped it over. His body tumbled inside. The hole was too small and shallow. She could barely cover his legs with the dirt. She used the leaves to hide the rest of his body.

"Father, you said it was just a nightmare, but it wasn't. Look how dirty my hands are. I only did what he told me to do. If it was a nightmare like you say, the shears would be sticking out of my chest."

The parents saw their daughter's eyes glittering wildly. Her fingers were blistered, and blood oozed from her broken toenails. They followed her outside. In the yard was the wheelbarrow, and inside were a shovel and a pair of shears. The tips of the shears were stained red. It seemed they hadn't gone in deep, judging from the amount of blood. The father flung the shears into the empty doghouse, and clasped the shovel to his chest, the blade pointing up. He knew the orchard so well he didn't need a flashlight. Neither did he want to risk waking the workers. The girl darted through the pear trees, swinging her arms in the dark. She talked feverishly.

"I did nothing wrong. He was the one who gave them to me. I'll go to the police in the morning. Would they believe it was self-defense? But how would they know that? Should we go to the highway then? Accidents happen there all the time. No, no, maybe it's better if we just leave him here. Who would notice he's missing anyway?"

Her parents grew short of breath, trying to keep up with her. The dew moistened their pants. Finally, the girl stopped before a tree. She dropped to her knees and dug at a pile of leaves. But there was nothing.

"That's strange! Maybe this isn't the right tree. Oh, it's that one! It's that tree over there!"

She ran to the next tree and dug up the leaves. But this time again, there was nothing.

"Did you mark the spot?" her father asked.

She grabbed the shovel from him. "I didn't need to. I know this place!"

She darted to another tree and dug at the base. But the man wasn't there either. The father pulled her to her feet and shook her by the shoulders.

"You can't go digging up every tree for six acres!"

"But I buried him under a tree that's already been picked!" she cried.

He clamped his hand over her mouth. Slippery with sweat, his hand reeked of metal. He hissed, "More than seven hundred trees have been picked so far! When the sun comes up, that number will only grow!"

She screamed. But the noise stayed trapped against his palm.

The sky was brightening. Soon the workers would wake. He exchanged a look with his wife, who stood behind the girl.

Her mother pointed at the empty hole and said anxiously, "Look, dear! This is all a nightmare, just a nightmare. So wake up now, please, won't you wake up?

The
Retreat

The drunken words spewed by a regular of Good Chicken were to blame. The meeting was supposed to take place at the Hanbit Academy of Mental Calculation at exactly seven o'clock. The academy director wrote the words *Taegwang Tenants Emergency Meeting* on the chalkboard and waited. It was twenty past seven, but still no one came. He walked toward the back of the classroom and surveyed his handiwork. What hadn't been apparent close-up was now obvious. The words slanted down from the second syllable, so that the last word ended up a handspan below. Even his sense of balance broke down as he grew old. When he was young, he used to hold two pieces of chalk between his fingers and drag them across the board, drawing double lines so straight as if they'd been done with a ruler. He still felt like a seventeen-year-old, who could run a 100-meter dash in thirteen seconds. He scolded himself for longing for his youth. There was still so much left to do.

He went back to the chalkboard and erased everything except for the first syllable. He tried again, his tongue poking out. He was making the last stroke when the door banged open, startling him. The shuffle of flip-flops approached. His writing turned crooked once more.

"Someone stole another tambourine. It's the fifth one already. What would anyone want with a tambourine?"

It was the girl from Billboard Karaoke on the basement level.

The director carefully erased the final stroke and made another attempt. Then he stood at the lectern and looked at the girl's exposed feet.

"You're late. You probably think you've got all the time in the world, but time doesn't wait for you. Don't have regrets when you're old like me. Live each day like it's your last."

She stared blankly at him from her seat and slapped her flip-flop against a bare heel.

Right then, Ms. Jang from Good Chicken dashed in, bringing with her the smell of fried food. She looked around the classroom. "They're not here yet? Don't they know what time it is?"

She had donned a plastic apron on top of her sheer fuchsia dress. The apron was splattered with grease and batter, and had faded so much it was difficult to tell what color it had once been.

"Ah, sorry! Game just ended," said Mr. Jeong as he rushed in, still wearing arm sleeves and his fingertips stained with chalk. "If you win twice, you've got to lose one. It's the only way they'll back off."

Mr. Jeong was the owner of Pintos Billiards on the second floor. His eyes were bloodshot from calculating hourly rates and watching cue balls bounce around the table all day.

Mrs. Park complained as she climbed the stairs. "I've got to drag myself up here like this, because they couldn't wait two days until the retreat? Am I the only one with a million things to do?"

Her grumbling was punctuated by pauses. The weight she had put on suddenly made climbing the stairs difficult. When she finally reached the third floor, she hung onto the academy door, catching her breath.

By the time the master of Goguryeo Taekwondo School jogged down from the fourth floor in his white uniform and indoor shoes, it was already 7:40.

At this hour, the academy was the only place they could gather. The child-size desks and chairs, arranged neatly facing the chalkboard until the adults had sat in them, were now askew. They stared at the academy director, who stood at the chalkboard with a stick of white chalk in his hand, and fidgeted to find more comfortable positions. The annual team-building retreat was the only time all the tenants came together, since each one had different business hours. They began to talk about the actual reason for their emergency meeting.

Just past midnight the day before, a man had stepped into Good Chicken. Ms. Jang, who had been frying chicken, heard the door open and poked her head out of the kitchen. He glanced about with bleary eyes and stood swaying in the same spot. His dress shirt had come untucked from his pants and was wrinkled, like a crumpled sheet of paper. She quickly removed her apron and ushered him to table #2.

"Oh, you've had a lot to drink."

She was used to drunk customers. They could be as aggressive as wild dogs, or as meek as babies. Good Chicken was a last stop for many, a place they dropped by for a nightcap after drinking all evening. At partitioned tables, men chugged beer, sitting slouched back in their seats.

The man ordered a half chicken with spicy marinade and a pint of beer, but Ms. Jang chopped up a whole chicken instead, dredging the pieces in flour and then dropping them in the pressure fryer. The chicken crackled as it hit the hot oil. While she fried chicken and poured beer, hands waved above the partitions to get her attention. She rushed here and there, serving more beer and pickled radish, and had her arm clutched by many. Sitting down next to the man, she tore the chicken into bite-size pieces and shoved them in his mouth. Most fell under his chair. The wooden floor was littered with cubed radish and coleslaw the other customers had dropped. The bits of food gleamed in the red light.

Mrs. Park from the skewer shop interrupted Ms. Jang. "Hey, we don't have all day! My skewers are about to turn to coal. Plus, how can you believe the words of a drunk?"

She stuck her index finger in her hair and scratched her scalp. Dandruff flaked out instantly. The academy director wrote the word *credibility* on the chalkboard.

"You think all drunk customers are the same?" Ms. Jang said, crossing her arms over her chest. "I guess the men who go to your shop are full of hogwash."

Mrs. Park jumped to her feet, sending her seat crashing behind her. "Oh, you can bet our customers aren't the same! Just like how you and I aren't the same, even though we both sell liquor. I don't powder my face like a ghost and play around with drunks for some measly change. I sell food and drink, I don't entertain men!"

Ms. Jang glared at Mrs. Park. "If I didn't know better, I'd say you're jealous!"

Mr. Jeong from the pool hall, who had been sitting between the two women, intervened. "Now what's that got to do with why we're all here? Let's hear what happened."

Once again the seat buried itself in Mrs. Park's fleshy rear end. The academy director underlined *credibility* and said, "Ms. Jang, please try to give a brief summary of what happened. Your customers will be coming soon."

Ms. Jang covered her mouth and laughed. "A brief summary? Oh, I don't know how to do that, but I'll try. Now where was I?"

"He dropped some chicken on the floor," Mr. Jeong said quickly.

The man drank beer, his mouth full of chicken. Pieces fell in his glass and floated in the foam. Ms. Jang attached herself to his side and said, "If you don't like chicken, I can get you something else. How about some fruit I bought this morning?"

The man grew almost cross-eyed. "I'm not drunk. You want to hear a secret?"

Clasping her face with both hands, he pulled her toward him until her face was inches from his own. The smell of chicken, beer, and tooth decay hit her.

"This is a secret. You can't tell anyone. Ms. Jang, you know I love you, don't you? This building's going to change hands soon. You know the amusement park nearby? That owner's buying this place. Then he's going to knock this whole thing down and build studio apartments."

Ms. Jang stopped talking. Everyone, including the director, was quiet.

"Maybe it's just a rumor," Mr. Jeong said, rubbing his chalk-covered fingers together. His fingertips were peeling from psoriasis.

"I thought so, too, at first. I assumed he was just drunk. But he didn't forget to take any of his change. Trust me, a drunk person never does that. I even called him this morning to make sure, and was he shocked! He denied everything. If he hadn't been telling the truth, there would be no reason for him to act that way."

"That's right," Mr. Jeong chimed in. "Most of the time, men just pretend to be drunk so they can cop a feel."

The chalkboard was crowded with the words boiled down from Ms. Jang's account: *amusement park, change hands, new construction, studio apartments.*

The taekwondo master, who, despite his small size, was nick-named Arnold Schwarzenegger because of his muscular body, finally spoke up. "I'm c-c-completely opposed."

His slight stammer lent his words weight. The director wrote in large letters, pressing the chalk hard against the board: *completely opposed*. It was something he did whenever he stressed important information to his students. Bits of crushed chalk clung to the letters.

"Then who'll talk to the owner on our behalf?"

Everyone looked at the director. He drew his lips into a thin line.

"I guess it would be best to speak to him at the retreat?" asked Ms. Jang. "He'll be in a better mood after a few drinks."

Everyone agreed. They dispersed one by one. The director straightened the desks again, but because he was upset, they kept going crooked. Even the writing on the chalkboard slanted down and was no different from his first attempt. The slanted writing bothered him.

Mrs. Park hurried down the stairs after Ms. Jang. "Now that I've had a good look while it's still light out, you're definitely no spring chicken! Thirty-four? Yeah, right! How old are you really?"

Ms. Jang whipped around and glared at Mrs. Park, who stood several steps above her, dressed in baggy pants. They were the sort with an elastic waistband, but it was buried deep in the folds of her flesh.

"You got something against me? You better watch it!" Ms. Jang cried.

"Don't get all riled up now! All your wrinkles are showing!" yelled Mrs. Park, hitching up her pants.

"Mind your own business," Ms. Jang snapped, continuing down the stairs. "I heard you buy cheap gingko nuts from China and pass them off as local. And don't you use expired chicken gizzards?"

Mrs. Park barreled down the stairs and grabbed Ms. Jang by the hair. "How the hell would you know? Did you see me? Did you see me do it?"

Ms. Jang shrieked, stumbling, as she was yanked this way and that. She reached back and scratched the older woman in the face and chest. Mr. Jeong and Arnold ran down the stairs to break up the fight. Mrs. Park tried to fight off the men, so that she could go after the younger woman, who fled down the stairs.

Mrs. Park stood in front of her skewer shop, which still reeked of varnish. Displayed in the front window were all sorts of skewers. These plastic replicas looked a lot fresher and tastier than the real thing. The renovation had been completed two weeks ago. Bright fluorescent lights had replaced dim tinted lights, and some of the tightly packed tables had been removed to create more space. She had even put in a bar where the grill would be prominently displayed.

Two years before, she had blindly trusted a newspaper ad about a skewer business being lucrative, and had opened a shop using the insurance settlement she had received from her husband's death. But within a few days of opening, she realized she was late in the game. There were over fifty skewer franchises in the country alone. Skewer businesses had once been hot, but were fading fast. All the shops looked the same with their wooden interiors and seating so cramped one's knees touched those of the person opposite. Even the menus were the same. Her franchisor also proved to be unstable. One day, the refrigerated truck that delivered supplies and key ingredients simply stopped coming. She called the headquarters, but the number was no longer in service. She couldn't get her deposit back. For several months she had no customers and just shelled out money for rent. Her oldest was in the ninth grade and the youngest in the sixth grade. She used all her savings to renovate the shop. She changed the interior and expanded the menu, developing a marinade from ketchup and chili pepper paste to suit the tastes of young people, even children. During the day, before the evening customers came, she opened a small window on one side of the front display, and sold skewers off a grill to passing children and housewives. Business was just about to pick up.

She stood outside her shop, looking up at her sign. She was on her feet every day, grilling skewers from ten in the morning to midnight. As they cooked, the marinade burned and stung her eyes. Her eyes were always bloodshot, and her face lost its suppleness from being exposed to smoke all day, like a piece of sausage hanging in a smokehouse. The scratches on her face and chest prickled. Though she had been the one to pick the fight with Ms. Jang, rage still boiled in the pit of her stomach. Just then, she remembered the skewers she had left on the grill. The pieces of chicken were like lumps of coal, scorched beyond recognition.

Ms. Jang ran a brush through her disheveled hair and discovered a fistful of hair had come out on the brush.

Don't let anyone look down on you. Don't show a single tear.

She was never the first to pick a fight, but if someone did, she didn't lose. It didn't matter if it was Mrs. Park or Mr. Kwak, the building owner. She's even grabbed drunks by the collar and forced them to settle the bill. Except for the fake tears she sometimes shed before men, she couldn't remember the last time she had genuinely cried. She opened her compact and coated her puff with powder. She looked in the mirror at the crow's feet around her eyes, like the cracks in a dried-up field. She pressed hard at the lines with her puff.

She felt most at ease here. Inside her dim fried chicken joint, she was forever thirty-four. To block out the sun, she had covered the window looking out onto the street with a tinted plastic sheet. There were no other windows. When the chicken was done cooking, the pressure fryer expelled steam through the outside exhaust vent. Two fans installed in the walls were always running, removing the stale smell of cigarette smoke, vinegar, and grease. The blades were sticky with grease, covered with a thick layer of dust, like iron filings on magnets. She closed up at two in the morning each night, went home, and slept until noon. She needed to shampoo her greasy hair at least twice. Her skin was pasty, since she had started wearing too much makeup from an early age. As she grew older, her makeup grew thicker. She headed to the shop by five to meet the truck that delivered raw chicken, flour mix, and marinade. To save on employee costs, she didn't provide take-out or delivery services. After donning her apron, the first thing she did was to make the batter and skim all the burned bits from the oil. Used oil tended to foam. She swept the floor and sometimes burned mugwort to freshen the air. It was time for the customers to start coming in. She pinned back her hair and put on her apron. The middle of the thick slab of tree trunk, which she used as a cutting board, was sunken in from the years of chopping. Nibbling her lower lip, Ms. Jang swung her cleaver and chopped the chicken into pieces, as if she were attacking it.

The director sat hunched at a desk in the classroom and ate the food his wife had packed for him. It was so bland it almost tasted bitter. But if he didn't stick to his diet, his blood sugar level increased right away. It was at a previous Taegwang team-building retreat that he'd discovered he had diabetes. There had been a long line of people waiting in front of the portable toilet, so he had gone searching for a private spot down the hill. Ants had swarmed toward his glucose-saturated urine.

That evening he had a late dinner because of the emergency meeting. His wife packed him both lunch and dinner, since he always had a lot of things to do, even after the other teachers had gone home. He swallowed the rest of his food.

Kwak, the owner of Taegwang Building, was a vigorous, healthy man in his mid-thirties. Though it was not yet nine in the evening, he was already drunk. He weaved his car through back alleys in order to avoid roadside checks. Only when he had parked in the small lot behind Taegwang Building was he able to relax. Drowsiness suddenly swept over him. He turned off the engine and climbed out of his black BMW. The back of the building was more run-down than the front. Muggy, foul-smelling steam blasted from the exhaust vent of Good

Chicken and wrapped around his legs. The garbage bags piled on one side of the lot gave off a terrible stench. Kwak walked to the front of the building and stood before the main entrance. Two men slipped into Good Chicken. The red interior light shone through the tear in the plastic sheet covering the window. Though it was dark, he could see the chipped and missing tiles on the outer wall. The letters that had spelled *Taegwang Building* had fallen off with the exception of one, which barely hung on. During the day, the sign was still visible by the dust that used to outline the letters.

Kwak jammed his hands in his pockets and slowly climbed the stairs. Billboard Karaoke, Good Chicken, and the skewer shop. Pintos Billiards, with a picture of a cue ball in every window, Hanbit Mental Calculation Academy, and Goguryeo Taekwondo School. Every one of these businesses was bringing down the building's value. He felt annoyed at the thought of going on a retreat with these people in two days. It had been his father's idea to hold an annual team-building retreat with all the tenants. Even after his death, he still exerted power over Kwak. His father had run a study hall on the fifth floor. After Kwak graduated from high school, his father sent him to study abroad in America, since no university in Korea would accept him with his grades. The subjects he ended up studying in America, paid for in American dollars, weren't very practical. He returned to Korea only when his father died. His father's entire wealth became Kwak's. The first thing he did was to shut down the study hall. He didn't want to spend the rest of his days like his father, sitting by the door, accepting small change from students or supervising the boys' and girls' sections. The students had called his father the Owl. At the start of every school year, the names of the students who had been accepted to prestigious universities were printed on a banner and hung in front of the building. His father had hoped Kwak's name would be included in that list one day. The banner used to appear regularly in Kwak's dreams. But when he had seen the wooden cubicle desks piled high outside the building, he finally felt free.

It's not that he hadn't considered repairing the building. He was no expert, but he knew the cost of fixing an old building like this would be a considerable task. Plus he'd still be left with the children's shouts that rang out from the taekwondo school downstairs all day long. What he wanted was to sell the building and use the money to build an elegant restaurant on the city's outskirts with a stage for live music.

He passed the bathroom, whose door was cracked open. The smell of ammonia stung his eyes. Kwak kicked the door, but it swung open again because of its rusty hinges. Frowning, Kwak walked up to his room on the fifth floor. The old building didn't have an elevator. Even if it had been a twenty-story tower, his father most certainly wouldn't have installed one to save on electricity costs.

The director of the academy called out to Kwak, following him up the stairs and standing close behind, while Kwak unlocked his front door. The director was a long-time friend of his father's. He had no sense of humor, just like his father. Kwak flipped on the light switch to reveal the spacious room.

"So I heard a strange thing today," the director said, his breath stale.

Kwak said nothing.

"I guess your silence means it's true, then? Are you saying we should accept it as good news?"

This time, too, Kwak remained silent. His whole body felt sluggish from the alcohol. He wanted to collapse into bed and sleep.

"Your father poured his blood, sweat, and tears into this building. If you end up selling it, you'd be going against his wishes."

Kwak sat down. There were trophies and plaques displayed in the glass cabinet before him. The plaques started with the words: "This individual has contributed to the development of . . ." Kwak cherished these accolades.

"Ajeossi, please stop beating around the bush. You still haven't realized I'm a simple guy? Let me be blunt here. You're two months late on the rent. I'm sure you know the rent here is a lot cheaper than anywhere in this area. I've let it go until now because you were my father's friend, but this building isn't right for an academy. What will kids learn from watching people go in and out of bars and the pool hall? You probably stayed because of the cheap rent, but I can't keep hanging on to this dirty run-down building just for your sake."

The director's pulse was starting to go up. He took a deep breath. "But you need to respect your father's dying wish."

Kwak's lips twisted into a sneer. "You can't help sounding like a boring book, can you? But you're not my teacher anymore. Try begging me instead, because that might be more effective. And quit using my father as an excuse. He's dead."

Slowly the director turned away. But inside him, the fire of a twenty-year-old that hadn't yet been extinguished flared up. He faced Kwak once more.

"Why would I expect anything different from you? Ever since you were a little boy, you did everything your father asked you not to do. All those times, I warned him not to raise you that way, especially since you were an only child. Even in 1984 when you beat up your classmate and got arrested, I told him to leave you in jail for a few days to teach you a lesson. But he didn't listen. I've seen countless punks like you, and I know how they end up. After you sell this building, you'll squander all the money. When you've blown it all and have nothing left, you'll finally see you're a nothing—a nobody. And only then will you remember these words."

Kwak stood up from his chair and strode toward the director. Nearly two feet taller, Kwak found himself looking down at the old man's smooth, bald head, blooming with liver spots. The alcohol and drowsiness loosened his tongue.

"For your information, it wasn't 1984. It was 1985. God, I'm so sick of your stupid lectures."

He grabbed the director by the collar of his suit and hoisted him up so that his toes just grazed the ground. Kwak released him with a push and strode back to his chair.

The director stumbled back, frantically windmilling both arms in the air, like ducks' feet paddling furiously underwater. He reached out for something to grab, but there was nothing. All he had to do was move one foot back to steady himself. He'd been extremely agile as a young man, able to do a front tuck and land on his feet, but now he didn't even have time to take a step back. He fell helplessly. Even as he fell, he was angry with himself. Once again, his sense of balance, broken down with age, was to blame. He toppled backward into the glass cabinet. The glass shelves shattered, and the trophies rained down on his face. He let out a deep breath.

Still in his chair, Kwak looked at the broken glass, the scattered trophies, and the director whose mouth was foaming. *Why won't the old man get up?* At last, the truth finally registered. He tried to shake the director awake, but it was useless. He picked up the phone and dialed 9-1-1, and then hung up right away. He locked his front door. For the next two hours, he stayed in his chair and wondered what he should do. All he had done was to shift the director's center of gravity. It was hardly news when an animal died in a jungle. But this place wasn't the jungle and the director was not some animal. No one would believe Kwak's innocence. Back when he lived in New York, he had seen a man get shot right before his eyes. The shooter had then taken the victim's wallet and run away.

He tried to pull the director up, but the skinny old man was heavier than he had thought. Rigor mortis had started to set in, and his chin and neck were becoming stiff. There was a small bump on the back of his bald head. Kwak lifted the director's sagging arm and put it behind his own neck, and wrapped his arm around the director's waist. He barely managed to get him to his feet. As he stood at the top of the stairs, he felt pure disgust for this building that didn't have an elevator. To avoid drawing attention, he didn't turn on the lights. As he crept down the stairs in the dark, he resolved to sell the building first thing in the morning. Fortunately, the taekwondo studio on the fourth floor was closed. He almost dropped the director a few times as he was going past the academy on the third floor. He glimpsed neat rows of desks and chairs through the open door. He was about to head down to the second floor when he saw someone urinating with the bathroom door open. He heard urine splattering on the tile floor. Just as he was about to pass by, the man called out to Kwak.

"Going somewhere, boss?"

Mr. Jeong stood outside the bathroom, zipping himself up. Kwak nodded without responding.

"Is that the director?"

"Ah, yes, we had a few drinks at my place."

Mr. Jeong drew near. "Let me help you then. Director, it's me, from the pool hall!"

Right then, a voice called for Mr. Jeong.

"Shoot, it's my customer. You sure you don't need any help?" Then he yelled toward the pool hall. "I'll be right there!"

Kwak's shoulders throbbed. Mr. Jeong hesitated a little, and then rushed back into the pool hall. On the ground floor at last, Kwak was about to step out of the building entrance when Mrs. Park from the skewer shop greeted him. Women tended to be more suspicious than men.

"You're closing already?" he said to her, as she lowered the metal shutters. His hair, damp from sweat, clung to his forehead.

She pointed toward Good Chicken. "I'm sure you already know, but we're not the kind of place that stays open late. We're a family restaurant. Though we do serve alcohol, if that's what the customers want."

Kwak hoisted up the director, who was slipping from his grasp. "Why don't you head on home? Your children must be waiting. As you can tell, Ajeossi is really drunk. I'm going to drive him home."

"Oh, his wife's sure going to worry," Mrs. Park said.

Kwak headed to the parking lot. The director's feet dragged on the ground. Ms. Jang, who had been pouring used oil down the drain, jumped at the noise. Even in the dark, she recognized them right away.

"Oh my, the director's had a lot to drink!"

Kwak headed toward his car. Ms. Jang muttered, "That's strange, though. He never touches even a drop of liquor."

In order to open his car door, he needed to hold up the director with one arm. A van slowly pulled into the parking lot. Because of the headlights, he couldn't see who was behind the wheel. He stood glued in place, narrowing his eyes in the blinding light. The headlights turned off and a man hopped out of the driver's seat.

"Mr. K-k-kwak!"

Judging from the stammer, it was the taekwondo master. Kwak opened his car door and maneuvered the director into the back seat. The director fell across the seat, so Kwak pulled him back up and propped him upright. He then said in a loud voice, "Ajeossi, I'm driving you home, okay? I'll wake you up when we get there, so close your eyes and sleep tight. You feel fine otherwise?"

The taekwondo master quickly climbed back into his van and moved aside to let Kwak pass. As he drove by, Kwak saw Miss Kim sitting in the passenger seat. In his rearview mirror, Kwak caught the master unloading bags filled with beer and snacks from the back of the van.

He had managed to get onto the road, but he didn't know where he should go. He had no idea where the director lived. Not once had he given the director a ride home. He glanced at the rearview mirror. With his lips pressed stubbornly together, the director appeared to be sleeping. Just three hours earlier, Kwak had been drunk, thinking only about going to bed. But now his buzz was gone and he was wide awake. Kwak turned down an alley and came out onto the main road; he repeated these actions again and again. He even drove out to the reclamation ground where apartment buildings were being erected, but it was as bright as day from the lights of the amusement park and adult entertainment businesses nearby. Luckily, he found an alley where the security light wasn't working. He shut off his headlights, put his car in first gear, and crept deeper into the alley. He opened his trunk to find something to dig with. All he could find was a broken ski pole. He stabbed the ground with it, but the ground was concrete. He looked everywhere, but there wasn't a single place to dig. After poking at the concrete with the ski pole, he lost his temper. "What kind of city has no dirt ground?"

Kwak pulled the director out of the back seat and loaded him into the trunk. In the cramped space, he looked like a baby curled up in a mother's womb. By the time Kwak returned to Taegwang Building, it was past four in the morning.

At that hour, Arnold, the taekwondo master, was tending the counter at Billboard Karaoke. The *open* sign had been turned off hours before. After midnight, the customers were let in through the lowered metal shutters. Taegwang Building was located in a secluded spot. Most customers requested alcohol. Karaoke rooms were banned from selling alcohol. Miss Kim, the owner of Billboard Karaoke, had converted one of the rooms so she could sleep there. Two nights ago, she had gone out, after leaving Arnold in charge. On his way back from the bathroom, Arnold had seen her walking next to Mr. Kwak. She'd been crying quietly while Mr. Kwak smoked a cigarette, his gaze fixed elsewhere.

A year ago, Miss Kim had taken over the karaoke business from her parents. The basement, where fresh air or sunlight never entered, had ended up ruining her father's health. Her parents moved to the country. In order to provide for their living costs and hospital fees, she began to sell liquor. When rumors spread that Billboard Karaoke stayed open until late and sold alcohol, business improved. Sometimes drunk customers grabbed her hand and wouldn't let go, but all the hassles stopped once Arnold started to help out. The door beside the counter opened and Miss Kim emerged from the room, dragging along her sandals. Arnold gazed at her pale face. He couldn't look directly at her. "M-make sure you g-get some sun at the r-retreat. And don't stay c-c-cooped up here during the day. C-come up to the taekwondo studio once in a w-while. Your body will break d-d-down if you don't exercise."

She grimaced. She felt drained, listening to Arnold stammer. She cut him off. "How many groups do we still have? I wish they'd go home already."

Arnold swallowed the words he wanted to ask: *Why were you crying that night?*

She has been aware of Arnold's feelings for her for some time, but she was never going to admit it. He couldn't have been any more different from Mr. Kwak. For the past three months, Mr. Kwak called only when he needed her. Once she had woken up in a hotel room to find he had already left without her. The day before yesterday, he had said he didn't want to see her anymore. "I can change," she'd told him. She had tried begging, and when that hadn't worked, she'd threatened to tell other people about their relationship. But he was hardly concerned. "Go ahead, see if I care. Who do you think will be worse off—me or you? Do you want to grow old, frying chicken and entertaining men like Ms. Jang?" A few hours earlier, Mr. Kwak had seen her in the van with Arnold. He would have realized she was selling alcohol illegally. He now had a good excuse to be rid of her.

When Kwak opened his eyes it was past ten in the morning. When he saw the shattered glass and scattered trophies, he remembered the events from the night before. The director was still in the trunk of his car. It was May. The May heat would speed up the decomposition rate. He just hoped the scavengers that feed on dead animals would stay away. He opened his window and gazed down at the parking lot. Tomorrow was the team-building retreat. Anyone with a corpse locked up in his trunk would have no mind to leave on a trip, but he decided to look at the situation differently.

About an hour up the Bukhan River from Nami Island, Kwak had a small cottage on the riverside, where he went boating and water-skiing in the summer. The retreat was to be held on a deserted island reached by motorboat from the cottage. It wasn't exactly an island, but more a mound that bulged out from the river. Kwak called that mound the back of a whale. The ground there was soft, composed of earth and clay. He could dig over a hundred holes.

That morning, the Korean teacher was the first person to arrive at the academy. The director, without fail, had always been the first to arrive and the one to unlock the door, but the front door was already unlocked, and there was a lunchbox on top of the desk closest to the door. The lid was on loosely, and the container was smeared with grains of barley and sauce that had gone sour. She wiped the desks with a clean rag and walked over to the director's desk. His black dress shoes were placed neatly under his desk. Changing into indoor shoes was the first thing he did when he came to work, and judging from the fact that he was in his indoor shoes, he hadn't gone far. She went to the chalkboard to grab the eraser. There were traces of words that had been left behind. She tried to erase them, but they persisted. *Completely opposed*, she read aloud.

The Korean teacher learned the director had not gone home the night before only when his wife called. "But he came to work this morning," she said. "He's stepped out for the moment, though."

He still wasn't back by noon. The day passed uneventfully. Both the director's wife and Korean teacher believed he had come to work, but left to run an errand. No one thought he was missing.

Mr. Jeong from the pool hall chalked his cue, estimating the angles between the three balls on the green felt table. Arnold watched him closely, a cue stick in his own hand. Mr. Jeong shot, but the white ball bounced off the wrong cushion. It was rare that he missed.

"You're saying the director isn't back from this morning?"

Arnold nodded.

Mr. Jeong pointed upward with his finger. "Did you ask Mr. Kwak? They were together last night."

Arnold bent over his cue. "Well, he came to work this morning. That's what the Korean teacher said."

Mr. Jeong took a sip from his yogurt drink. "Maybe he went to the bathhouse to relax and ended up falling asleep from all the drinking last night."

Arnold followed the white ball around the table. "But he's never like that."

Mr. Jeong adjusted his grip on the cue. "Every clock stops sooner or later. More often if it gets old."

As Kwak was going down the stairs, he saw Mr. Jeong and Arnold in the pool hall. Mr. Jeong pointed up toward the ceiling and Arnold shrugged in response. The night before, both men had seen Kwak half-carrying the director. Just then, Mr. Jeong seemed to glimpse Kwak standing outside the door, but Mr. Jeong quickly turned away, pretending he hadn't seen him.

Kwak scrambled back up to his room. All the tenants of Taegwang Building were witnesses. He opened his window and had a cigarette. He gazed down at the parking lot. A woman was peering into Kwak's car. She raised her head, looking toward his fifth-floor window with narrowed eyes. It was Ms. Jang from Good Chicken. Kwak hurriedly ducked out of sight. *That's strange. He never touches even a drop of liquor.* What she'd said the night before rang through his head.

The tenants of Taegwang Building met at the taekwondo studio on the fourth floor. They sat scattered around the padded floor.

Mr. Jeong said worriedly, "If the director doesn't show up tomorrow morning, our businesses are finished. He was the only one who could present our case to Mr. Kwak, but if he hasn't even called his wife . . . Anyway, since we're all here, why don't we go over who's bringing what tomorrow?"

"I'll fry up plenty of chicken," said Ms. Jang said. "I'll pack some soju and beer, too."

Mrs. Park scratched her head. "Then I'll take care of the rice, side dishes, and kimchi."

Mr. Jeong wrote down each item in his notepad.

"We'll use the school van, and I'll cover the gas," said Arnold. "And don't you worry about driving. I'll make sure we get to our destination in one piece."

He was flushed from the drink he'd had earlier with Mr. Jeong. He didn't stammer when he was drunk. Mr. Jeong checked all the items to make sure they hadn't left out anything.

"That's not important right now," Mrs. Park said. "What's going to happen to us?"

Ms. Jang let out a deep sigh. "Isn't it obvious? Mr. Kwak will sell this building. He's been going out a lot lately. Something's obviously up. The problem isn't if he's selling the building or not, but when."

Mrs. Park turned pale. "I couldn't sleep a wink last night. I spent all my savings on the renovation and now he's selling the building? And they're going to pull it all down to build an officetel? What about our security deposit? What about everything I spent on the renovation? I'm going to lose everything and be forced out on the street."

Mrs. Park pulled down her sleeve and wiped her face. Ms. Jang reached out to clasp her hand. Mrs. Park didn't shake off the younger woman's touch. Ms. Jang's face crumpled and wrinkles broke out across her features, but no tears fell. She couldn't remember the last time she had cried.

"But at least you've got kids," Ms. Jang said. "How about me? I've never had a baby. All I did was age. I fried chicken and put up with drunk men, so that I could build a client base, but they're going to tear down this building now? I wanted to buy a house in the country. I wanted to live out the rest of my life quietly. I paid the security deposit when I leased my shop, so shouldn't I get it back when I leave? Mr. Jeong, I guess you're in the same boat, because what's a pool hall without regulars?"

Regular customers were the lifeblood of pool halls. If they moved to a new location, they would have to start from scratch.

Arnold snickered all of a sudden. "All this headache because of one man! Is it fair we have to go through this because of one person? Is money really everything? Christ. We wouldn't have this problem if he just disappeared."

At his words, everyone's face turned pale. Miss Kim saw goose bumps appear on her own skin.

"After all, anyone could have an accident," muttered Arnold.

The girl read murder in their eyes. In every gaze lurked the sharp blade of an axe.

"That's right," said Mrs. Park and Ms. Jang together in a small voice. "Anyone could have an accident."

Miss Kim gripped her knees with both hands and made her body small.

Right then, the studio door opened and Kwak stepped inside. "I see you're making preparations for tomorrow?"

The gazes of all five people whipped to Kwak's face. He saw in each stricken face the embarrassment and hostility of someone whose secret had been discovered. Kwak didn't have the nerve to join them on the floor. It seemed the first stone would be cast at any second. Kwak tried to dispel the awkwardness in the air and laughed loudly.

"Don't bother taking any meat and liquor. It'll be hard lugging it up there. Why don't I call ahead and tell them to get everything ready?"

He felt as if they had shoved him out of the studio. He ran up to his room. He fastened all the locks on his door. He had cleaned up the broken glass, but the trophies were still lined up one side of the room, since he hadn't ordered the replacement glass. The tenants knew what had happened last night; he was sure of it. He sat on the floor and polished the trophies with a dry cloth. He made plans in his head for the following day.

They would head to the Bukhan River by car, unload at his cottage, and take the motorboat to the island. Since it was the weekend, the river would be swarming with water-skiers, but only Kwak knew where the island was. He and the tenants would get in the motorboat and it would flip on their way to the island. But he was worried about Arnold and Mr. Jeong, who had served in the navy. The trophies shone. No, the accident had to happen on their way back from the island. By then, everyone would be drunk. While they drank, he would slip away and rig the boat engine. He would hide his life vest in the boat, and right before the overheated engine exploded, he would jump into the water and put the life vest on. While everyone panicked, the boat would sink. The rough waters of the Bukhan River would swallow the boat and its passengers.

The tenants of Taegwang Building had gathered in one place. A sign on the door of Good Chicken said the shop would be closed for vacation. Ms. Jang was wearing large, dark sunglasses to hide the wrinkles around her eyes. Since she had woken early, she kept yawning. Mrs. Park's feet hurt from her new running shoes. Inside the cooler were marinated meat, vegetables, and ice. A plastic crate filled with soju and beer was loaded into the van. With his camera, Mr. Jeong from the pool hall snapped photos of Ms. Jang standing in the shade. Kwak pulled up next to the van in his luxury car. It was past nine in the morning, but the academy director still hadn't arrived. But they couldn't keep waiting for him. If they continued to delay, they would be stuck in traffic for hours.

"What a shame the director couldn't join us," Ms. Jang said.

To Kwak's ears, her words sounded like an accusation. He thought to himself, *Oh, don't you worry. He's coming with us.*

They decided to take a group picture with the van as a backdrop. To get everyone in the frame, they stopped a young man walking by on the street.

"Going on a trip? Lucky you!"

The passerby took the camera and backed up a few steps. Mr. Jeong, who was standing next to Ms. Jang, put his hand on her shoulder. The young man laughed. "How about a smile? Everyone looks so stiff! Say *kimchi*!"

They did as the young man said. They all opened their mouths and smiled awkwardly at the camera.

The
Woman
Next
Door

A new neighbor's moved into number 507. I'd just taken out the laundry and was about to hang it on the clothesline. The washer is junk now. Whenever it goes from *rinse* to *spin*, it gives a terrible groan and shudders, as if it might explode any second. Over the years, it's shifted about twenty centimeters from its original spot. Since it's done nothing except *wash*, *rinse*, and *spin* for ten years, no wonder it's in bad shape. I pat the top of the washer and mutter, "Yeongmi, I know you're tired, but let's get through it one last time." The washer wrings out the water and barely sounds its end-of-cycle buzzer.

Yeongmi is the name I've given the washer. It's also my name, though it doesn't get used a whole lot anymore. To a washing machine, the motor is the same as a heart. A repairman who once came to fix the washer said so. He'd said the motor's life had reached its limit. It managed to finish its job today, but I don't know how long I can keep it going this way.

Once my husband caught me talking to the washer. Seeing nobody else on the balcony, he'd asked, "What are you doing?" So I'd played dumb and said, "What does it look like? I'm doing the laundry." How can a banker who has to calculate sums down to the penny understand? If I'd told him the truth, he would have thought I was crazy. According to him, my head's stuck in the clouds. That's why I'm always floating around in space, never touching solid ground. If he knew I'd gone so far as to give the washing machine a name, he'd probably faint. "It's finally happened—a malfunction in your software." Eight years ago, I worked at a bank too. Back then I never thought I'd be talking to a washing machine one day. It's not that I have anything against my husband. It's good for a banker to act like a banker, isn't it?

The soy sauce stain on my son's shirt didn't come out. I forgot to soak it beforehand, that's why. When I sort what can be hung from what has to be re-washed, only one of my husband's dress shirts makes it to the clothesline. My husband says things that show how much he doesn't understand: "The washing machine does the laundry and the rice cooker cooks the rice, so what do you do all day?"

Movers are lifting furniture up to the fifth floor with a ladder hoist. There isn't much. After all, you don't need a whole lot to fill an 800-square-foot apartment. And don't get me wrong. I'm not the type to snoop around. But is it a crime to look? It's not like I'm spying on people with binoculars. All the furniture looks new. I can't stand shabby old things with peeling paint. The person who used to live in 507 brought cockroaches with him when he first moved in, and soon even our home became infested. It's natural for any woman who's been married a decade to eye new appliances, especially when her own are old and shabby.

The furniture may be new, but it's not for newlyweds, that's for sure. One look at the bed says it all. The mattress is standing on its side, but you can easily tell it's a single. This resident—obviously alone with these new things—who could it be? The appliances are the latest models: a washer with a transparent lid, an immaculate gas range, never-before lit. My gas range, which has to have its switch pressed several times before it lights up, can't hold a candle to that. Who is this person? If my husband were here, he'd say something for sure, like how I'm becoming nosy because I've got too much time on my hands.

•

"Hello."

Right away I know it's the new person in 507. She looks like she's in her late twenties. Or maybe even in her mid-thirties? Don't they say it's hard to guess a woman's age these days? In each hand is a large plastic bag from the department store two bus stops away. They look heavy—the plastic handles dig into her hands, creating purple welts. I'm in the middle of carrying my son's bike up to the fifth floor, which is the top floor. Our apartment complex doesn't have bicycle racks, because it was built back when I was in high school. Rumors of redevelopment have been floating around for the past ten years, but still, nothing. But my husband keeps insisting this apartment is a great investment. Since it was built so long ago, trying to find parking around here is madness. If they were to make room for bike racks, about two parking spots would have to go. So racks are out of the question. If I don't want my son's bike to get stolen, I have to carry it all the way up every time. It weighs at least twenty kilograms, more than my six-year-old son. He'd said he wanted to ride the bike, but he's already lost interest, and has been whining for a pair of rollerblades for the past few days. You can't just go buy anything a child asks for; you shouldn't spoil your kids. This is the only issue that my husband and I see eye-to-eye on. I have to hook the seat over my shoulder to carry the bike, and by the time I reach the second floor, my shoulder is stiff and sore. Then it's only curses and frustration that spur me on.

The woman must have come up behind me. She wouldn't have been able to pass because of the bicycle, but she doesn't look a bit annoyed. And then to have the patience to greet me, with her heavy bags and all—isn't that something? All I can do is bow awkwardly, hunched over. Cleaning products like scouring pads, rubber gloves, and a box of powdered detergent poke out from the bags. She opens her door while I'm chaining the bike to the stair railing and calls out, "Jal butak deuleo yo."

It's a rare thing to hear these days: I entrust myself to your care. I mean, isn't this something a new employee would say to her superior on her first day? But I'm not her boss, her elder, or even her landlord. I'm just her neighbor.

"You know, there's a supermarket nearby with a cheaper, better selection . . ." This is what I offer as a friendly greeting.

Jal butak deuleo yo. Soon enough, I would grasp the full meaning of these words.

My husband stops undoing his necktie and worries again. He says my reckless trust for strangers is as dangerous as a child alone by the water. He wasn't always like this. The bank he works for merged with another bank and as a result, many employees were laid off. He didn't lose his job, thank God, but he compared that uncertain period to the torture of hanging from an iron bar, trying not to fall. The generations that had to take mandatory P.E. exams in school know well the agony of doing chin-ups or hanging from a bar for a long time. The anxiety from those several months left a coin-sized bald spot on the crown of his head.

My husband seems uneasy that she lives alone. "Without a family of her own at her age—isn't it obvious what kind of woman she is?"

"But you'd see what I mean if you met her. She seems very down-to-earth. People like that are so rare these days."

I've said things like this before, but he's turned out to be right every time. Triumphant, he would then reproach me: "How can you be such a poor judge of character?"

"What does she do, anyway?"

Naturally I don't know a thing about her. While I set the dinner table, the words he spits out from the bathroom pierce my back like darts.

"You better not lend her any money."

•

Standing in front of a hot stove frying fish in 34-degree August heat is the worst. The dried corvinas I had put in the freezer all have their heads wrenched up. Some have burst bellies. It's because the ice trays had been thrust on top. Even fish don't turn out the way I want them to. The fish cook unevenly, since not all the parts are on the grill. Just as I'm flattening their raised heads with a spatula, the doorbell rings. It's the woman next door. She steps into the front hall, flicking her gaze around our apartment. I can't help feeling embarrassed, since everything is old and scratched up. My son's toy blocks and grimy stuffed animals are scattered all over the place, and what about the dingy wallpaper smeared with his fingerprints? Just then, the washer spins the laundry with agony, as if it's wringing its heart. But listen to this woman.

"Oh, everything is so cozy here! I don't know how long it's been. I used to live in a house like this. Pots with permanent stains . . ."

The warped drawers are hanging open, exposing their contents. To my shock, the woman heaves a sigh, pursing her lips to hold back tears. After gaining control of her emotions, she finally speaks.

"Is it okay for me to call you Onni?"

Big sister. I'm so flustered I forget to invite her in. She speaks again, as if she just recalled why she's come.

"I was wondering if I could borrow something . . ." She hesitates and then mumbles, "A spatula."

A spatula? I'm stunned once more. Although I've lived here for six years, no one's ever come to borrow a spatula. It's totally out of place, as foreign as, let's say, the name *Remington rifle*. Not once has a spatula come up in conversations with my husband. And would I ever need to mention it to my six-year-old son? So of course it would sound alien to my ears.

The woman points at my right hand. In my hand is the spatula I was flipping the corvinas with. Needless to say, I've also given it a name. Frying things can get so tedious sometimes. There's some greasy fish meat stuck on the end. I hurriedly flip over the corvinas and hand it to her.

"Thank you, I'll bring it back right away," she says apologetically.

A cheap 1000-won spatula with a burnt plastic end? I'm the one who feels bad. I call out to her as she's disappearing out the door. "Make sure you wash it first! It probably stinks like fish!"

Just that morning, my husband had looked at me, shaking his head. "You act like you know everything about her and you don't even know her name?"

Remembering his words, I rush out into the corridor in my bare feet. "By the way, what's your name?"

Her voice comes to me through her open front door. "It's Myeonghui!"

She seems to be in the kitchen, flipping something with the spatula. After a slight pause, she says, "*Myeong*, as in *bright*, and *Hui*, as in *feminine*. Myeonghui."

•

Myeonghui is a single, twenty-nine-year-old who teaches composition, four days a week, at an afterschool academy for elementary students.

"So did you learn anything about her?"

My husband's a little twisted sometimes. I'm not a detective and Myeonghui isn't a criminal. He mocks women's friendships. He says our friendships are like aluminum pots, boiling over one moment and turning cold the next.

There are still more than ten corvinas left from the bundle I'd bought. My son is already complaining it's always fish. It's only after I place one on the grill that I remember the spatula, but a ramen ladle is hanging from the spatula hook instead. I rummage through the shelves, but can't find it. The fish is starting to burn.

"Okay, okay. I'll flip you over, hold on a sec."

I lower the heat and even search the master bedroom. But there's no way the spatula could be there. I crawl on the kitchen floor, peering at the gaps between the floor and sink. My whole body is covered with sweat. My knees slip several times.

"Onni, it's me. Can I borrow the spatula again?"

Myeonghui, who's come in at some point, is gazing down at me. Spatulas aren't tiny like beans. So it would be impossible for it to fall in a crack, wouldn't it? I try to flip the corvina with a pair of metal chopsticks, but it breaks into two chunks.

Myeonghui doesn't ring the doorbell anymore. She tries the doorknob and if it's unlocked, she opens the door and lets herself in. I'm not so uptight. If someone opens up to me, I open up, too. Again last night, my husband said women were truly incomprehensible creatures. He asked how in the world we could have become so close in one week. I blurted, "As long as you're a banker, you'll never understand. You have no right to criticize her. Plus, you haven't even met her."

"Haven't met her? I carried a sack of rice up for her just now. This is ridiculous. You're actually defending a stranger you've known only seven days instead of the man you've been married to for ten years?"

"So what do you think? I'm right about her, aren't I?" I wanted my husband to like Myeonghui.

"How can you tell by just looking at the hardware?" he said with a smirk.

Obviously, Myeonghui hasn't returned the spatula after borrowing it the day before. So what's she talking about, asking to borrow it again? I don't want to accuse her of not returning a spatula that barely cost 1000 won. At the same time, it isn't good for boundaries to be so unclear from the start. Just as my husband says, you can't go trusting just anybody, right? Can I trust Myeonghui?

"Don't you remember, Onni? I returned it with some fried zucchini yesterday. You hung it right there on that hook."

The hook Myeonghui is pointing at is the same hook I always hang the spatula from. Seeing me so confused, she begins to laugh. Then she asks, "You've already brought in the laundry? You never sit still, do you?"

The clothesline on the balcony is bare. That's when I remember the laundry; I'd forgotten to take it out of the wash. I hurriedly open the washer lid. Inside, the clothes have dried into a clump. When I tug at my son's trousers, the other laundry follows, all strung together. Myeonghui laughs. I laugh, too.

Myeonghui brings me a present. She's wrapped it in pretty wrapping paper and even attached a bow. But I know what it is right away.

"Oh, Myeonghui."

I nearly cry. I sense my husband eavesdropping on our conversation; he'd been watching TV in the bedroom with the door closed, but the volume had been turned down all of a sudden. Myeonghui tells me to open it. It's a spatula. The part used for flipping is stainless steel and angled just the right amount to prevent your wrist from straining, and the handle is made of silicone to resist heat. I'd seen it at the department store, but hadn't bought it because it was too expensive.

"I was picking one up for myself and I thought of you, so I bought two."

How could I have suspected Myeonghui of not returning my spatula . . .

"But Onni—"

"What is it—do you need something?" Now I can just tell by her voice.

"I think my fluorescent light burned out, and something's wrong with the door, too. Can I borrow your screwdriver?"

•

It seems my forgetfulness is no laughing matter. In the morning Myeonghui came to borrow the screwdriver again. She'd returned it last night shortly after using it, but when I opened the toolbox inside the shoe cabinet, it wasn't there. I'd been on the phone at the time. I'm the type of person who can't do two things at once. I was the same way when I worked at the bank. Girls who could yak on the phone while punching numbers into a calculator or stamping receipts never ceased to amaze me. It'll probably turn up in the wardrobe or my son's toy box. Maybe I even tossed it in the trash. It happens all the time. You hold a piece of tissue you're planning to chuck in one hand and the car keys in the other. After tossing the keys in the garbage, it's only when you try to start the car with the tissue that you realize your mistake.

My husband calls me at lunchtime. He was waiting for his grilled tuna special to come out. It sounds like chaos inside the restaurant. Amid the stainless steel bowls clanking and crashing in the background, he raises his voice. "Why's there a screwdriver in my briefcase?"

There's no time to make excuses, for he calls out to the server, "Excuse me, there's lipstick on the cup. A new one, please!" Then in the next breath, "What else are you going to put in my bag tomorrow?

For God's sake, don't put Seonghwan in, because he'll just run around the bank all day."

For some reason, I'm the one who gets angry. "Seonghwan? What are you talking about—a new gum or brand of cigarettes?"

With the sound of his laughter, the line goes dead.

Seonghwan is our son. I feel as if I'm going to forget that, too. Right then I realize he still hasn't come back from kindergarten. He's usually home by 12:50, but it's already 1:20. I throw on my slippers and run down to the apartment entrance. In the playground under the blazing sun, my son is on the swing and the person pushing him is Myeonghui. Then I remember. Since yesterday, he's been out for summer break.

Myeonghui and I worry about my forgetfulness together. "Onni, stress might make it worse. Don't obsess over it."

But when I boil the kettle dry until it's scorched black, she seems to think the situation is a bit more serious.

"There's a famous poet who trains his memory. Why not use this chance to memorize the capitals around the world?"

I have trouble sleeping. At four in the morning, I get up and walk back and forth between the bedroom and kitchen to make sure I turned off the gas. Awakened by the rustling, my husband throws a fit. I lie down after making sure the gas is off, but I begin to suspect I've left the door open. When I get up and check, the door is locked.

Since I can't sleep well at night, I'm drowsy during the day. My son spends more and more time with Myeonghui. Occasionally their laughter seeps into my dreams.

Myeonghui and I usually run our errands together. She's given me a small upright shopping cart as a gift. She has the same one. We usually go to Huimang Shopping Center, which opened a year ago. Not even half a year later, the nearby supermarkets both small and large were forced to close. One or two survived, but it seems they're barely holding on by selling cigarettes or liquor late into the night.

When I'd told Myeonghui the first time I took her to Huimang, her response had been completely unexpected. I thought she would at least sympathize with the markets that were forced to close, but she'd just shrugged while examining the expiration date on a package of instant tripe-stew. "Onni, why do you shop here?" she'd asked.

Huimang's prices were cheaper, but more than anything, you got prize coupons—one for every 10,000 won you spent. When you collected a hundred coupons, you could redeem them for a pair of rollerblades. Rollerblades are the latest craze around our complex. The sight of my son, gliding about the apartment courtyard on rollerblades, dances before my eyes.

"See? It's survival of the fittest. There's nothing you can do."

The interior of Huimang is full of mirrors. Everything is ridiculously distorted in the bulging convex mirrors. In obscure spots, signs warn that shoplifters will be charged a hundred times the cost of the stolen item.

Myeonghui, who'd been picking out scouring pads, looks at me out of the corner of her eye. "Onni, isn't it hot?"

Although the air conditioning is running, it doesn't seem to be very effective.

"You want to cool down fast?"

Myeonghui slips the steel wool pad she'd been holding down my shirt. I can hardly breathe. I quickly glance around. Fortunately, the cashiers at the three registers are too busy punching in numbers.

Looking at my pale face, Myeonghui snickers. "Oh, don't be so uptight. It's just for fun."

Turning her back on the cashiers, she replaces the scouring pad from my shirt back onto the shelf.

"Not so hot anymore, right?"

She looks into the convex mirror and sweeps up strands of loose hair. "Those signs are there just to scare you. They're like scarecrows. But of course smart birds never fall for them."

My legs are still shaking even after we leave Huimang. "Have you ever stolen anything?" I ask.

"Only when I was really young. I used to work at a supermarket and I would see women who stole all the time, cheap things like scouring pads and gum, but I pretended I didn't see. If you make a scene over something like that, you'll only lose your customers. So even though you see them leave with things in their pockets, you just let them go. One lady would come dressed in a trench coat and steal big things like jars of honey. But these women were regulars who were responsible for most of the sales."

Myeonghui and I are like sisters. We're very open with each other and get along without any problems. We even play around like little kids. I don't talk to washing machines and spatulas anymore. But sometimes she's like a complete stranger. She's very different from me. Using the same spatula and same shopping cart don't make us the same. For one, she's very fashionable. She wouldn't be caught dead wearing things like sweatpants, even at home. Shuffling around in cheap flip-flops, shorts, and a stretched-out shirt—I can't compete with Myeonghui.

Yesterday, I saw my husband coming out of her apartment. I don't know when they became close. Naturally, she's started to call him Hyeongbu. Brother-in-law. This isn't so unusual, since she calls me Onni. He was holding a screwdriver. He said he'd just replaced her fluorescent light.

"Didn't you say women are like aluminum pots? Boiling over one moment and turning cold the next?"

There was no way my husband could have missed my sarcasm. But far from getting angry, he grinned and said, "The hardware, obviously, and the software seem pretty good. She even calls me Hyeongbu."

I'd been a little worried he might not like Myeonghui, so it's a good thing they're getting along.

The bathroom door is open a crack while I'm on the toilet. It's hardly the first time I've left the door open. My husband walks past and slams the door shut. I hear what he says. "No shame, I tell you!"

For someone who used to sneak peeks through the crack in the door, what does he mean by shame? It's not like I leave the bathroom door open and urinate in front of just any man. What more do I have to hide from a man I've lived with for ten years? There's nothing left to hide, like a pocket turned inside out.

Since it's bedtime, I'm just in my slip. The nights have been over 30 degrees Celsius for the past few days. With a cigarette clamped between his teeth, my husband asks, "Why do you always wear granny underwear? You know the kind with lace? Can't you wear those for a change?"

Lace lingerie . . . what could be less economical than those? You can't even put them in the washer. They need to be hand-washed, and if you're not careful, they'll snag and get ruined. So why would I start wearing expensive lingerie like that all of a sudden?

While replacing Myeonghui's light, he must have snuck a few peeks at her lingerie hung out on the balcony. I've seen them before, too. Delicate mesh slips like dragonfly wings, the material so fine they're easily hidden inside a fist. So what does he mean I have no shame? I've never hung my underwear in plain view and invited men inside the apartment.

Above the stove hangs a spatula. The same one hangs above Myeonghui's stove. I've named mine Myeonghui. I touch the spatula—the symbol of our friendship.

●

Myeonghui and my family are like one family now. Whenever I make stew or season greens, I make Myeonghui's, too. On some weekend nights, the three of us have a few drinks together. I don't know where she's heard such funny stories. She makes us laugh to the point of tears. She and my husband seem to understand each other well. They talk about stocks and shares, even mixing technical terms like *syndicate* and *franchise* in their conversations. As for me, I have no interest in that kind of talk. Eight years ago, I worked at the bank, too. Although I was never late or absent, I never became an exceptional teller. If they were to talk about how milk production doubled after letting cows listen to music, or how hard the vegetation in a forest must work to get sunlight, I'd also join in. But when my husband and Myeonghui talk about things I have no interest in, I make tea or peel melons, nodding occasionally, pretending to be paying attention.

•

I lost the house key. When leaving for Huimang, I was positive I'd locked the door. Myeonghui also remembers up to the point where I locked the door and twirled the key chain around my pinky. My forgetfulness is a big problem. Where could I have dropped it? I search the flowerbeds and walk all the way back to the store with my gaze glued to the ground, but I don't see it. While I stand anxiously in front of my door, Myeonghui calls the locksmith. The locksmith arrives on a motorcycle and takes less than two minutes to open the door for us. By then, my son's ice cream has melted in the grocery bag. He comes up from the playground and screams as he chucks the ice cream. "Stupid Mommy, stupid Mommy."

Sensing my anger, he darts off without slipping on his shoes. It's off to Myeonghui's again. He eyes me as he clings to the ends of her skirt, using her as a shield.

"Come here. You better come here by the time I count to three."

But even when I count to three *three* times, he doesn't budge. The tactic doesn't work anymore.

Myeonghui scolds him, purposely wearing an angry expression. "If you say something mean like that again, a horn will grow on your bum. You understand?"

My son's black pupils glitter in his grimy face.

"I'm serious. A boy I knew ended up with a horn *this* big on his bum!"

Left with no other choice, he reluctantly comes out from behind Myeonghui. Without looking at me, he mumbles as if he's reciting lines. "Mommy, I'm sorry. Please forgive me."

I don't know when Myeonghui's words began to carry more weight. I start to know, then don't know.

"What's going on inside that head? Take a good look in the mirror. No wonder you can't think straight. You look like a lunatic."

My husband changes the lock. Myeonghui seems more upset than me. I have to admit my feet look pretty filthy, with dirt between my toes and my cracked heels like a turtle's shell. Since I'd been running around in my flip-flops, there's no way they'd stay clean.

"Where's your head at? You're like a person playing with a ball, except without the actual ball."

My husband doesn't look me in the face anymore. Why does this man refuse to look at me?

•

Myeonghui thrusts something at me. She's even laminated it.

"I didn't know if I should. But you know how I feel . . ."

The capital of the United States is Washington, Canada is Ottawa, Australia is Canberra, Ethiopia is Addis Ababa, Burundi is Bujumbura . . . Tiny writing fills the whole page.

"A teacher from my school helped me. Better safe than sorry, right?"

Thinking of Myeonghui's efforts, I stick it on the fridge with a magnet.

My husband goes to get a drink and sees the list on the fridge.

"Addis Ababa? What the hell is this? Why do you waste your time on these stupid things? You retain such useless information that you end up forgetting the stuff you actually need. What are you planning to put in my briefcase today? What surprise do you have up your sleeve this time?"

My son, who had been lowering his chopsticks to the corvina, starts with fright and backs away.

"What is it? Did you find a hair or something?"

My gaze runs over the whole plate, but there's nothing wrong, except that the lower part of the fish is a bit burnt. He points at its mouth with the ends of his chopsticks. The tongue, fried in oil, is a dark gray. Pushed out of its mouth, it lies limply on the edge of the plate, looking like a fat caterpillar.

"I'm never going to eat fish again, Mommy. Auntie's fish doesn't look like this. I like nice fish."

I take out the rest of the corvinas from the freezer. My fingertips go nearly numb from tugging the fish out of the twine. All of them have their tongues sticking out. The tongues seem too large for fish. Why do they need tongues anyway? Not to taste or to talk. Are they only for pushing food into the esophagus, like the shovel of a bulldozer? The fish seem to be sticking them out only to taunt me. Stupid Yeongmi, stupid Yeongmi. I pull out each tongue and snip it off with scissors.

•

The owner of Huimang is watching me a little too closely. Even if she doesn't, I don't like her bulblike eyes that gleam with suspicion and nosiness. They're eyes that catch everything without seeming to, eyes that would light up like a 100-watt bulb with the flick of the switch. If it weren't for the prize coupons, if it weren't for the rollerblades, I wouldn't come here at all. Plus, I know she's cheating me with the scale. I get two kilograms of tomatoes from her. Then I go to the snack aisle to get crackers for my son. I can't help picking up and putting down various packages, since I try to find ones with less sugar. But the owner, who'd been sitting in the produce section, is suddenly behind me. As soon as our eyes meet, she retreats hastily back to produce. Then in another aisle, I'm putting a box of laundry detergent into the shopping cart when I glance back and meet the eyes of the owner once again. How could she be suspicious of someone like me? I hurriedly pay for my things and leave. If I just collect two more coupons, I can get the rollerblades.

Whenever I stand in front of the washer or fry fish, I now memorize the capital cities around the world. I've already memorized over fifty different capitals. I hope this works. I've replaced the kettle with a new one that whistles when the water starts to boil. The washer is struggling to do the spin cycle today. The theory behind washing machines is quite simple. *Spinning* uses centrifugal force. The repairman told me, so it should be right. The reason the drum, which can hold six and a half kilograms of laundry, doesn't fly out is because its protective box prevents it from escaping. But you never know if the washer that could no longer handle the centrifugal force would crash through the balcony window one day. Patting the washer lid, I whisper, "What happened? How did you come to this?"

It seems my husband and Myeonghui got off work at the same time. Through the window, I see them walking side by side as they cut across the apartment courtyard. They walk up to the entrance and stop. Then my husband turns and begins to walk toward the playground by himself. Myeonghui comes up to the fifth floor first. I hear her door open and close. Around ten minutes later, my husband rings our doorbell.

A couple of days ago, I'd heard her say to him, "I'd like to make a deposit of around ten million won at your bank. Could you help me choose a plan that comes with tax benefits and a high interest rate?"

She'd probably stopped by his bank to make the deposit. Considering his bank isn't even nearby, I should be grateful she went out of her way. That's probably why they ended up coming home together. And they probably pretended to come home separately, so that I wouldn't get suspicious. After all, my husband believes my head is full of daydreams, and he doesn't believe in friendships between women. I'm sure he's being careful so that my friendship with Myeonghui doesn't end over a small misunderstanding. But our friendship isn't like aluminum pots.

∙

My face in the bulging surveillance mirror looks distorted and ugly. Without makeup, it seems especially sallow, and because I didn't get enough sleep, my eyes are bloodshot. Just as my husband said, my mind really seems to be off in space. I feel as if I'm walking on sunken ground.

Myeonghui says it's just my nerves, but I'm certain the owner of Huimang is suspicious of me.

"Onni, try to relax. You're just being paranoid. I'm worried you're going to drive yourself crazy."

Is she right? Am I just paranoid? Myeonghui is looking inside the ice cream cooler with my son. She often gives him what he wants. Just a couple of days ago, she bought him a box of expensive cookies that came with a cheap toy, and slipped an ice cream cone in his hand. I keep telling her not to do that. I tell her it would only spoil him and create bad habits, but she doesn't listen.

I come to the aisle with household goods. A sign warns that stolen goods must be compensated a hundred times the original price. Myeonghui had called it a scarecrow. I laugh to myself and repeat what she'd said. I touch a steel wool pad the way she had. There isn't a single person in sight. Turning my back on the checkout counters, I quickly slip the scouring pad into my bra. I feel a thrill run down my spine. When I look behind me, the owner is glancing half-heartedly between the aisles.

"Hey Light Bulb Eyes! Catch me if you can. I'm right here!"

The owner doesn't scare me. To balance things out, I slip another scouring pad into the other side of my bra. My breasts become extremely full. I shine those breasts in the bulging mirror. If the owner is suspicious, she'd be running up to me by now, but no one has noticed. I guess Myeonghui is right. I'm just tense because I haven't been getting enough sleep.

Myeonghui approaches, pushing the shopping cart. My son holds her hand and in his other hand, there's a box of cookies that comes with a toy. If I get one more coupon, I can redeem all the coupons for a pair of rollerblades. As soon as I mention the rollerblades, my son begins to jump up and down with excitement. I pay for my things and collect the last coupon. As we're about to step out of the store, the owner blocks my path.

"I need to see everything inside your bag."

It's only then that I realize I'd forgotten to take the scouring pads out of my bra. I swear I didn't plan on stealing them. I have two new ones at home. It was only for fun.

"What kind of people do you take us for?" Myeonghui yells.

The people on the street look at us. We follow the owner back into the store. She hasn't noticed the scouring pads stuffed inside my bra, has she? She takes everything out of the bag and places it on the floor. One by one, she checks each item against the receipt. A crowd begins to form around us. They're all familiar faces. After all, I've lived in the neighborhood for six years.

Myeonghui says to the owner, "You're going to be sorry! You're accusing innocent people here!"

"Explain this pack of gum, then!" the owner cries, holding the gum up to my nose.

It's a pack of Juicy Fruit. I've never bought that gum before. Instead of me, it's Myeonghui who shouts.

"Do we look like people who would steal a measly pack of gum that costs three hundred won? Do you really want to kiss your business goodbye?"

The owner refuses to back down. My senses start to grow dim. Their voices buzz in my ears.

Myeonghui calls my husband. I don't know how she knows his work number by heart. My son, terrified, begins to cry. She clasps his hand and wipes away his tears.

I didn't steal that pack of gum. But I'm not sure if my hand grabbed it without me knowing. Sweat is running down my whole body. My skin begins to prickle and burn as the scouring pads chafe against my flesh; it might even start peeling.

My husband arrives. The dress shirt I had ironed this morning is a bit wrinkled, but seeing him away from home like this, he looks very smart. He shakes me, his hands clutching my shoulders. "Yeongmi! Yeongmi! What happened? Yeongmi, talk to me!"

I don't know why this man keeps calling my name like this. Surely, he doesn't think I've forgotten my own name.

Myeonghui starts to cry. "I don't know why Onni did it. It's all my fault."

My husband pats her shoulder. He doesn't even look at me. He's ashamed, no doubt. He's probably wishing he didn't know me. My husband is not the man I once knew. The shoppers glance at our faces as they pass by. I sink down beside the ice cream cooler and gaze blankly at my husband's face. He's talking to the owner. He and Myeonghui look like people who've known each other for a long time. When did they become this close? Isn't it women who turn hot and cold like aluminum pots?

"The capital of Austria is Vienna, Lebanon is Beirut, Lesotho is Maseru, Syria is Damascus . . ."

I don't know why I'm thinking of capitals right now. I start to mumble the words as they come to mind. I can't stop.

Myeonghui approaches. As soon as she bends toward me, she grimaces. Then I hear her. I hear the words she spits out, softly, like a curse.

"She's finally lost it."

I don't stop. My words build speed.

"Australia is Canberra, Burundi is Addis Ababa, America is Maseru, Austria is Washington, Japan is Kyoto . . ."

My memory is still pretty good. I recite smoothly without stopping.

Myeonghui cringes. Actually, it looks like a sneer. Why is she laughing at me like that?

Maybe Myeonghui never returned the spatula she borrowed from me. She may have put the screwdriver inside my husband's briefcase, since I keep his bag in the front hall cabinet. Anyone can burn the kettle and forget the wet laundry. Even our house key—she could have hidden it. One by one, I begin to recall all the things she's borrowed from me. This memorization exercise seems to be working.

Spatula, screwdriver, bottle opener, umbrella, key, garlic press . . .

Myeonghui, my husband, and Seonghwan look like one family. My husband and son—is she planning not to return them as well?

Myeonghui, the woman next door. Who is this stranger?

Flag

1

The power went out late last night, at ten past midnight. While people were still sleeping, the electrical appliances stopped working. The children who woke were cranky; they missed the hum of the refrigerator and the whir of the fan, sounds as comforting to them as a lullaby. Housewives who opened the refrigerator to prepare breakfast found blood dripping from the frozen pork they'd left to thaw, the meat turned a dark red. The ice cream bars had melted, leaving wrappers full of mush around the sticks, and the marinated spinach smelled sour. It gets so humid in July that food spoils in no time. Everyone was calling the 123 hotline.

Even up to the early eighties, power outages were common. Students cramming for their exams often studied by candlelight. Sometimes these candles caused fires. Since 1997, though, all this has become a thing of the past.

This outage wasn't widespread. The affected area was limited to Building D of Kwangmyeong Apartments and Towers 1, 2, and 3 of Rose Village. It could have been a worn-out line or even a bird perching on a high-voltage line. Birds on high-voltage lines are safe as long as they touch nothing else. But if they nod off and touch another line, *zap*, they're finished.

I looked at my map and checked the utility pole in question: #021/8619E. I stepped into the side street with the poles marked 8619E. The street went down a steep hill with a sixteen-meter pole every fifty meters. It wasn't yet ten, but the sun beat down, poised over the vents on the roof of Kwangmyeong Building A.

Preoccupied with reading the number tags on the poles, I reached the bottom of the hill before I knew it. Behind me were the eight poles I'd gone by. I had a habit of calculating the distance by counting poles. Three hundred fifty meters later, I finally stood before #021.

I used to work in Gyeonggi Province until they transferred me here. Back there, not a day went by without an outage. And the cause? Magpies. They would build their nests on top of the transformers and come in contact with the line, or a porcelain insulator would break off. Maybe to magpies, utility poles looked like oak trees, sturdy enough to hold nests that would last a lifetime. So not only did I replace transformers and repair lines, but I also had to move their nests into trees. But where would you find magpies here in the city? City children would never see a magpie except in a picture book about birds.

Climbing utility poles was a piece of cake. At my old technical high school, they called me Monkey Boy. We had to go up and down the fifty practice poles rigged up on the school grounds, and I set the speed record.

I strapped on my leather tool belt and was about to start climbing when I felt something spongy underfoot. It was a pair of black leather shoes, pooled with water. Though the backs were crushed in and the heels worn, the shoes were placed neatly together, as if they'd been removed by a front door. A drunk certainly didn't leave them behind. I felt a drop of water. Was the rain starting again? I looked up. About two meters off the ground, a suit jacket hung from the pole's first peg, water dripping from its hem. It had been raining on and off until early morning.

I climbed, my gaze locking onto each metal peg that zigzagged up the pole. The streetlight loomed above, staring down at me like a cyclops. High above the suit jacket on the other side of the pole hung a damp pair of men's trousers. On the next peg up, a white dress shirt with rolled-up sleeves flapped in the wind. The breeze must have dried it out during the night. Above that hung a sweat-stained undershirt and above that, a necktie, still knotted, as if it had simply been loosened before being removed. Next, I met a pair of socks swaying back and forth in front of my face like tired balloons. When I tilted my head back to look toward the top, I saw a pair of men's black pinstripe briefs, waving like a flag in the southeasterly wind.

He had taken off his shoes, hung his suit, and then removed the rest of his clothes one by one as he made his way up the pole. In the end, he'd even shed his briefs, hanging them at the very top. Sitting atop the pole without a stitch of clothing, he must have resembled Adam, the first man. He would have been tense, no doubt, taking care not to touch another line. This isn't something a drunk would dare attempt. Besides, the first peg was set far above me, and I'm pretty tall for a guy. I'm positive he was sober. Maybe he was from a technical school, too.

I climbed up past the two transformers and streetlight; the 6600-volt line now stretched below me. I loosened my tool belt and strapped myself to the pole. Luckily, the transformers hadn't burned out. It must have been the metal buckle from the belt; the wind must have brought it in contact with both lines and tripped the automatic shut-off.

The street was empty. There was an elementary school nearby; I could hear the pump organ and children singing. I climbed all the way to the top. I saw the street I'd walked down and the school playground, hidden by a stone wall until now. Little kids in sky-blue gym uniforms were doing sprints in time to a whistle. I leaned back in my harness, set my feet against the pole, and gazed down at the scene sixteen meters below, now laid out flat like a blueprint. In an apartment building across the street, a fifth-floor window opened and a young woman with long hair peered out. Our eyes met. Flustered, she disappeared and the window banged shut. The organ wheezed every time it hit a G. The children sang, or rather screeched, at the top of their lungs. With a fingertip, I lifted the fluttering pair of briefs from the pole. On my way down, I deactivated the shut-off. The man's clothes, which I had removed on my way up, now littered the ground.

The inside pocket of the suit jacket contained a small notebook. I searched his pockets, but found no wallet. The rain had soaked through the pocket lining and left yellow splotches on the notebook, making it look like an antique world map. The grid-lined pages were filled with dates and miniscule handwriting, which I had trouble making out because the ink had run. But one thing was clear—he led a busy life. Three whole pages were crammed with names and dates of birthdays and wedding anniversaries. The next section was left blank. He had then used the remaining pages for what seemed to be a journal, but in many places the wet pages clung together. I did my best to separate them, but they ended up torn. I eased myself against the pole and read, skipping the parts that were difficult to make out. From time to time, I tilted my head back and glanced up toward the top of the pole.

Having shed his skin, where could the man inside have gone?

2

APRIL 3

On a building rooftop, a huge billboard stands on two steel columns. *Paradise on Earth. Visit Hawaii Today.* A Hawaiian maiden smiles down at the street. She wears a floral-print bikini and a string of flowers around her neck—a lei, they call it. Spread out behind her is the Pacific Ocean, the water sparkling with the coral reefs below. Young men with tanned bodies ride surfboards, balanced precariously on pointy waves. I can almost taste the sweetness of the coconuts clustered at the top of the trees.

The bus moves in fits and starts. I stand clutching a plastic strap and look out the window at the billboard. My right hand is wedged between the rear ends of the people standing behind me. In that hand is a briefcase, and in the briefcase are catalogues with business cards stapled to the covers, along with some nicely packaged gum and candy. My arm went numb a while ago.

Every time the driver slams on the brakes, the women shriek. Every time the bus tilts, the breasts of the woman behind me rub against my back. Every time we come to a bus stop, I find myself pushed farther back by the new arrivals, and every time a body blocks my view out the window, I crane my neck to find an opening. When the next stop is announced, someone rushes for the door and bumps my head. My glasses are knocked loose and dangle crookedly off my nose. I don't mind, though.

Every day for the past two years, whenever I've passed through this congested area, I've looked up at that billboard. The advertisement was just one travel agency's ploy to entice tourists to Hawaii. The ad colors have faded from two years of exposure to the sun and the exhaust fumes of all the cars stuck in traffic. The paint is peeling and even the lei around the girl's neck has lost its luster. But her smile remains the same, just as it did two years ago when I first saw her. I've been looking up at her ever since, whether hunched up like a turtle in my down parka, peering over steamed up glasses, or oblivious to the rainwater trailing down my umbrella onto my shoes in the rainy season.

One day, that girl started to smile at me.

APRIL 29

The third Chrysler Korea dealership is located at a busy downtown corner. The sides facing the two main streets are fitted with enormous floor-to-ceiling glass. It's only when you get closer you see a little *enter* sign on the automatic sliding doors, like a tiny blemish. From sunrise to sunset, light spills in through the windows. As I wait for the crosswalk signal to turn green, I look across to where I work. The dealership looks like a greenhouse.

Whenever I sit at my desk, I can't help making eye contact with the people walking by on the street. There is a cluster of buildings nearby: City Hall, two department stores, a bus terminal, and several banks. Here, I can't even perform ordinary acts, like blowing my nose or tightening my belt. You never know when someone might be watching. The entire setup—the desks, chairs, every single flower-pot—revolves around the cars on display, not the people who work here. What amenities come to mind when you think of an office? Well, you won't find them here. Not a single picture hangs on the wall. You don't want people looking at art instead of the cars.

I polish the windows until it's time for the morning pep talk. A day doesn't pass without them getting dusty and smudged. In my three years here, I've mastered the art of cleaning windows. I've yet to figure out how to become a top-notch salesman, but I know if you wipe the glass with moistened newspaper and then remove the remaining moisture with a cloth, the glass becomes so clear a bird is likely to smash into it. The showroom window is as big as the screen at the Taehan or Piccadilly. Written high up in fancy swirls is the phrase *World-Class Luxury—Chrysler.*

Someone had thrown up outside the showroom window during the night. The backstreet around the corner is lined with small, windowless bars that have names like The Red Rose, Casablanca, Ruby, and Winter Wanderer. It must have been a customer from one of those places, trying to catch a taxi. There was vomit splattered all over the bottom of the window. I sprayed water onto the glass and carefully wiped away every last trace.

Inside the showroom, a luxury sedan is waxed to a brilliant luster. It sits on a round platform and there's a device underneath that makes it turn around and around all day long. The effect is amazing. Car buyers can't take their eyes off it, at least until it goes all the way around. For the price of that car, you could buy yourself a small apartment on the outskirts of Seoul. I've been here three whole years and I still haven't sold that Chrysler.

Maybe my luck will change today.

MAY 3

Sometimes when there's no one here, not even Miss Kim the receptionist, I'm the one who watches the office. Then I get up on the platform and climb into the driver's seat. Still wrapped in plastic, the genuine leather seats have the new-car smell and the gear stick moves smoothly. The shift knob, with an oak wood-grain finish, is the size of an egg and fits perfectly in my hand. I know every single word in the brochure for this car. A salesman has to know all there is to know about his product. When no one's around, I'll chant the phrases of the advertisement. "The ultimate high-speed driving experience—feel yourself become one with the road." There's even a gyroscope half-set into the dashboard. It turns constantly when the car is in motion, and the driver can almost feel the earth go around. Cream-colored airbags, front and side, for both driver and passenger. In my mind, those airbags have gone off over a hundred times.

The morning meeting starts before I can finish polishing the glass. Each day begins with a twenty-minute pep talk. This is the one time of day when all forty or so salesmen come together. After that, everyone's day ends at a different time. We stand in rows, dressed to kill. This meeting is for show, for other eyes only. For example, the average height of our forty plus salesmen is 178.6 centimeters and the women on their way to City Hall or the department store for work are sure to look. I hurry into the meeting and stand in the back.

Just before we hit the floor, we gather in the back lounge, which consists of two benches outside the men's bathroom. Here, you'll find everything you can't find in the rest of the dealership, like ashtrays and wastebaskets. You can have a smoke, learn the latest way to knot your tie, or drink coffee out of paper cups from a machine. Getting kicked out of a building by security for soliciting, or slipping brochures under windshield wipers at an underground parking lot, only to run into a salesman from another company who's doing the same thing—these are the kind of tales I get to hear while I fix my tie in the latest style and put mousse in my hair.

May 11

I recognized her right away.

I've always worked Sundays. We're supposed to take turns, but when their Sunday comes around, the other employees weasel their way out. And their excuse? Weddings or funerals. I've covered for them a few times, and now they just take it for granted. Not that I have a family or girlfriend to spend my Sundays with. And it's not a complete loss when I'm the only salesman working, because everyone who walks in is my customer. Once I even sold two compacts, and though my commission wasn't a whole lot, it was still pretty good. I raised the metal screens covering the 4,000-square-foot dealership and went inside. I flipped the switch for the platform and started buffing the windows. The morning flew by before I was even half-done.

I was breathing on the glass, scraping at a stain with my fingernail, when a woman's reflection fell across the showroom window. She had parked on the street right outside the showroom and was gazing at the car on the revolving platform as if in a trance. I hurried into the dealership, rolled down my sleeves, and put on my suit jacket. We'd been trained to dress neatly to keep up the reputation of Chrysler. She had on cat-eye sunglasses that looked really good on her slender face. In her arms was a Maltese sporting a red bow. The woman put her nose to the window and peered at the car. She was so close to the glass it kept fogging up. She chewed her bottom lip. It seemed she was having trouble deciding whether to come in or not. She took a step toward the entrance and the doors slid open. She took a step back and the doors slid shut. I shuffled some papers at my desk and tried to look busy. The doors kept opening and closing. Finally, she came in and took off her sunglasses.

"Hello, may I help you?"

My voice, resonating with confidence, sounded good even to my own ears. I picked up that little trick, listening to the other salesmen speak in their deep, polished tones.

The woman had an unusual way of walking: only her hips moved, while everything above seemed to hover motionless, like a vision floating on air. Her face was very familiar. I may not be a top-notch salesman, but I know the basics. The number one rule about selling is having a good memory. Before I knew it, I was pointing my finger at her, practically shouting.

"'Paradise on Earth. Visit Hawaii Today.' That's you, isn't it?"

She was the Hawaiian maiden on the billboard. There was no way I wouldn't recognize a face I'd stared at for a good ten minutes every day. Faith can move mountains, as they say, and the girl from the billboard had taken pity on me and decided to honor me with a visit. I'm embarrassed to admit it, but that's what I was thinking. She gave a sheepish smile.

"Someone actually recognized me. And I'm not even famous."

It really was her—the Hawaiian maiden in the flesh. But unlike the brown-skinned model on the billboard, the woman before me was fair. I had imagined someone short and plump, but she was my height and so thin her cheekbones stuck out. The billboard artist had painted a more voluptuous version of the actual woman. She smiled brightly at me, just as she had from the billboard. She drew closer to the car and ran her palm along the curve of the hood.

"It's beautiful," she mumbled, as though to herself.

"Would you like to sit behind the wheel?"

She hesitated a bit, but then handed me her dog and climbed in. The car continued to rotate with the woman at the wheel. She pressed the buttons on the dashboard, one by one. The windows went up and down, the driver's seat moved back and forth. Each time the car came back around, I could see her examining every last feature.

"So, what's Hawaii like? Is it really paradise on earth?"

"There were too many people and a pickpocket stole all my money," she said breezily as she turned the steering wheel.

She opened the mini fridge in the backseat and even pulled out the ashtrays. Meanwhile, her dog licked my tie. I sensed she wasn't going to buy the car. From my three years of experience, I'd learned enough to tell the difference between someone who was serious about buying and someone who wasn't. We called it "getting the vibe." I wasn't getting the vibe this time. Or was I wrong?

"I'll think about it."

She took her dog back and stepped out of the dealership. Even when she was standing outside, she peered into the showroom window a few more times. She headed to her own car. It was a Le Mans GTI, a model discontinued in 1995. The car accelerated out of sight.

MAY 26

I was outside, polishing the showroom window, but the manager must have been watching me for a while. Before stepping inside, he said, "You know, being good at cleaning windows isn't everything." I made a note to myself.

MAY 28

I saw her again today.

I got off at Seoul Station and took a cab to the Hilton. The Namsan Loop was filled with couples taking romantic strolls. The young taxi driver kept straddling the median line because he was looking out the window so much. Thinking I should make a trip to the bathroom before heading up to the eleventh floor, I wandered here and there until I ended up on the basement floor. Stage lighting escaped through the open door and illuminated the wall in front of me. In the spacious lobby, which was labeled the Crystal Ballroom, a poster announced "Yi Kangja Fall/Winter Collection." The ticket table was deserted. I stood by the door and glanced into the ballroom. People watched the fashion show, while dining at round tables draped in white tablecloths. Under the brilliance of the stage lights, models walked out in time to the music. They struck a pose at the front of the T-shaped catwalk, turned, and strutted back. All wore dark eye shadow, similar to the kind of makeup a singer named Kimera had sported—was it ten years ago she'd come to Korea? The fall line ended and winter wear appeared, displaying leather and fur.

She had on heavy eye makeup, but this time, too, I recognized her right away. A silver fox-fur coat came down to her ankles. I recalled what a customer had once told me. If a fox suffers high stress levels, the fur loses its sheen. And so, electrocution is the preferred method, since foxes have to be put to death in a way that doesn't damage the pelt. Her coat shimmered under the blue stage lights. She was mesmerizing. I asked a staff member near me what her name was.

"You don't know Yi Minjae? She's a top model these days."

When I got to the eleventh floor, I was an hour late. I knocked on the door of Suite 1105. I tried the handle, but it was locked. It seemed the middle-aged woman who had introduced herself as Mrs. Han had gotten tired of waiting and gone home. When I thought hard, I recalled her mentioning her husband was returning from the United States either yesterday or the day before. She had told me many times not to be late. I lost my chance to sell the car on the platform.

JUNE 3

I must have walked a total of at least five blocks. It's been days since I planned to replace the soles of my shoes, but I still haven't had a chance to get to a repair shop. For the last three years, I've bought more shoes than I've sold cars. I was working an underground parking lot, slipping car brochures under windshield wipers, and was just coming up to ground level when my cell phone rang. It was Sanghyeok.

"Man, it's been a long time. You remember me, right? The one with the zit face, always getting in trouble? The student rep even shaved a cross on my head a couple of times. Ha ha ha, I guess only an idiot wouldn't remember me. Anyway, Seongjin gave me your number."

Sanghyeok said he was getting married the day after tomorrow. Friendly threats spewed from the phone. I had no excuse since it was a holiday; if I didn't show up, our friendship was over. After I hung up, I realized I hadn't seen Sanghyeok for over ten years. The last time was probably at our high school graduation, but I couldn't recall his face. As if there wasn't more than one kid with bad skin and bad haircuts.

At Sanghyeok's wedding, we didn't stick around for pictures and headed to a bar. The drinking continued even after the bride and groom left for the airport.

"Hey, Seongjin, long time no see. It's already been a year since I saw you, right?"

Seongjin seemed to have kept in touch with our high school buddies. A chunky guy squeezed in next to me. I was watching the music video of "Thriller" on the wall TV. Michael Jackson, made up like a zombie, was dancing with other zombies and prowling the night streets. I tried to sing along, but couldn't remember the lyrics. Suddenly, Chunky smacked me in the back of the head.

"You retarded or what?"

The glass I'd been holding tipped over and I spilled beer on my crotch. Feeling my head, I looked up, but just like with Sanghyeok, I didn't recall his face.

"You probably don't recognize me, because I put on a shitload of weight."

He stayed glued to my side and bullied me into remembering him, telling one anecdote after another of the trouble he'd caused in high school.

"All coming back now, isn't it? Oh, this one you'll really remember," he'd say, smacking me in the head every now and then.

Our group dwindled as we hopped bars for more rounds until it was just the eight of us.

"Leave the finishing touch to me," said Chunky. "Trust me, you won't believe this place."

We hailed two cabs and crossed the Han River Bridge. We climbed out of the cabs and walked down a backstreet, stopping in front of a yellow sign that said HERE'S LOOKING AT YOU. This sign would stay in my mind long after I had sobered up the next morning, like a road sign at a dead end. A metal screen was pulled over the door, but when Chunky rattled the screen, a man let us in. We swarmed down the stairs. The ones in front tripped and fell. We laughed and talked boisterously like a group of high school boys. The hall was lined with frosted glass doors. We surged into one of the rooms. A panoramic photo still from *Casablanca* covered the far wall. Chunky draped his arm around a girl who had hurried into the room and hollered for Madam Kim. An enormous middle-aged woman came in, swinging her breasts. The flesh spilling out of her clothes was like lard. Her thighs, wrapped in black fishnet stockings, showed through the high slit in her skirt, and her flesh bulged from the stockings in diamond patterns. Right then, girls crowded into the room. As the disco ball spun, fragments of light fell on the large table. A girl who had climbed onto it grabbed my hand and tried to pull me up. As I was trying to stand, something like a hammer hit me in the back of the head. I collapsed onto the table.

When I finally woke from a raging thirst, I found myself in a small hotel room, with Chunky snoring beside me. The rest of the guys were also passed out in their wrinkled suits, piled up on top of each other. Their snores sounded like a chorus sung by a group of off-beat, tone-deaf children. I went into the bathroom and drank straight from the tap. My mind cleared a bit only after I had washed my face with cold water. The room wasn't big, but it was clean. My head throbbed. I felt it and found some gauze stuck on it.

In the dark, I found Seongjin and shook him awake. He rummaged through Chunky's suit pocket and took out a pack of cigarettes and two 10,000-won bills. We found our shoes and stepped out into the hall. The plush carpet, the color of red bean soup, absorbed the sound of our footsteps. Just then the elevator doors opened and a couple stumbled out. A drunk, balding, middle-aged man leaned heavily on a woman, his arm slung around her shoulders, as she led him down the hall in search of a room. The woman had on cat-eye sunglasses. Sunglasses in the middle of the night? Though their backs were turned, I could see everything in the full-length mirror before me. I recognized her, even in the dim light. It was Yi Minjae.

Right outside the hotel, an aging janitor was lugging a heavy cleaning cart to sweep away our vomit from the night before. Across the street was the Han River. We sat along the riverbank and had a cigarette.

"My God, we're turning thirty next year—can you believe we're still at it? Maybe the night's to blame. Or maybe we're just used to living like this? I guess old habits die hard."

The voice traveling up my vocal chords was not my normal voice; it was the deep salesman voice I used when talking to customers.

Seongjin's laughter mixed with the sound of the water. "Hey, you sure nothing went wrong after Jaebeom threw that pint glass at your head?"

I smoked my cigarette to the filter. "You mean Chunky?"

Seongjin lit another cigarette for me. "So you finally remember? He was so pissed you didn't recognize him. Said he knew a way to make it all come back. Man, we got so wasted."

We used Chunky's money to have some soup to cure our hangovers and said goodbye.

The early morning bus sped along with three passengers on board. The billboard appeared in the distance. We quickly passed it. I twisted around, draping my arm over the back of the seat, and watched the ad grow smaller. The bus stopped, waiting to turn left. Right then, I saw the maiden's pupils move. It seemed she was cautiously looking for someone, afraid of drawing attention. Her pupils moved ceaselessly like rolling marbles until they froze at a certain spot in the intersection. Our eyes met. Then she smiled brightly at me. What? How could a woman in a picture smile? I blinked hard and shook my head. Was it because of last night, because I'd been hit in the head? The bus went around the building. When I looked up again at the billboard, she was gone. All that remained was a white silhouette, as if someone had cut her out from the ad.

My front door was cracked open. I was positive I had locked it. I had even turned the handle to double-check. There was water on the tiles, and the smell of the sea lingered in the air. Nothing was leaking or dripping. I peered at the water marks. They were wet footprints.

There were wet prints also on the living room floor. I placed my foot on top of a footprint. They were made by a person with small feet. The water seeped into my sock. The footprints led to the master bedroom. I gently pushed open the door. A woman was lying facedown on my bed. Her tanned back gave off a purplish tint, and every breath made her shoulder blades stand out sharply and then go flat. She turned over, breathing heavily. Her long hair was plastered to her face like ivy, but there was no mistaking who she was. It was Yi Minjae.

Yi Minjae slept for a long time. I went out into the living room and waited for her to wake. I didn't think it strange that she was in my apartment, sleeping in my bedroom. She came out into the living room. Her eyes were a little puffy, but it was definitely her. She walked toward me, moving her hips in her peculiar way.

"I don't know what kind of woman you are."

I was a bit angry because of what I'd seen at the hotel.

"I'm not Yi Minjae," she said with a bright smile. "I'm the woman on the billboard you see every day. Come with me. Just promise you won't grow tired of my smile."

Yi Minjae, I mean, the woman on the billboard, stroked my shoulder.

It was the bus driver who shook me awake.

JULY 18

I raised the metal screens and stepped into the dealership. I flipped the switch for the platform and went to the bathroom to get some water to clean the showroom window. During the night, someone had thrown up by the window. I filled the spray bottle and was stepping out of the bathroom when I saw somebody sitting in the driver's seat of the car on the platform. It was Yi Minjae. Her hair was dyed blond and came down to her shoulders. She looked like a Barbie doll. She saw me and smiled brightly.

I got the vibe as soon as I saw her face. "So, you've made up your mind?"

"Do you think we could test drive it?"

"We sure can, Miss Yi. I'll go get the key."

She had moved into the passenger's seat and was examining the glove compartment. I climbed into the driver's seat. As soon as I started the car, the dashboard lit up and the gyroscope began to turn.

"By the way, the fox-fur coat looked really good on you."

"You mean you came to the show? I didn't think you'd be into something like that."

"Oh, I just happened to see it. But that isn't the only place I saw you. I saw you somewhere else, too."

Her face stiffened right away. "Careful now, don't mess with me. You want to sell this car, don't you? Then just open the showroom window so we can go."

"Sure thing, Miss Yi. All clear for takeoff."

I stepped on the gas. It was only after the front wheels had come down the platform that I remembered the window. I first needed to disable the window sensor, but I'd forgotten the glass was there, because it was too clean. It was my fault for polishing the windows so much. The car went right through and shattered the huge pane. There wasn't enough time to step on the brakes. Glass poured down the roof of the car and Yi Minjae shrieked as she covered her face with her hands. The car hurtled across the sidewalk and crashed into a streetlight. With the blare of the horn, my vision turned white.

When I came to my senses, my face was wrapped in the airbags that had deployed from the front and side. The airbags were cream-colored, just like in the brochure. Then I remembered Yi Minjae in the passenger seat. Her face, too, was wrapped in the airbags.

Yi Minjae fractured her collarbone from the force of the airbags. When I went to see her, she was in a neck brace, watching TV in a half-reclining position. As soon as she saw me, she started screaming and hurled the bouquet of roses I had brought.

Because the demo car was insured, Yi Minjae's medical bills and the cost of replacing the bumper were covered. But I had again lost my chance to sell that car.

It's congested here as always, and like any other day, I look up at the maiden on the billboard. The next stop is announced. Someone rushes for the door, bumps my head, and knocks my glasses to the floor. People step on them as they swarm toward the door. The left lens cracks into five pieces, but I don't mind. Through the cracked lens, I now see five maidens.

3

The rain-soaked suit shrank as it dried. I folded all the clothes into a neat pile and stored them in a cardboard box. The shoes had started to mildew, so I tossed them into a recycling box. I tacked a note on the electric pole the man had climbed: "Whoever is looking for his suit and personal belongings, please make all inquiries to the following address: Taegwang Apartments, A207. Tel: 345-2100."

Once in a while, I would receive a prank call, but as time passed, even the prank calls stopped. I walked by the pole and saw that an art school ad covered my note. To keep my note out of everyone's reach, I climbed the pole once more. At the very top, I placed the paper with my contact info and climbed down.

I started to pay closer attention to the calls my company received. I thought he might try climbing a pole again and set off another power outage. But they were usually inquiries concerning bills and payments. Blackouts were rare in 1997, but even more so in 1999. When I go out to eat or find myself downtown and notice extremely clean windows, I have an urge to go inside. If I wanted to, I could walk inside and introduce myself to the man working in the restaurant or shoe store. Recently I saw his shoes again—the pair I had thrown out. A Filipino man picking up the recycling bins was wearing them.

I'm still waiting for his phone call. But I know a snake that has shed its skin doesn't come back for what it has left behind.

My habit of calculating the distance by counting electric poles has been replaced by the impulse to climb to the top of a pole. I, too, want to place something of my own there. But so far, I've managed to fight that urge.

Your
Rearview
Mirror

He stands on one of the twenty round display pedestals spaced throughout the department store. To his left is a Marilyn Monroe, wearing a see-through blouse and flowing skirt over layers of petticoat, and to his right is another Monroe, wearing a loose, black dress like those once worn by pilgrim women. The Monroes are striking the famous pose, the one where the actress tries to hold her skirt down as it flies up, ballooned by the gush of air from a New York subway vent. The Monroes were born in an injection-mold factory in Guro. Their heels are raised, and thick screws are drilled into their feet, fastened tightly to the pedestals. Positioned between the mannequins, the man listens to the same music all day. The top-40 hits are on repeat and will play nonstop until closing time. It takes forty-five to fifty minutes for the same song to come on again, but there's no way to tell which track begins the album. At one point, his ears have started to pick up the lyrics to the hip hop and dance tracks that had initially only sounded like noise.

Between his feet are the holes the screws have left behind. In order to take the mannequins down to change their clothes, the screws had to be constantly loosened and tightened, which ended up stripping the holes and making the screws go right through. This pedestal, now useless, was assigned as his post. So he stands on his platform, just like the Monroes who stand atop theirs along the edge of the store, dressed in the latest fashion. He no longer places his feet where the screws had once been after he began to feel as if they were still there, piercing his feet. When the song that had been playing when he first climbed on comes on again, it's time for his break. For ten minutes, he can stretch, go to the bathroom, or drink coffee from the machine to chase away his drowsiness. He wipes his sunglasses with a piece of tissue. It's dusty inside the store. In the fall, bits of thread cling to his pants from the static.

He has spent the last two years on this cheap, plywood pedestal. During that time, it has snapped four times under his weight. From it, he has a clear view of the entire 3,600-square-foot Cosmos Shopping Center. It sells mostly clothing, but there are other businesses tucked inside the department store, such as a music store and a gift shop. In the middle of the man's field of vision is the main apparel section. Garments that resemble the robes of an emperor hang from shiny, stainless-steel racks. What appears neat and straight at ground level looks crooked from above.

There are surveillance cameras around the store that slowly turn left and right. Three monitors placed before the man play images captured by these cameras, but there are certain areas that don't show up, like right below the cameras, or to the left of the camera when it's facing right or to the right when it's facing left. He calls these the *blind spots*. Blind spots in a car's rearview mirror create a great deal of problems for new drivers. They're usually the cause of accidents that occur when a driver suddenly slams on the brakes or changes lanes. Even with a curved rearview mirror, some spots still don't show up. To avoid this problem, the man stuck a small convex mirror called a *blind-spot rearview mirror* to his side mirrors. But drivers aren't the only ones to experience blind spots. They're created wherever there is light and shadow. At the store, everyone calls him Mirror Man.

Cosmos Shopping Center is situated at the heart of Myeongdong. Every day, hundreds of customers surge in and out. From his vantage point, he observes the scene with folded arms. On the opposite side of the entrance, his coworker, Jeong, stands on another pedestal. The man's mirrored sunglasses reflect a different scene each time he turns his head. Pillars, clothes pinned up like butterfly specimens, garment racks, the tops of people's heads as they shuffle through aisles—these reflections flit by on his lenses like a panorama. His gaze is about to move on to the gift shop when it's pulled back to apparel. The image of a woman hovers over his sunglasses.

With her back to him, she looks up at a gray dress mounted on a pillar, its sleeves and pleated skirt spread out to display its shape. The woman's own dress, made of spandex, hugs the curve of her small bottom. She has a long waist and neck, and not an ounce of fat on her body. He glances over at the mannequins. Unlike these, which strike the same pose all year round, the woman doesn't stop moving. A strand of hair falls over her forehead; she tucks it behind her ear, and moves her head in time to the dance track. The gray dress she's admiring is the biggest fashion trend these days.

Last year, it was all about the "sheer" look. Clothes made of material like dragonfly wings had glittered like fish scales under the lighting, hurting his eyes. Now, gray drawstring pants and pleated skirts have started to take over the store, and the "dragonfly-wing" clothes have been banished to the clearance rack on one side of the store, sporting *40% sale* tags.

The woman walks slowly to the shoe section, her gaze drifting over the display. She picks up a shoe and examines the sole. She then goes into the lingerie section and flips through the sales rack, and walks around the whole store, only to come back to the pillar with the gray dress. There's something odd about her that he can't pinpoint—she sticks out from the rest of the shoppers, like a triangle among squares. She strolls around the store again. Her gaze moves over objects absentmindedly, and her gait is as leisurely as someone going for a walk, except she always ends in front of the same pillar, like a mountain climber circling the mountain slowly on her way to the top. She stands before the gray dress as if in a trance, and then quickly glances around the store. The man looks away toward the music store. When she turns her head back toward the dress, he fixes his gaze on her once more. She moves away from the pillar. This is all she has done while the same song came on twice. She buys nothing. Instead, she looks at her watch as if she has just remembered something and then rushes out the door.

She comes back when every trace of sheer clothing has disappeared from the store, and the whole floor is a sea of gray. It's been nearly a month. It's the same day midterm exams are over for middle-school students, and the store, as well as the streets, is swarming with girls in uniform. The automatic doors stay open, without having a chance to shut. Girls wearing backpacks and holding corn dogs smothered in ketchup head toward the gift shop. The man's eyes move after them. Most items tend to disappear at times like these. He feels uneasy about the girl with dirty running shoes, who's chewing gum and standing by herself before a CD rack. She picks up a CD and puts it down, not budging from the spot. She blows a bubble and it pops, sticking to the side of her mouth. She unsticks the gum with her tongue, pushes it into her mouth, and chews so hard her jaws shake.

But there are too many girls to watch just one. He even skips his ten-minute break. For lunch, he has some instant noodles at a food cart and then returns to his post.

There are some girls in the lingerie section who seem suspicious. With their backs turned, they stand close together, whispering and exchanging furtive looks and smiles. Underwear takes up so little room and is frequently stolen. He looks at the monitors, but he can't see what's in front of the girls. They're standing in a blind spot. He glances toward the music section, but the girl who'd been standing before the CD rack is gone. His gaze moves over the whole store for her and then freezes on the pillar with the gray dress. He recognizes the woman at once. Just as she had a month ago, she looks up at the dress, as if in a trance. She stands close to the pillar, getting jostled and shoved by the students. A careless girl smears ketchup from her corn dog onto the woman's back, but the woman doesn't even notice. She doesn't seem interested in anything else. As the crowd sweeps her along, she glances absentmindedly at the other objects. He keeps losing sight of her in the crowd, but she's easy to find among the clusters of short, dumpy girls in uniform. She glances at her watch and hurries to the cashier. A long line stretches from the sales counter. Even while she waits, she keeps turning to look at the dress. She places two strapless bras shaped like seashells on the counter.

He walks toward the pillar. The whole store is empty; it's past closing time and everyone is gone for the day. There is still a warmth in the air, and the noise that filled the store all day rings in his ears. The gray dress is nothing special. If it had a unique design, one of the Monroes would have it on. He doesn't understand what the woman likes about the dress. A price tag stamped with the Cosmos logo dangles on the inside of the dress. The price is half of what he makes in a month.

The automatic doors open and the smell of rain drifts in. The rain is coming down so hard it splashes in through the open doors. Cold air hits the hems of his pants. The doors don't close. He climbs down to examine the sensor and sees her standing right out front. Wet hair sticks to her face like squid legs, and her long skirt, which her umbrella couldn't completely shield, is soaked up to her thighs. She sweeps up her loose hair, gathers the ends of her skirt, and wrings out the rainwater. It's right after opening time, and because of the rain, there are no other customers. The employees, dressed in their blue uniforms, have left their stations and are drinking coffee together in a corner.

Once the woman has passed the music store and lingerie section, she stands before the pillar, just as he expected. Her wet clothes cling to her body, accentuating her thinness. She slowly looks around the store. Her gaze stops on his face for a moment and moves on. Because there are no customers, Jeong isn't at his usual spot and is standing in front of a salesgirl instead, telling jokes with exaggerated gestures. A violin piece called "Zigeunerweisen" is playing. The woman traces her steps. She passes the lingerie section and stops in front of the CD rack. The violin melody is leading up to the "The Gypsy Bridge" section, the finest part of the entire piece. The rack is filled with CDs arranged in alphabetical order. She turns slowly, a hand brushing over the album covers. Suddenly, there is a disc in that hand. She joins her inner wrists together and crosses them to form an X. She drops, and then raises them, while rotating her hands at the wrists. At first, he sees what looks like ten, twenty hands spinning in the air, then a blur, like the whirling blades of a fan. He holds his breath, watching her hands slow down and speed up, in time to the violin. Then, like a flower bud unfurling, her fists open slowly, pinkies first, and the CD that had just been in her hands is gone; her empty white palms gleam under the fluorescent light. Everything happened so fast—the instant it takes for a sword to slice through the air, for a dragonfly to light on a blade of grass and then take off. The violin melody is still at "The Gypsy Bridge" part, but for him, it feels as if ten years have passed through his body. His eyes dart around the store. The salesgirls are gathered around Jeong; his voice rings out and a few girls laugh hysterically as if they're about to collapse. The automatic doors open. The woman pulls out her umbrella from the stand. The umbrella opens. She steps out into the rain. The doors close. She heads toward Myeongdong Station and disappears from view.

Only after she's gone does the man realize the CD at the top of the rack is missing.

She comes to the store every twenty-eight days. Each time, she lingers by the pillar with the gray dress and each time, she steals something. A pair of hairpins embedded with tiny pieces of cubic zirconia. A rayon scarf. A handkerchief. A pair of socks. But he pretends he doesn't notice, and so she keeps coming back. In his pocketbook, he marks the days she comes. If his calculations are correct, she should come in today.

Because final exams were held that morning, the store is packed with schoolgirls even before lunchtime.

"Why the hell are there so many exams?" Jeong mutters.

From their pedestals, Jeong and the man scan the store, their arms folded across their chests. Because the girls have swarmed in at once, the store roils like the inside of a boiling kettle. Jeong gives a low whistle. One whistle meant something was fishy and repeated whistling meant there was evidence. Jeong motions with his chin. The man looks, thinking it's probably a schoolgirl, but it's the woman. She's at the pillar again. This time, though, a salesgirl is handing her the gray dress that had been displayed on the pillar. The woman disappears behind the changing room curtain. Shortly after, she steps out in the gray dress. It fits her perfectly, as if it had been custom-made for her. She turns slowly before the full-length mirror, studying her reflection. "Wow, you look like a model." The salesgirl fusses over her. The woman points at one of the Monroes. The salesgirl brings the same outfit the mannequin is wearing and the woman goes back into the changing room again. She can't seem to make up her mind.

The clothes she tries on pile up on the rack. As the salesgirl removes yet another garment from its hanger, she begins to look annoyed. Just then, another young woman asks the salesgirl a question, and smiling again, she goes to help the new customer.

The woman disappears into the changing room once more, but when she comes out, she isn't dressed in her own clothes. Instead, she is wearing the gray dress. She moves toward the store entrance, weaving through the people walking in. The man hears Jeong's rapid whistles. Just as the automatic doors open and the woman's body is about to slip through, he steps in front of her. He has no other choice but to seize her, since Jeong caught her red-handed, and the dress is considered to be valuable. He slips a hand under her arm. Underneath the thin material of the dress, her skin is warm and soft. She tries to shakes off his grip, but soon stops struggling and follows him without a word.

On the shelves are piles of defective products that need to be sent back to the factory, as well as garments that customers have asked to be mended. The clothes smell musty. The woman sneezes as soon as they enter the storage room. The rainy season hasn't started, but it rains often, and there is white mold growing on clothes placed near the ground. They're probably crawling with vermin invisible to the eye. Naked mannequins are heaped behind boxes, their torsos, arms, and legs all separated; not even one is properly assembled. In the past, he has assembled countless mannequins and has even helped the salespeople dress them. It was harder to change clothes on the Monroe mannequins than the other ones, which frustrated the employees. But the Monroes catch the customers' attention. Once the man has even danced with a mannequin for fun, holding it close to him, but he'd felt its cold, rigid body every time he moved. The man releases his hold on the woman.

"You saw the warning, didn't you?" His voice echoes in the room. "Shoplifters will be charged fifty times the cost of the stolen item."

She doesn't reply.

"I'm sure you've seen it. I'm afraid I can't let it go. Not this time. Plus, my colleague caught you in the act."

She flinches.

"Why'd you do it? But I guess if nobody ever stole anything, I'd be out of a job. Who can I call?"

Still she doesn't reply. Instead, she gazes up at him. Close up, she looks different. She is thickly made up, like a wax doll, and her eyes are as deep as a well. A well that would hold chilled water.

"Since you won't say anything, you leave me no choice."

She obediently hands over her purse. The contents reveal lipstick, compact powder, and a feminine hygiene pad amongst various odds and ends. Some women tend to shoplift every time they're on their period. Perhaps she, too, is one of those; after all, she did come to the store every twenty-eight days. Even in the midst of the smells of dust and mold, he catches a whiff of her sweat and perfume. The perfume smells good. The price tag dangles from the neckline. There is no ID or business card in her purse. Instead, he finds a transparent lighter with a red fabric flower suspended in the fluid. He sticks a cigarette in his mouth. As the flame shoots up, the flower flutters inside the fluid. *Las Vegas, where a beautiful girl is always waiting.* Written below that on the side of the lighter is a phone number.

"How about this? If you return the dress, I'll let you go. But just this time. Next time, I won't be able to help you out."

Her clothes are still hanging in the changing room, just as she'd left them. She changes in the storage room and is about to leave through the back door when she turns and comes back. She sticks something in his pants pocket. It's the Las Vegas lighter.

According to his calculation, she should come to the store on the 25th. But a week goes by and she doesn't appear. In that time, the season has changed, and knitwear has started to invade the store. Before the month is up, every last trace of the gray dress will disappear. The pillar is often reflected on his sunglasses.

He calls the number on the lighter. A boy who sounds like he's in the midst of puberty answers. "Are you coming by car?" he asks. When the man says he'll be coming by subway, the boy says, "Hold on." He calls out to someone, asking where the man should get off if he's taking the subway. "The nearest stations are Yongsan and Hannam. But you'll have to walk for a while. Head toward Itaewon. When you reach the main street, you'll see a sign." He then adds, "At the door, ask for me—Fifty Won. You know, like what you'd need for the payphone."

Las Vegas. Just as the boy said, the neon sign is easy to spot. It flashes on and off from a high-rise building, attracting attention. Las Vegas spelled out in Korean would blink in orange and disappear, and then the English would blink in purple. The man ends up taking a taxi instead of the subway. He's too anxious to transfer trains and then walk. Although the neon sign flashes on top of the building, Las Vegas is deep underground. When he grabs the handle as thick as a loaf of bread and pulls open the front door, he sees carpeted stairs leading below. A slow song oozes up the stairs the color of red beans. At the very bottom is a glass door. He pushes it open to find himself in a large ballroom. On a circular stage in the center of the room, men and women embrace each other, swaying gently like mollusks to a 4/4 beat. A mirrored disco ball turns slowly, scattering shards of multicolored light on the floor. All around the room, dancers clad in bikinis dance on platforms, and round tables covered in white linen surround the stage. Instead of getting a table, the man sits at the bar. He doesn't even know her name. Even her features are a bit vague in his mind. A pale face like that of a wax doll, a mannequin-like figure, pupils as deep as a well. With this description alone, no waiter would be able to find her.

He is about to raise the small red lamp to signal a waiter when the music ends. The people dancing on the stage return to their seats and the lights dim. A spotlight beams down. Just then, a woman comes on stage, pushing a wagon. It's her. He recognizes her, despite the thick stage makeup. The people cheer. She's wearing a bow tie around her bare neck and a silk hat on her head, and a bundle of feathers is attached to the bottom of her sleeveless leotard like the tail of a bird. Each step sends the feathers swishing like a fan and each movement makes the sequins on her costume sparkle and catch against each other. Instead of greeting the crowd, she gets down from the stage and stands in front of a drunk man in the audience. He is chewing on a strip of squid jerky, the end of his necktie tucked into the breast pocket of his shirt. He looks up at the woman with glazed eyes. As soon as her hand brushes against his shoulder, a white dove appears and flutters into the air. People gasp. She walks over to another man with mincing steps and strokes his shoulder. She raises her white-gloved hand and uncurls each finger to release another white dove.

The water she pours into a page of newspaper folded into a cone disappears and she correctly guesses the card an audience member is holding. The show builds momentum. While she is getting flowers in a pot to blossom, a waiter wheels a silver box the size of a medium fridge to center stage. A human form is outlined on the doors. Each compartment has holes for the head, hands, and feet to fit through. A drum roll sounds. Her eyes skim the crowd. They stop on the man's face. The bartender mixing drinks behind the bar pushes the bewildered man forward. The people sitting at their tables turn to look at him. Reluctantly, he walks toward the stage. The woman looms closer. The audience's applause rings in his ears. She looks up at his face and whispers, "Trust me."

He steps into the box. The three doors close one by one, and he sticks out his head, hands, and feet, just as she instructs him. She puts a red handkerchief in one of his hands. She turns the box once. He watches her. She faces the audience and brandishes a machete. He has seen this trick before. She turns the blade flat and sticks it in near his chest. As soon as the blade comes in contact with his chest, it shrinks like a spring. Someone whistles. The middle compartment of the box pushes out like a drawer and he is thrust to the edge of the box where he gets squashed in the small space. His body twists into an S shape. But to the audience, his body will seem as if it has separated.

"Can you wave for us?"

The man flutters the handkerchief. He wriggles his toes, too. The drawer is returned to its original position and the woman chants the magic word. The compartment doors open and he steps back onto the stage. He is covered in sweat from nervousness. He walks back to the bar, accompanied by applause. Pulling the wagon behind her, she shakes the bundle of feathers on her bottom and disappears backstage. The disco ball begins to spin again and a dance track plays. The stage fills with drunk people once more.

When he has emptied two bottles of beer, he hears a rasping noise. The woman is wearing a cloak that comes down to her ankles, but the back of her cloak bulges out from the feathered tail on her costume. He now understands the secret behind her fluid hands, like a flower bud opening, as she stole CDs or handkerchiefs from the store.

"Thank you," she says, her husky voice drifting out from between small red lips.

She takes a seat on the stool next to him. When the bartender smiles knowingly and places an empty beer glass before her, she narrows her eyes at him. The man orders another beer and pours it into her glass.

"You've come to my rescue two times now," she says, sipping her beer. "You see, it looks like I pick a random audience member, but it's all planned. I only realized after the show started that the person I work with wasn't there. Can you believe it? He didn't even call me to let me know he couldn't make it. That's when I saw you. My name is Choi Sun-ae, by the way. Here, they call me Luna."

Choi Sun-ae, who stands to go back on stage, whispers into his ear. "Not just anyone can become a magician's assistant. It only works between a father and daughter, brother and sister, or husband and wife. Or lovers."

Now, Choi Sun-ae no longer comes to the store. Instead, he goes to Las Vegas. She works twice a week at Las Vegas and twice a week at Fantasia, which is a block from Las Vegas. Every time she switches locations, she loads her equipment into a van. The back of the van, with its seats folded down, contains all kinds of magic props, as well as three white doves inside a birdcage and several sequined costumes with feathered tails. As his visits become more frequent, he naturally becomes her assistant, and when she chooses him from the crowd, he even pretends to look awkward and uncomfortable. Before the show, they practice backstage in the dressing room.

"There are basically two techniques in magic—deception and sleight of hand."

The man steps into a box. Choi Sun-ae shuts the door and puts on a large padlock. When she chants a short magic phrase and opens the door, the box is completely empty. There's a space beneath the box that's invisible to the audience. After he goes into the box and the door is shut, he quickly opens the secret trapdoor at the bottom and hides his body in the small space. But because of his size, it's not easy to shut the trapdoor seamlessly.

"I'm an only child. Mom was Dad's partner, but after she died, I naturally took her place. It wasn't hard. He was a magician before I was born. I grew up playing with his magic props, instead of with toys. Dad spent all his time off stage developing new magic tricks. I'll show you his secret notes some day. I've been performing at clubs since fifth grade. It was fun to spin plates and do tumbles, but when

I entered middle school, it was hard to catch up to all the studying. Of course, I lost interest in books. I barely graduated. If I'd been a boy instead of a girl, what do you think would have happened? Dad wouldn't have had a partner then."

Choi Sun-ae, who has been chattering away, clamps her mouth shut. It's at times like these her eyes get that deep-as-a-well look, so deep a bucket wouldn't be able to reach the bottom.

•

He and Jeong are standing in the CEO's office. The office is on the top floor of the Cosmos building. When they had knocked on his door just moments before, they had found the CEO dozing, slumped against the high-backed chair. He sits up straight and sighs.

"You!" he says, pointing at the man. "How long have you worked here?"

It would be exactly three years by the end of the year.

"I guess you start to go through the motions after three years. How about you?" he says, jutting his chin out toward Jeong. Jeong started a month after the man.

"Yup. Three years is long enough for rust to grow on a rearview mirror."

He gets up from his chair and walks over to the window. He gazes down at the Myeongdong streets.

"There's a gaping hole in my business because of you two. I don't think you realize there are plenty of people who'd love to take your place."

Jeong and the man write formal apologies. The CEO tries to intimidate them by threatening to cut 20 percent of their paychecks for three months if they don't shape up. It's two in the morning when the man gets home after the shows at Las Vegas and Fantasia. So of course he's fighting to stay awake in the mornings, from the moment he climbs onto his pedestal. Although he has managed to hide his drooping eyes with his sunglasses, his concentration has dropped and all he does is wait for closing time.

As the man is shutting the door behind him, the CEO calls out in an annoyed voice that if they want to get paid, they should work for it.

In the bathroom, Jeong and the man chain-smoke.

"Sometimes I feel like I'm nothing but a rearview mirror."

Jeong is venting, but he sounds like he's ready to crawl into a hole. Jeong is dating Miss Lee, one of the salesgirls.

"Let's see who quits first."

Jeong stamps out his cigarette on the bathroom floor and gets back onto his platform.

·

It was a weekday and because the store had just opened, things were slow. There were about a dozen customers at most. Still, they should have been prepared. The man dozed off and Jeong was chatting with Miss Lee, looking down from his pedestal. Right then, the CEO, who had come downstairs to inspect the store, saw a girl in a large trench coat. They should have known as soon as they saw the trench coat—it was autumn, but the temperature got as high as 25 degrees Celsius at noon—but he noticed her only when the CEO grabbed her wrist with both hands as she tried to escape, crying, "Shoplifter! Shoplifter!"

When they took off her trench coat, objects spilled out onto the floor. How could so many things fit inside a coat? The man was amazed. Four CDs, a small purse, two pairs of jeans, a pair of dress shoes, a belt, a box of days-of-the-week panties. The CEO yelled at him and Jeong, asking what the hell they had been doing while she was cleaning him out. Her parents came in. She was in her last year of high school and was planning to take the university entrance exam very soon. On the verge of tears, they claimed she had stolen from the stress of studying. The CEO demanded she be reported to the police or they pay fifty times the total amount she stole. They chose to pay. The paycheck the man received at closing time was 20 percent less than usual.

•

The shutters are lowered over the entrance and display windows. The whitish heads of the mannequins seem to be floating in the dark. He and Choi Sun-ae park the van in the lot across the street and take the long way to the store. It's 2:10 A.M. when they get to Myeongdong after the last show at Fantasia. They pass a few drunk people on the way from Euljiro 1-ga Station to Myeongdong Station. The wind carries smells of urine and vomit from the alleyway. If there is anyone around, Choi Sun-ae will signal him by whistling. He can find the keyhole for the shutter with his eyes closed, since he and Jeong take turns opening and closing the store.

He unlocks the shutter in one try and flips open the alarm cover. He punches in the security code and disables the alarm. He lets Choi Sun-ae in and then follows her, closing the shutter behind them. It gets darker the deeper they walk into the store where the security lights don't shine. He fumbles in the dark. The dust that has settled on the floor rises and tickles his nostrils. His hands keep bumping into clothes hangers and he almost trips and knocks over a CD stand. They have to come and go without leaving a trace.

"It's okay, I'll do it," she says.

Choi Sun-ae takes the lead. She stands in front of the pillar. She feels for the rack below and pulls something out. He stands between the mannequins and keeps watch. Choi Sun-ae picks up hairpins, a broach, and a dozen pencils as she walks toward the doors. Objects disappear inside her cloak. She stoops and goes out into the street. The man, about to follow her out, casts one last look at the mannequins. *Sorry, I'm off.* He reactivates the alarm, lowers the shutter, and locks it.

Choi Sun-ae has taken the dress she has admired for so long. Spreading it across her knees, she smiles like a child. She pulls out small objects from her cloak and lays them on the van floor. She is triumphant, as if they were precious booty she had won.

"They won't notice a thing. And even if they did, who cares? I took just as much as they took off your paycheck."

They sit in the back of the van and eat instant noodles. In an hour, the sun will come up.

•

As the squid jerky became stale, it took on the smell of the ink from the bag, but Choi Sun-ae chews happily on a strip. Her face reveals both the artlessness of Choi Sun-ae and the dazzle of Luna.

"Luna is the goddess of the moon. The first time I went on stage with my dad, the owner of the club gave me the name. But it was only much later I found out who she really was. A college student who'd been watching my show came backstage to see me. He told me Luna loved a shepherd and she put him to eternal sleep so that he'd never leave her. Luna has another name, but I forget it now. I think she and I are alike. I mean, can't you tell by my obsession with this dress?"

Choi Sun-ae is wearing the gray dress. The pleated skirt looks good on her narrow hips. After watching the scenery and prattling for some time, she sleeps, nestled up against her chair. They should arrive in Busan in about forty minutes. He wants to be awake when they cross the city border.

Choi Sun-ae has found work at the nightclub of a new hotel in Busan.

"The hotel's called the Mirabeau. I made my decision as soon as I heard it. The Mirabeau—doesn't it sound great?"

She's excited. Now, he will become her official partner. Her magic props will get shipped once they find a permanent address.

Rain starts to fall. It quickly becomes dark. The cars turn on their headlights. The bus driver pumps the brake pedal a few times and slows down. He glances at the rearview mirror and proceeds to change lanes. But the cars in the next lane honk and cling to the side of the bus like insects. The bus swerves. It tilts a little to the left and the tires skid. *Would our kids play with magic props, too, instead of toys?*

He looks toward the front windshield where the wipers are sweeping away the rain. Above the windshield hangs a small picture of a young curly-haired girl on her knees, praying, with the words *Please keep them safe* . . . It's something many drivers put up in their buses. Suddenly, the man's body is hurled to one side, and the image of the girl whirls through the air. The scenery outside the window stretches like taffy and the marsh below the embankment surges up. He is tossed in the air like laundry in a washer.

He opens his eyes as if in a dream. Blood is trickling down his cheek from his eye. The seats hang overhead. Those in seatbelts are upside down, still strapped to their seats with their arms and legs dangling limply. The bus has flipped over. The man's right foot is caught in a vent. Frantically, he looks around for Choi Sun-ae. It's impossible to see out through the big crack on the front windshield. Moans come from all over the bus. He turns his head and notices the large rearview mirror on the side of the bus. It's bent, and there are cracks spread across it like a spider's web, but in it he can see the inside of the bus: the shattered windows, heaps of broken glass, curtains fluttering upside down in the wind, the crumpled seats dangling precariously as if they could drop any second, the bloodstained seat covers stamped with the words SAMCHEONRI TOURS, and arms and legs, as motionless as mannequin limbs.

He also spots Choi Sun-ae's gray skirt in the cracked mirror. He tries to free his foot, but it doesn't budge. He wipes away the blood that's flowing into his eye and looks at the rearview mirror again. He can't see her face, but it's definitely her. The gray skirt is flipped up and her legs are draped over the back of a seat. His gaze travels up her legs and stops at her crotch. There, unlike the rest of her slender frame, which has virtually no body fat, is a distinct lump. A lump of flesh that can't be hidden with tight underwear—the unmistakable bulge of male genitals. Suddenly, there's a splintering noise and the seat hanging over him smashes down on his head. Everything goes dark.

He comes to on a metal cot in a white, eight-bed hospital room. His nerves responded to the needle the nurse stuck him with, and he woke up with a yelp. Vials in a stainless steel container rattle as they're wheeled away. He sees the freshly painted white ceiling and yellow fluid dripping from a plastic bottle. A tube snakes from the bottle to his left arm, held in place with tape. His leg, in a cast up to his thigh, hangs suspended in the air.

Each time he had opened his eyes, he had heard the wail of the ambulance drawing closer. The blue sky had grown higher and bluer as the weather cleared, and people were carried away on stretchers. The ambulance went under the overpass. He thought he saw the words WELCOME TO BUSAN through the crack in the closed curtains of the ambulance.

"Did you have a nice sleep?" A middle-aged man sitting up in a cot across the room greets him.

"I don't think I even dreamed," he says. It's only then that he registers the white bandage bound tightly around the older man's head. There is blood seeping through the gauze.

"You were out for four days. Now that you're awake, I finally have someone to talk to. Were you with anyone on the bus?"

He hazily recalls the words *Please keep them safe . . .* that had spun in the air. But the inside of his head feels like a jumbled-up puzzle.

"Did anyone die?"

"Nope. If the bus had kept rolling down the hill, no one would have survived. But there was a cow that was out grazing, and the bus hit it on the way down. That cow basically acted like a doorstop and stopped the bus."

"So only the cow died?"

"Two cows, not one. Turns out it was pregnant. How's your head? Doesn't it hurt?"

He touches his forehead and realizes there's also a bandage around his own head. He then recalls the red seat that had crashed down on him.

·

A week passes before he's able to wheel himself out of the ward. The nurse in the lobby buzzes the women's ward on the sixth floor.

"I'm sorry, but there's no patient by the name of Choi Sun-ae."

He asks if there were patients who had been transferred to other hospitals.

"No, we're the closest hospital to the accident and anyone who was injured was admitted here."

There were some who suffered only minor injuries and were already released. Could she have been one of those people?

He is still trying to piece together his memory. Just the day before, the name Choi Sun-ae had suddenly come to him. But the other pieces associated with this name eluded him. As the seat fell, its metal leg had stabbed him in the forehead. The doctor said his memory loss was the result of trauma to the brain, and although each case is different, his memory should return eventually. All at once, he remembers a distinct image instead of a word: two legs reflected in the shattered rearview mirror.

·

He is now able to go to the bathroom by himself. Piece by piece, his memory is coming back. He remembers standing between two Marilyn Monroes a year ago. As he is rounding a corner, he bumps into a young man. The young man walks very slowly, while holding onto an IV stand. His long hair, which comes down to his shoulders, is disheveled, and his face is badly bruised and cut. It's a face that can look either seventeen or thirty-two years old. The young man smiles brightly as soon as he sees him, his eyes sparkling behind swollen lids.

"Excuse me, but do I know you?" he asks, gazing into the young man's face.

The young man's face stiffens and his eyes grow as dark as a well. "I'm sorry, I thought you were someone else. You look exactly like someone I know." He moves the metal stand forward and gingerly takes a small step.

"Were you on the bus that crashed?" he calls out.

The young man, continuing in the other direction, shakes his head without looking back.

Though it was for a mere second, the young man's eyes seem all too familiar. But his thoughts are only of a girl named Choi Sun-ae. Who on earth is she?

Then a new word flashes in his mind. He cautiously tries it out on his tongue. After a few attempts, he blurts it out. *Mirabeau.*

Flowers
of
Mold

From the fifth floor, the playground looks like a small pond. The heavy downpour from two days before has created muddy puddles that refuse to dry up. There are pools of rainwater everywhere—under the opposite end of the seesaw the woman straddles, even under the monkey bars the child hangs from.

The woman is shelling kidney beans. Every time she twists open the shells, speckled beans peep out, nestled neatly in a row. If a bean happens to pop out onto the sand, she quickly reaches for it, raising her bottom in the air. Then her end of the seesaw rises a little to find its balance point.

The child is catching his breath before swinging from the third bar to the fourth. If he wants to land on dry ground, he has no choice but to go all the way across. His pants are slipping down, and his shirt rides up to reveal a patch of pale skin.

The woman sits hunched over with her back toward the man. From his vantage point all he can see is her plastic container on the sand. Soon the container brims with beans.

"Are you planning to cook rice with beans tonight?" he asks, but his voice doesn't reach her. "Who could forget that taste? The creamy texture? You mind if I have some?"

Standing by the balcony window, he keeps smacking his lips. He can picture the downy fuzz covering the bean shells to the very fibers that get stuck under her thumbnails. Luckily the woman hasn't noticed him watching. She is deep in concentration, like a student solving a math problem. The child still hasn't crossed the monkey bars. With his teeth clenched, he continues to hang from the bar.

From his back pocket, the man takes out a little notepad, curved from having been pressed against his rear end. Bits of food have dried between the pages, which stick together when he tries to turn them.

Bean shells, seesaw, monkey bars, boy, puddles.

The man writes down a few words that will help jog his memory. Later, the shells she chucks will become the only clue in identifying her garbage bag from the others. He doesn't know which unit out of the ninety she lives in. Luckily there's only one apartment building.

On the news that morning, the weather person gave the forecast in a yellow raincoat while holding up a yellow umbrella. A low pressure system was moving in and developing across the western coast and all of Gyeonggi Province. Scattered spring showers were expected the entire week. She added that this early summer heat wave in April was the result of El Niño. If the heat and humidity continue, the man's work will become difficult.

He wakes to a woman's shrieks. It's a little past two in the morning. Glass shatters on the floor. Frantic footsteps echo throughout the apartment. A woman is screaming at the top of her lungs, but he can't make out her words. His wardrobe and stereo system are placed against the wall, which is all that separates his room from 507. He gets up from his bed, walks over to the wardrobe, and listens. The front door of 507 opens, banging against the wall. Someone slips and lands with a heavy thud. A pot lid immediately follows, rattling noisily in the hallway until it eventually stops.

"Don't you dare come around here again!" she yells. The door slams and the bolt turns sharply.

He tiptoes toward his front door and looks out the peephole. The corridor is as dark and gloomy as a cavern. Soon it will be time for the newspaper boy to come charging in with the morning paper. Nearly half an hour later, footsteps finally start down the stairs. The shoes don't seem to be on properly; they sound like clogs. He waits until the footsteps have left the building.

When he steps into his tiny storage closet, his shoulders get wedged between the walls. The sickening smell hits him full force. The humidity is already making his garbage rot. He takes a plastic bucket down from the shelf, puts on rubber gloves, and creeps down the stairs. To avoid attracting attention, he doesn't turn on the landing light. Even in the dark, he knows these stairs like the back of his hand. The L-shaped stairway has a total of seventy-two steps—eight steps and then a landing, continuing in this pattern all the way down. The second step going down from the third to the second floor is higher than the others. At first this step caused him a lot of trouble. He even sprained his ankle once, but now he automatically adjusts his footing whenever he reaches this spot.

Large rubber trash bins the size of small bathtubs line the flowerbed outside. Shadows fall across the maple leaves the streetlights don't reach. There's no one in sight. The man pushes off the lid and steps up on the flowerbed ledge. There's only one bag inside the bin since the garbage truck already came that morning. Because the bin comes nearly up to his chest, he has to bend over all the way to reach the bag. The smell at the bottom turns his stomach.

His bucket barely holds twenty liters. In the beginning he hadn't used a bucket. The next morning on his way to work he'd discovered the garbage had leaked, and a trail from the stairs ended right at his front door. The garbage bag is heavy. Even though he lifts it with care, putrid stuff drips onto his slippers.

It's a good thing he didn't get rid of the small bathtub. When he first moved into this run-down, fifteen-year-old apartment, he repapered the walls, redid the floors, and replaced the bathroom sink. The porcelain tub and toilet were full of cracks. The navy blue tiles were mildewed and chipped with not a single tile intact. Some were missing entirely. One night after he washed his face and pulled the stopper to empty the sink, the dirty water that should have drained away poured onto his feet. It was a leak in the water pipe. While the plumber replaced the sink with one that wouldn't get dirty so easily, he advised the man to get rid of the tub. The plumber kept pestering him: why did he insist on keeping a tub in this tiny bathroom, now that more and more people were opting for showers? The man ignored the plumber's advice and kept the tub. However that night after the plumber left, the man regretted his decision. Though he was not tall by any means, water would slosh around his hips and overflow whenever he took a bath. The tub was so short that soaking his whole body was out of the question. If he tried to immerse his shoulders, he had to stick his feet out of the tub and place them on the taps, and if he tried to immerse his legs, he had to hang his rear end out of the tub. Before the man started this whole business, the bathtub was a real headache, just as the plumber warned.

He places the garbage bag in the bathtub. It's already starting to smell different. When summer comes he will have to stop. Even now, his 525-square-foot apartment reeks of rotten fish, though he disinfected everything with bleach and sprayed lemon-scented air freshener. Garbage spews from a rip in the overstuffed bag. He leans into the tub and struggles to untie the stubborn knot. Taking off his rubber gloves, he tries to undo it with his bare fingers, but it's useless. He straightens and massages his sore back, cursing whoever tied the knot. He knows he shouldn't blame someone for tying a garbage bag so tightly it doesn't easily come undone. People never consider that their garbage might be opened. After all, that's what he thought, too, until that incident.

·

The waste management program, which required everyone to use standard plastic garbage bags, started on January 1, 1995. The man was in bed all day after a drinking binge the night before. The doorbell rang. He wasn't expecting anyone. After a few seconds, it rang again. He looked through the peephole, but the lens was so cloudy he had no choice but to open the door. Women who identified themselves as members of the apartment strata council crowded the doorway. There were over ten of them. Those who couldn't fit in the narrow space spilled down the stairway to the fourth floor.

An older woman, her face flecked with liver spots, nudged a young woman beside her. The young woman blurted, "Are you learning acupuncture by any chance?"

It was only then he recalled the unopened box on top of his wardrobe. After purchasing acupuncture tools and a manual from a pushy salesman who had come to his office, he hadn't opened the box once. How was it possible these strangers knew about his acupuncture set?

The young woman stared at him, her gaze unflinching. He did receive a monthly newsletter from the acupuncture association.

"Have you been snooping through my mail?" he blurted in a fit of anger.

"We found him!" the women shouted in unison, and then began to whisper among themselves. "See? I told you it'd pay off. But we haven't seen this one before."

The woman with the liver spots pushed the young woman aside. "So it's the guilty dog that barks the loudest! And we've got one guilty dog right here!"

A heavy garbage bag was passed from person to person up the stairs until it reached Liver Spots. She tossed it at the man's feet. It burst open. Through the rip, he saw patches of the phrase *Market delivery available* written in red. It was his garbage from two days before. There was no doubt about it.

"Do you know the trouble we went through to find you? We combed through every piece of stinking trash like we were picking lice. They're right when they say persistence will pay off, because we finally came across this!"

Liver Spots held up an envelope and shook it in his face. The words *Acupuncture Association* were written in Chinese characters and the man's name and address were typed neatly in the bottom right hand corner. The envelope was dirty, as if flecks of kimchi had been stuck all over it.

"Don't pretend you didn't know you had to use proper garbage bags. That's not going to get you out of this."

A shout came from down the stairs. "It's because of people like you our country's in this state!"

"Ever since I crossed the Taedong River with my father, I've been through all kinds of hell," Liver Spots said, her voice trembling in anger. "But never, in my whole life, have I been forced to dig through someone else's trash!" She let out a deep sigh.

The man vaguely recalled hearing about the waste management program.

"Don't let this happen again."

One by one, the women filed down the stairs. The young woman who had been standing next to Liver Spots started to follow the rest of the group down, but stopped.

"You live alone, right? Try to understand. It's not just once or twice something like this has happened. I mean, how much can garbage bags cost that people are dumping their garbage secretly at night? Garbage trucks won't collect something like this."

Liver Spots shouted from a few stairs down. "What are you doing? Hurry up! We have to go through the other bags."

"The fine is 100,000 won," the young woman said as she headed down the stairs. "We'll let it go this time, but that lady—she has arthritis. If you make her climb five flights of stairs again, you won't get off the hook so easily."

Garbage spewed steadily from the rip. A trail of putrid discharge had leaked from the bag, dotting up the stairs to the man's front door. He put on rubber gloves and picked up the garbage strewn about his entrance. Rotten potatoes and rice covered with green mold crumbled in his hands. He gagged repeatedly. Though the garbage was his own, it seemed completely foreign to him. He discovered crumpled-up letters; they were already somewhat flattened out. It was clear the women had already gotten to them. When he pictured them passing around his letters, snickering among themselves, anger surged through him. Even his own handwriting seemed alien.

"The man you're planning to marry isn't right for you. I knew him long before you did. I've often seen a hidden side to him, a side you're not aware of. But you haven't taken my advice and you've gone ahead and picked a wedding date. Today I saw you standing side by side, handing out invitations around the office. Why can't you see him for who he is? Is it like what you say—that love is blind? It's not too late.

I love you more than life itself—"

Not a single letter was finished. Completely drunk, he had written letter after letter until early morning. In the end he hadn't sent any of them. As soon as he picked up the bag, a soju bottle cap fell out of the rip and bounced off the ground. The noodles he had boiled to have with his soju had gone straight into the trash untouched. They were bloated, stuck to another unfinished letter.

•

The knot in the garbage bag finally loosens. As soon as the bag is untied, a fistful of trash spills into the tub. Strands of hair are tangled up in dust and cigarette butts. The man brings a folding chair, sets it up before the tub, and sits down. He puts on his rubber gloves again and pores over every piece. He recently replaced the fluorescent light in the bathroom with a 100-watt bulb, and it's blinding. The hair is easily over twenty centimeters long. He pulls the strands taut and examines them under the light. He picks up a cigarette butt burned right down to the filter, and peers at the teeth marks on the end of the filter. Looking at the contents splayed in the tub, he crosses his legs and spreads open his notepad on his knee.

April 23. OB Lager bottle cap, Pulmuone soy bean sprouts, Shin Ramen, Coca-Cola, Chamnamu soju . . .

The notepad is crammed with lists that look like items to find in an I-Spy book. He is more focused than a watch repairman who's removing a part from a broken watch with tweezers. He inspects each thing meticulously, stopping occasionally to scrawl something down.

Kool menthol cigarettes.

His writing is barely legible, since he holds the pen by its end so that he won't get his notepad dirty. Two instant udon noodle containers are stacked together, the kind that come with all-in-one soup mix and freeze-dried shrimp.

Ottogi Vermont Curry.

He also finds the peels from the potatoes and onions that would have gone into the curry.

When he dumps out a twenty-liter garbage bag, the tub fills up halfway. The slimy cabbage leaves and potato peels slip through his gloved fingers. Foods rich in protein smell the worst. The foul stench of fish heads, entrails, and chicken bones is unbearable. A pink rubber glove surfaces with a chicken bone stuck to it. It's a right-hand glove with the words *Mommy's Helping Hand* printed on the wrist. The man flips through the pages of his notepad and finds the page that has a record of a left-handed rubber glove he had fished out a couple of days ago.

March 23. Cheiljedang Beat laundry detergent (750 g), Kool cigarettes, Coca-Cola, Nongshim Big Bowl Noodle (shrimp flavor), Mommy's Helping Hand rubber glove (pink, left hand).

The brand and even the color are the same. When everything fits like this, there's no question about it. The garbage is from the same house.

She enjoys drinking OB Lager and Coke, smokes Kool cigarettes, and likes to eat shrimp-flavored instant noodles. She is also left-handed and has long hair. But it might not even be a woman after all. It could be a man with long hair. Making inferences is easy. Since things like diapers, chocolate, and candy wrappers haven't turned up, it's safe to assume there's no child in the household.

From last winter to now the man has gone through over a hundred garbage bags. He gradually learned the different tastes and lifestyles of the ninety households in the building, though what he learned doesn't amount to much. Two kinds of people live in these cramped 525-square-foot suites: young married couples and single people like himself, or elderly couples who have married off their children and sold their big house. It's always the younger people who get suckered into buying the newest products advertised on TV. They're more open to trying different things—things in flashy packaging and beverages made with exotic tropical fruits. They also tend to go for items that are pricey, considering their quantity or size. He sometimes compiles statistics from the data he has gathered: The women in this building use a higher grade of dishwashing soap with aloe that is gentle on the hands, and perhaps because many of them work, they use two-in-one shampoo and conditioners. They also tend to use sanitary pads with wings.

The man scoops everything in the tub back into the bag. The volume is considerably smaller, now that the liquid has drained. After he reties the bag, he carries it back down to the ground floor and puts it in the bin. He takes his cigarettes out of his pocket and sticks one in his mouth. If only he could have looked through *her* garbage, he could have discovered what she was really like. Then, he could have learned of her weakness for the color cobalt and attraction to articulate men who dressed neatly.

She quit her job when she got married. In order to see her one last time, he went to the newlyweds' housewarming party, though he didn't feel like it. Sporting an apron and her hair pulled back into a ponytail, she squeezed in beside him as if it were the most natural thing to do.

As drinks started to flow, someone asked her, "Miss Kim, no, I guess we have to call you Mrs. Park now, what made you fall for Mr. Park?"

Giggling, she replied it was because of the cobalt-colored dress shirt he'd been wearing.

Park, two years his junior, had graduated from the same university. Park didn't change a bit, even after marrying. He still holds the same position in the accounts department. The man, however, moved up fast and now sits right behind Park at a coveted location with a view of the whole office. Every time he looks up and sees Park's starched shirt and neat, wrinkle-free suit, he remembers her long, white fingers hitting the computer keyboard. He'd hear Park entertain their co-workers with stories by the vending machine.

"Damn it, she's always buying cobalt-colored shirts. Now I shudder if I even hear the word *cobalt.*"

He even caught Park coming out of a restaurant with a new female staff member. The woman has no idea what kind of man she has married.

As he is going up to his apartment, he bumps into the paper boy who is rushing down the stairs after having finished the morning deliveries. The boy plugs his nose in disgust, curiously eyeing the man's gloved hands. The boy is also wearing a red rubber glove on his free hand. A rash can develop on the inside of the wrist from sticking your hand in and out of the narrow metal mail slot. To ward against this, milkmen and newspaper boys have started to wear rubber gloves on one hand. The boy strides down the dim corridor. Even though the man uses bleach to rinse the tub and tiles, his apartment still reeks. The sensor lights the boy had triggered switch off one by one as the timer runs down. It's already past four in the morning.

When the doorbell rings he's in the middle of trying to piece together a torn-up bill he had laid out on the floor. He'd found the scraps in the garbage the night before. The bill, now held together by tape, is still missing some pieces. There are times when he finds bills that haven't been crumpled up. He's really lucky if they're dry, but even if they're covered with food scraps, he doesn't mind. If he irons it after a quick rinse under the tap, he can make out the print without too much trouble. However, whenever they're ripped to shreds like this, he has to put everything together like a child's jigsaw puzzle. The name starts to emerge ever so slowly. Kim _____hoon. The doorbell rings as he's looking for the missing piece.

Whoever rang the bell seems to be leaning against the front door. He tries to push open the door, but the door doesn't budge; it's probably a man, judging by the weight. Only after several attempts to shove open the door does the person seem to notice. Still, it takes a while for him to step away. It's a complete stranger, so drunk he can barely hold himself up. He has a large bouquet of roses is in one hand, and his dress shirt, pulled out of his pants, hangs over his thick legs like a tablecloth.

"Don't worry."

The massive body falls on him. He braces himself, struggling against the dead weight, like a monkey caught in the grips of a giant bear. He can tell the fellow easily weighs over a hundred kilograms. The stranger looks down at him and mumbles again.

"Don't worry."

His foul breath hits the man in the face. The stranger keeps mumbling unintelligibly, crushing him still. When he plays the words over in his mind, it seems the fellow is saying "I'm sorry."

The stranger manages to open his eyes, which begin to roll in different directions, making him look cross-eyed. Suddenly they focus, registering that the man is in his undershirt. His eyes flash with rage.

"What? Who the hell are you? What are you doing here?" he shouts, trying to force his way into the apartment.

The man pushes him back. "Hey, what do you think you're doing? Do you know what time it is? You have the wrong apartment!" But he doesn't stand a chance against this giant.

"I can find this place with my eyes closed. Where is she? I know you're in there! Stop hiding and come out!"

The fellow stops shouting and backs up abruptly. He begins to retch uncontrollably. Vomit hits the floor and splatters all over the man's dress shoes, which are sitting by the front door.

"Isn't this 507? Samgwang Apartment, Unit 507?"

The fellow becomes more coherent as he sobers up. The light in the stairwell hasn't been working for a long time. Whoever lived in 507 before must have hit it with his furniture as he was moving out.

The doorbells for 507 and 508 are right beside each other. In the dark the fellow had pressed the wrong bell.

"Goddamn, I'm really sorry."

Looking from the man to the mess he created, the fellow stumbles toward the stairs and flops down on the ground.

While the man cleans up the vomit, the fellow presses the doorbell of 507. The apartment is empty. For the last couple of days, the man hasn't heard a peep from the unit. If someone was there, it would have been impossible to ignore all the commotion. The fellow continues to push the bell. Electronic cuckoo sounds chirp inside. When the door doesn't open, he shouts and pounds on the door with his huge fist that's like a boxing glove.

"I said I was sorry! Please open the door!"

Kim ____hoon. Even though he searches every corner of the floor, he can't find the missing piece. It probably got thrown out in another bag. He found these pieces in the bag with the kidney bean shells. He riffles through the pages of his notepad.

Bean shells, seesaw, monkey bars, boy, puddles.

Inside the garbage bag, there are crinkly plastic candy wrappers and a fistful of chicken bones. He can tell the woman doesn't mind preparing foods that require a lot of time and effort. He finds an old toothbrush with the bristles harshly flattened.

The doorbell rings again. It's the fellow again. He shoves the bouquet of red roses he'd been holding into the man's chest.

"Could you give her these? It's her birthday today."

He staggers down the stairs, bumping into the wall. The man counts the roses. There are thirty in all.

For a few days now a pair of yellow socks has been hanging on the clothesline on the balcony of 507. The heels and toes have dark smudges the detergent couldn't remove. Three days have passed, but he still hasn't run into her. There's no sign of life next door. On his way home he circles the building on purpose, using the back path, and looks up at 507. The glass balcony door is shattered, all except for a few pieces still dangling in the frame. Only their units, 507 and 508, have the lights off. People at his office have been staying late. Once tax season passes they should be able to get off at the regular time.

The roses that he hung by the window have started to wither, the petals curling and blackening at the edges. A single wall is all that separates 507 from 508. He moves everything to the opposite wall. Half the morning goes by as he takes his wardrobe apart, moves it over to the other side, and then reassembles it. He drags his bed over to where his wardrobe used to be. He lies down on his side facing the wall. He runs his palm over the wall, which is twenty centimeters thick at most. When he puts his ear next to it, his senses sharpen at the smallest sound. If he leaves his room door open, he can hear everything, even footsteps coming up the stairs. But to his disappointment, the steps always stop before continuing up. Just like dandelion spores suddenly blown in by the wind, curiosity had started to sprout within him. He thinks he hears the sound of a key being inserted into a keyhole and the bolt sliding back into the doorframe. That instant, the mail slot cover on his front door snaps open and a red rubber glove shoves in the morning paper.

From the bus stop he takes the long way and uses the back path again. He looks up at the balcony of 507. He sees the bare clothesline minus the yellow socks and realizes with a jolt that the woman is finally back. But when he rushes up, not a single sound comes from her unit. He has temporarily stopped his garbage work. He had always worked with the bathroom door shut, worried about the stench that might escape. But the sealed-up bathroom became an echo chamber, amplifying every drop of water that fell from the tap, so that it was impossible to hear any outside noise.

After an early dinner, he waits for the woman to come home. He stretches out on his side on the bed, facing the wall. He lies close to the wall, his groin pressed against it. Afraid that the woman would slip past him again, he even resists going to the bathroom. However, the pressure in his bladder forces him to get up. When he comes out of the bathroom, he discovers a maggot squirming on the floor. Summer is coming, but it's still too early for maggots. He had mopped every corner of his apartment with bleach several times. Writhing gently, the maggot moves toward something. He picks it up with a tissue and flushes it down the toilet.

He finds another one in a crack in the bedroom doorway. The man crawls from the room to the kitchen, looking everywhere. He crawls toward the window where he hung the bouquet and discovers a continuous stream of maggots crawling along the edge of the wall. Some drop to the floor, curling up instantly into balls. A horde of maggots is writhing inside the cellophane. He opens the balcony door and hurls the bouquet into the back lot overgrown with weeds.

In the morning while he's shaving, he senses that someone is outside the front door. He runs into his bedroom, then dashes to the front door, struggling to put on his pants. In his hurry, he ends up taking longer. He has to meet her. He has to tell her about the drunk fellow, about the roses. He thrusts open the front door, but the corridor is already empty. The clicking of heels is fading. Urgently he leans over the railing and looks down the stairwell at the railings that zigzag all the way to the bottom floor. He sees a flash of yellow, like a butterfly that has taken flight. Is it the yellow he glimpsed from the yellow socks that had been hanging on her clothesline? He looks down at his own feet and realizes he forgot to put on his shoes. He'd stayed up waiting until three in the morning. He hadn't heard any footsteps come up to the fifth floor. When did she come home? Or maybe she'd never left the house in the first place. Maybe she'd been cooped up inside all this time.

Only a trace of her perfume lingers in the empty stairwell. It's a light, fresh scent, unlike the perfume called Poison once so popular with the female staff at the office. He inhales deeply, making his lungs expand like balloons. What kind of woman is she? He realizes he wants to get to know her.

When he lifts up the mail slot cover, he discovers another flap behind it. He shoves it open as well and sees the inside of 507 through the rectangular opening. His cheek, flattened on the cement floor, turns icy. There is a pair of indoor slippers placed neatly by the door. They are mustard-colored with crudely embroidered flowers on the instep. He slips his hand into the slot and gropes for them, but it's difficult, because he can't see what he's doing. He needs to leave for work in about ten minutes. He wriggles his arm further and further in until he's in up to his armpit, causing the flap to pinch his skin. It's a slow process; he has to take his arm out, look inside to estimate the distance, and then put it back in again. After some thought, he fashions a metal clothes hanger into a long hook and slips it into the slot. He hooks the slipper and pulls it toward him. Finally the slipper is in his hand.

The one-size-fits-all slipper is worn out. She has small feet, judging by the flattened faux-fur insole where her heel has rubbed. The vinyl on the instep is peeling and its color has faded. Although it looks mustard yellow, it probably was a bright yellow once. He hides the slipper in the back of his closet.

"Shit, late again."

He purses his lips and then heaves a sigh. To his surprise, he finds himself whistling. He bounds down the stairs and all the way to the bus stop.

Half a month passes. Now that the woman has returned, he has resumed his garbage work once again. The garbage truck empties the bin every other day, so if he skips even one day, he may never find her garbage. On the fifteenth day the other indoor slipper turns up. The nearly empty bag is tied loosely so the knot comes easily undone. For half a month she probably turned her home upside down, trying to find its pair, until she finally gave up and threw out the lone slipper. There are purple fruit stains on the embroidery. He retrieves the other slipper from his closet and places them side by side. The difference in their color is noticeable, and bits of cotton and foam stick out through the worn soles. He pulls out the rest of the contents from the garbage bag. Used tea bags, thick orange peels, Diet Coke cans—all diet foods. Next, he lifts up a plastic package, tightly rolled up. It's an empty pouch of fabric softener, mimosa scent, the same floral perfume from the corridor. It smells fragrant in the midst of the rotten stink, despite the slippery grains of spoiled rice stuck to the packaging. At the very bottom of the garbage bag is a three-tiered, fresh cream cake, untouched and gone bad. A fluffy layer of mold is already blooming on the top. Grape stains cover the patches where the milky cream has rubbed off, and a red outline marks where a cherry had been. It looks like she picked out only the fruit from the cake. He unfolds every little piece of paper, even an aspirin wrapper. One train ticket to Gurye. In his mind he sees her climb Mount Jiri. Her yellow socks become streaked with dirt. A seven-digit number scrawled on a slip of paper—maybe a phone number? He also finds a past due notice for a pager. Once he has wiped off the cream, her name and pager number materialize. *Choi Jiae. 012-343-7890.*

He stands in the middle of a large grocery store, holding a yellow shopping basket. In it he has placed mimosa-scented fabric softener and a jumbo container of bleach. Products rarely purchased are covered with dust. In front of the cosmetics counter is an employee, heavily made up like a mannequin. She latches onto passing customers and hands them questionnaires, repeating the same words over and over again.

"We're promoting our new product. You'll receive a free gift just by filling out this short survey."

Every year, companies launch dozens of new products. Even at his company, those in product development are anxious to come up with a hit product like Nongshim's Shrimp Crackers. In order to develop products that guarantee consumer satisfaction, thousands of surveys are distributed throughout the entire nation. He has a thorough knowledge of his neighbors' different tastes and patterns of consumption. Once he read about a sociological discipline called "garbology," which examines the waste of residents in a certain area to learn about their behavior. Looking through a garbage dump is a far more reliable way of getting answers than collecting information through a vague survey. Garbage never lies. *You want to know the real answer to a riddle? Garbage.* This is what he thinks as he wanders down the supermarket aisles.

The drunk fellow is sitting on the top step of the fifth floor. He looks up with bloodshot eyes and recognizes the man at once. The man has to wait on the landing until the fellow moves aside, since his huge body is blocking the way. He extends his chunky, bearlike paw and clasps the man's hand. A large cake box sits on the step.

"I'm sorry, I couldn't give her the flowers. I didn't even see her."

"Yeah, she went on a trip."

"Then I guess you saw her?"

Grimacing, the fellow scrubs his face with his hand. "No, I heard through a friend. Oh, this here . . ." he says, catching the man glancing at the cake box. He hands it to him. "I'm sorry to bother you again, but you mind giving this to her? She just got back, so she won't be going anywhere for a while."

The man has no choice but to take the box with just one hand, since he's carrying his groceries in the other. When the box slips a little, the fellow's bloodshot eyes widen.

"Hey, be careful! You might squish the cake."

At the words *squish the cake*, the fellow's broad face squishes up, too.

"Is it a fresh cream cake? With fruit, like cherries or pineapple on top?"

"She's crazy about fresh cream cake. I'm a huge fan myself," he snickers. "You think we'll ever eat it together again?" he mumbles, as if talking to himself.

The fellow nods goodbye and begins to make his way down the stairs. The cake is heavy. While the man is opening his door, he hears a curse come from the third floor. The fellow must have tripped on the higher, second step.

"Excuse me," the man calls down the center of the stairwell.

Several levels below, the fellow's broad face emerges over the railing.

"You know . . ." the man starts to say.

The fellow has no clue that she doesn't like fresh cream cake. It could have even been the cause of their breakup. But how could he tell the truth without giving the wrong idea? If he confesses he digs through other people's garbage, the fellow will think he's crazy. And if he says that she told him herself, the fellow is bound to grow suspicious.

"What if something happens?"

The fellow gives him a blank stare.

"I mean, what if I don't run into her?"

The fellow smiles brightly, revealing yellow teeth. "Then you go ahead and eat it!" His laughter grows distant.

The woman is on a diet right now. She doesn't hate the guy; she just hates his enormous body that weighs close to a hundred kilograms. She's sick of eating fresh cream cake, and she's sick of his mistaken belief that she also shares his love for this cake—it's the reason they broke up. If only the fellow had dug through her garbage, who knows? They might still be together.

·

Inside the man's fridge, the cake is slowly spoiling. He still hasn't run into her. They have narrowly missed each other each time. Whenever he scrambles out into the corridor after her, she is already gone, leaving behind a trace of mimosa-scented fabric softener. He opens his address book. *Choi Jiae. 012-343-7890.*

"Did somebody page me?" says a bored voice on the other end of the line, chewing gum.

"I'm supposed to give you a cake, but you're impossible to run into."

She blows a bubble and the gum pops. "What are you talking about?" She chews again.

"I live next door to you, Miss Choi."

"That's it, I've had enough," she snaps. "A man man kept calling, leaving weird messages and now this! I'm not, what's her name, Choi Jiae. I've had this number for over a month now."

The door of 507 is wide open. He takes the cake out of the fridge and rushes inside. A middle-aged couple is repapering the walls. With all the furniture taken out, the unit looks bigger than he imagined. The smell of adhesive stings his nostrils. A man with a strip of pasted paper in hand is climbing a ladder. He glances toward the entrance.

"Can I help you?" his wife calls out. She smiles at the man, holding a brush dripping with paste. "Do you want your walls repapered? We offer very good prices."

The man moves out of the doorway as two workmen carrying a large sheet of glass come up the stairs. They go out to the balcony and remove the broken shards and start to put in the new pane.

·

The drunk fellow is in the back lot looking for something. He raises his crimson face when the man calls out to him. The man steps into the lot. Overgrown weeds come up to his knees.

"I'm sorry. I ended up eating the cake. It took a whole week to finish it."

The fellow is out of breath. In his hand is a broken branch.

"She moved out," the man continues. "But I guess you already knew that?"

The fellow nods, whipping the overgrown weeds.

"Then what are you doing here?"

"Last summer, we went on a trip to Jeju Island," the fellow says, his eyes taking on a far-away look, as if he's reminiscing. "You see, Jiae likes the ocean."

It's not the ocean that she likes—it's the mountains.

Fixing his gaze into the distance, the fellow keeps mumbling. "We bought a dol harubang there. You know the Jeju souvenir—the stone statue with holes punched in it like pumice? The night we got into a fight, she went crazy and threw it out the window. It should have landed somewhere over here. I've looked everywhere, but I can't find it."

They search, but it's not easy to find a little statue in a thicket of weeds.

"Then why don't we look again from opposite ends?" The man searches for a stick.

"You sure you're not busy?"

He picks up a branch and walks over to the other side. "I've got lots of time."

He whacks the grass as he examines the ground. He glances up to see the fellow wipe his red face with his sleeve. It's sweltering. At noon the temperature hits about 28 degrees Celsius. *Tonight's going to be the last time. Just once more and I'm calling it quits.* He takes off his tie and shoves it in his suit pocket. He unbuttons the top button of his dress shirt that's choking him. *But there's no other way to know. You know why? Because the truth is rotting in the garbage somewhere.* Savagely, the man beats the grass.

Toothpaste

A giant billboard stands atop a high-rise tower. A maiden in a floral-print bikini with a lei around her neck smiles down at the intersection twenty stories below. Stretching out behind her is the Pacific Ocean, where a motorboat cleaves through the greenish waves and copper-skinned young men balance themselves on surfboards, bending their bodies like bows. The fruit at the top of the palm trees is the size of rugby balls.

He stands clutching a bus strap and looks out the dusty window at the billboard. The laughter and raucous sounds of a foreign language ring in his ears. The water looks clear, but if you waded in, shards of coral would pierce your bare feet. The bus doesn't budge. Once apartment buildings started to go up on this reclamation ground, the road, which runs parallel to the coastline of the West Sea, wasn't able to handle the sudden increase in traffic volume. Today's high tide was at 4:10 A.M. The water is starting to recede already, backing away from the breakwater. Once again, the bus didn't arrive on time that morning, and the station swarmed with twice as many passengers as usual. The bus suddenly cuts into the left-turn lane, and a woman standing close behind slams into him with the force of a heavy suitcase. His hand is wrenched from the strap and he falls, his face mashing against the window.

For the past year, whenever he's passing through this congested area, he has stared up at the billboard. He keeps staring, until he can read the writing at the bottom. *Paradise on Earth. It's Closer Than You Think.* The left-turn signal comes on twice, but the bus is still stuck in the intersection.

The girl on the billboard smiles her same smile in the sleet and in the winter rain, and he looks up at her, whether he's dressed in his fall suit still reeking of chemicals, or in his down parka and leather gloves. Someone behind him has already claimed his plastic strap when he'd let go. He keeps his gaze fixed on the billboard, all through the bus's lurching. The ad was already old when he saw it for the first time a year ago, with colors fading from direct exposure to the sun and the paint peeling in places. Even the maiden's smile has lost its luster.

Foam is poking through the rip in the nylon seat. Once the bus is able to escape the intersection and enter the freeway, it will speed all the way to Seoul Station. He peers through the tangle of arms that block his view. The bus is now right in front of the tower. He can no longer see the top part of the billboard, but can make out the smaller print. Various destinations and their prices are stamped on the maiden's thighs.

Bankok/Pataya - 5 Days - 499,000
Boracay - 5 Days - 749,000
Langkawi - 5 Days - 649,000
Hawaii - 5 Days - 999,000

These unfamiliar destinations are like the different items on a menu at a French restaurant. Day and night, the maiden casts inviting glances at passersby, saying, "For a million minus a thousand won, you can come to Hawaii and spend five days with me."

What the man is actually looking at is the high-rise rooftop, blocked by the billboard and spotted only by the helicopters and low-altitude airplanes flying above. He had spent most of his thirty months of military service atop a 25-story tower in Yongsan, behind rooftop billboards just like this one.

Before stepping into the building three to four times a day, he'd stared up at the gigantic billboards. Dressed in full military gear, he'd had to tilt his head all the way back to see the red convertible, with a blonde woman in the passenger seat wearing an off-the-shoulder top. Countless times in his mind, he'd gotten in the empty driver's seat and sped along the road. He stepped into the elevator and took it to the very top. He then needed to climb the emergency stairs. On the wall where the stairs suddenly stopped, a sign bore the words No Admittance. Attached to the wall was a steel ladder leading to a square metal hatch in the ceiling. When he pushed open the hatch and poked out his head, he saw gigantic water tanks and exhaust fans turning ceaselessly. Surrounded by colossal billboards, the rooftop was like a cardboard box without a lid. Beams crisscrossed on the backs of billboards, and rusted pegs protruded. There on the roof, hidden by the billboards, the man guarded anti-aircraft missiles in two-hour shifts. Beatings and punishment were meted out endlessly. Groans escaped his lips every time the club struck his behind, but they were absorbed by all the outside noise. At night, the moon rose in the square night sky. When he got off duty and stepped out of the building, the beautiful golden-haired woman was still there in the sports car. It was from this period he began to suffer from a mild case of claustrophobia.

The bus finally rounds the tower. Since he isn't holding onto a strap, he falls as people are swept to one side. As his face hits the window, spittle flies out from between his lips and lands on the glass. Out of one eye, he sees the rearview mirror stuck on the side of the bus. Reflected in the convex mirror is a girl's face. Though her face is distorted, he notices her right away, amid all the unfamiliar faces. It's a face he's seen before. People press up behind her, but she holds herself up by pushing against the back of a seat. Her face is devoid of makeup, and there are dark smudges under her narrowed eyes. The bus finally enters the freeway and he manages to straighten himself up. When he glances at the rearview mirror again, the girl is gone.

•

A crumpled Coke can bounces off his foot and flies forward. When he steps on a discarded ice cream wrapper, the melted content spews out and soils his shoe. Sun Villa is situated next to its twin, Moon Villa. A warning in red is posted on the stone wall: *Those Caught Littering Will Be Fined.* As if to mock these words, foul-smelling garbage bags are piled up beside the wall. The man cuts across the villa courtyard, which reeks of urine. It's only been a year since completion, but thin cracks, like plant roots, run up the walls of the building.

The man purchased this apartment outside Seoul for various reasons. He'd first seen the advertisement for the pre-sale villa units in the morning paper. Amid tedious advertisements with phrases like *high investment value, a low price per square foot, 15% finishing options, equipped with top-grade gas range*, and *twelve mineral springs*, this particular advertisement had caught his eye.

Open your window to the West Sea. Every evening, be treated to the sunset. Take the #24 from Incheon and get to Seoul in 40 minutes. Have a seat. Relax all the way to Seoul.

On the day he moved in, he slid open the window that faced west. Instead of the horizon of the West Sea, he was greeted by the view of someone else's balcony, crowded with laundry. Except the laundry wasn't on the balcony; it was hanging over the railing above a street so narrow that a white undershirt grazed his nose every time it flapped in the wind. This apartment tower across the street blocked his view of the West Sea. Until late at night, pop songs and the clamor of machinery from Songdo Amusement Park drifted into his bedroom, and on rainy or cloudy days, the air carried the smell of animal waste from the park zoo. Sometimes when he passed his window, he made eye contact with the people watching television in the living room behind their balcony. He hung a large print of the Hong Kong nightlife over his window. The photograph portrayed neon signs that said *Coca-Cola refreshes you best* and *Dry, Drier, Driest*, which was probably a Dry Gin ad. Since then, it was always night outside his window, glittering with bright lights.

The small window of the guard booth slides open and an old security guard sticks his head out. "Hold on, I've got a letter for you!"

While the guard searches for the letter, the man leans against the aluminum booth and gazes up at the villa windows. The laundry draped over the balcony is hovering in the dark like ghosts. He is reminded of back alleys in Hong Kong where people would string laundry on a bamboo pole and hang it over the street. He'd learned only recently that people here hung their laundry over the balcony because their apartments hardly got any sun. The guard rummages through the desk drawers and even riffles through a stack of paper.

Then as if he'd just remembered, he pulls out a folded envelope from his back pocket.

"I found it a few days ago in the courtyard."

He spits toward the dark flowerbed. The envelope is marked with a boot print and is damp from the humidity. It's addressed to Park Seongcheol, a name that's identical to his own, except for the middle syllable. The bottom consonants are so tiny that the characters look like circus performers balancing precariously on a unicycle. He stands under the security light with his briefcase wedged between his knees and rips open the envelope. Insects flutter around the security light. It rained off and on for the past several days, so the ink is smudged and has bled through the paper.

"I went through a lot of trouble to find your address. I spoke to HR at your company, but they wouldn't tell me. In the end, I had to lie. I said I admired your work, that I worked for a magazine and wanted to interview you. Where do I start? Of course I know it wasn't all your fault. After all, we were both spring chickens back then. But everything went wrong for me after that. I wilted before I could even blossom. All because of you, Mr. Park. Don't waste your gift on useless things. I've told a lot of lies, but I'm not lying when I say I was your admirer once."

The man holds the letter up to the light and reads it several more times. He can't understand it. He feels as if he's reading a news article where the beginning and ending have been removed. Judging by the writing, he's certain a woman had written it. He turns over the envelope, but the name and address of the sender are missing.

"Sorry, but I don't think it's for me."

The old guard is watching television with his feet propped on the desk. "I searched the whole villa for two days."

The man glimpses a tiny bathroom inside the booth. The guard hacks and spits into the toilet.

"I realize there's no one by the name of Park Seongcheol, but look—Sun Villa, Building B, 201—isn't that you?" the guard says, pointing at the address on the envelope.

He sucks in his sunken cheeks, sending his mint candy clacking against his teeth. Each time he opens his mouth, the smell of mint, unable to mask his stale breath, hits the man in the face.

"But I told you my name isn't Park Seongcheol," he says.

He tosses the letter on the guard's desk and climbs the stairs to his apartment.

There is dried toothpaste smeared on the side of the kitchen sink from this morning. His desk is strewn with tubes of toothpaste. Since the product name hasn't yet been chosen, the word *toothpaste* marks each white tube. They have about twenty days to come up with a TV commercial concept and script. Through the wall he hears the clatter of plates from the apartment next door. He squeezes toothpaste onto his brush, puts it in his mouth, and paces the living room. Ever since a large stain formed on his bathroom ceiling from the apartment upstairs, he has carried out his morning and nightly routines at the kitchen sink. Not much has changed from his days in the army seven years ago. Just as before, he finds himself enclosed in a cramped, square space. From here, he can't even see the moon. With his mouth full of toothpaste foam, he walks to his desk and scrawls a few words into an open notebook. *Gum disease, bad breath, cavities, triclosan, control, refresh, kiss*—though featuring a kiss in a toothpaste commercial became a cliché a long time ago. Foam drips onto the floor from his mouth. He rinses, spits, and then squeezes toothpaste on his brush once more. The mint flavor makes his tongue and mouth go numb.

·

He gently pushes open the heavy, padded door to the screening room. The light from the hallway spills into the dark room where thick curtains have been drawn to shut out the light. The dust swirling over the screen is illuminated for a moment, and Mr. Kim, standing beside the screen with a pointer in hand, grimaces and covers his eyes with his hand. Images flash on the screen, as the film makes its way from the feed reel into the projector. His hunched shadow wavers on top of the screen.

When he got off the bus at Seoul Station, he was already late for work. The words from the advertisement—*get to Seoul in 40 minutes*—were true only if you were traveling in the middle of the night when there was no traffic, or when you were racing along the freeway at 120 kilometers per hour. Because of his frequent tardiness, he once nearly had to submit a written apology.

Even this morning in Incheon, his bus had come late. It had then started pulling out of the terminal with people hanging out the door. A few who had managed to climb onto the steps were forced off. When the doors couldn't close, he had no choice but to come down and wait for the next bus. He sprinted the two blocks from Seoul Station to his office building. He almost got run over by a car darting out from an alley.

He trips over a cord and frantically puts out his hands to break his fall. Every gaze that had been glued to the screen is now on him. With his own eyes still not adjusted to the darkness, he gropes along, searching for a place to sit. The screening room floor is sloped like a movie theater. He manages to find a seat in the back. Light from the projector penetrates the face of Mr. Kim, who stands brandishing his pointer.

Toothpaste commercials parade by tediously on the screen. A woman with curly hair bites into a green apple with a loud crunch. The brand appears across the screen with a close-up of the woman's red lips. She runs her tongue over each white tooth that gleams like porcelain. Words flash across the screen: *So clean.*

Stacks of advertisements are heaped on the tables. Under the company's mandate to not waste office supplies, the employees are forced to reuse the backs of old advertisements. The man writes the word *toothpaste* in big and small letters on the back of an ad. Another toothpaste commercial appears on the screen. A woman and man, both young and beautiful, dash toward each other from opposite directions. Closer and closer. When his whole page is crammed full of *toothpaste*, the word suddenly feels alien. It even feels like an onomatopoeic word, like *ouch* or *tweet*. On the other side of the paper is the face of a well-known actress. Her hair is wet, as if she has just stepped out of the shower, and she's holding a glass brimming with cold beer. He doodles on her face with a marker, scrawling stringy hair like that of corn on her chin and under her nose, and covering one eye with a patch. He even colors her teeth black. If his memory serves him right, she was once voted the female celebrity with the most winning smile.

"She'll still be smiling, even if you pull out all her teeth."

It's Chae, his colleague, who's taken a seat next to him. He snickers at the picture. "Try selling beer with a model like that."

This time, he draws a scar on the actress's cheek. He's adding stitches to the scar when a hand snatches up the paper. Mr. Kim glances at the disfigured face of the actress and turns over the paper. On the back page, the word *toothpaste* is written countless times in both small and large letters; they squirm like insects. Mr. Kim taps the desk with the pointer, something he always does before delivering a statement. He has a knack for saying the right thing at the right time.

"Thanks for the reminder. I almost forgot we're working on a toothpaste commercial."

Laughter breaks out around the room, and he walks slowly back to the front, which slants downward like the bottom of a soup bowl. The take-up reel finishes winding the film and keeps turning, making a noise like a cicada. Someone gets up to turn on the light, but Mr. Kim holds up a hand. A white square hovers on the screen. Mr. Kim raises his voice.

"That's right, our assignment this time is toothpaste. Of course I would love to work on commercials for Volvo, Coca-Cola, or McDonald's, since those brands practically sell themselves." Abruptly, his tone changes and he mutters quickly, "How hard can this be? Toothpaste is toothpaste. What's toothpaste? Something you use to brush your teeth. Do you need to use it to know what it does? No, it's obvious. If toothpaste prevents cavities, why do you think dentists are still in business?"

"Are you saying we should do false advertising?" calls a voice so thin it sounds ready to crawl into a hole.

Instead of responding, Mr. Kim collapses his pointer and slips it into the inside pocket of his blazer. Mr. Kim never rambles, always opting for a concise response.

"Have you walked down the toothpaste aisle recently? There are more than a dozen different brands alone. Fights gingivitis, cavities, plaque, bad breath, blah blah blah. They're all the same. What you're doing is helping consumers choose from a mountain of different brands out there. Through a tasteful, hopefully charming ad."

Mr. Kim had come up with a hit soju commercial twenty years ago. Many people still recall the animated commercial that began with the cha-cha-cha tune, featuring its drunk, red-nosed character. But in real life, Mr. Kim doesn't touch a drop of alcohol. He gestures at someone in the front row. From where the man is sitting, he can only see the back of the person's head. When Mr. Kim gestures again, a woman with long hair stands up.

"This is the face—the new face that will bring life to this commercial! We're targeting younger folks this time. Those between nineteen and twenty-five. For that reason, we couldn't go with established models, since they're probably appearing in other commercials. Even the toothpaste company wanted someone new. Now that you've gotten a look at the face of our product, I'm sure the juices are flowing. Miss Choi, why don't you introduce yourself?"

She steps forward hesitantly and stands beside Mr. Kim. The top of his half-balding head comes up to her ears. There are a few snickers around the room.

"Nice to meet you. I'm Choi Myeong-ae."

Because of the dim lighting, he can see only the outline of her face. Someone sitting by the window gets up and tugs the curtain cord. As the curtain is drawn to one side, her pointed chin and tightly closed lips materialize. She has her gaze fixed on a certain spot on the floor, eyes narrowed from the sunlight. Whistles and cheers erupt from all over the room. She turns a little red. He's seen her before. He's sure of it.

The staff files out through the door until only he, Mr. Kim, and Choi Myeong-ae are left. Mr. Kim opens the door to the archives room at the front and whispers to Miss Choi, gesturing here and there, while she nods occasionally. The man takes his time straightening the paper on the table and glances again at her. He's certain he's seen her somewhere, but he just can't remember where. Miss Choi follows Mr. Kim to the padded door, making eye contact with the man as she walks past.

"Have we met before?" he says, hurrying up to her. "We have, right? How did we meet again? We've talked before, haven't we?"

She takes a step back, as he keeps pressing her. "I think you've got me confused with someone else. We've never met before."

Mr. Kim peers into the screening room and gestures to her to come out.

Miss Choi smiles at Mr. Kim and says, "I guess I have a common face."

As if it were the most natural thing to do, Mr. Kim puts his arm around her shoulders and looks between her and the man. "Tão Bom, quit fooling around and come up with a catchphrase by the end of the week. Something decent we can actually use!"

No one on the ad design team is called by their real names, but by their nicknames, based on a word from a tagline they developed, the product name of a past hit commercial, or of one where they hadn't hit the mark. The man went by "Tāo Bom." He'd noticed the tiny tremor in Choi Myeong-ae's cheek when Mr. Kim had called him that. But just as suddenly as her expression had changed, she's now back to looking prim and composed.

"Come on, let's go grab a bite," Mr. Kim says.

At his words, she moves closer to Mr. Kim and links her arm through his. They walk down the hall, the sound of her heels echoing after them. She is wearing a short black dress that hits above her knees. Buttons run down her back, all the way to her tailbone.

"I swear there's something funny between those two," says Chae, who had been smoking in the hallway. He scratches his disheveled hair and gazes after Mr. Kim and Choi Myeong-ae. "All those buttons. It must be hard work doing them up on her own and then undoing them all again."

He half-listens to what Chae says and gropes along his foggy memory. He's certain they've met before, but he just can't remember where. He shouts after her as she draws farther away.

"I know we've met before! It'll come to me sooner or later!"

He can't tell if she heard him or not. They disappear around the corner.

•

"Someone broke the light bulb again," the security guard says, recognizing him. "It's the third one now."

The old guard is standing on a plastic stool, changing the bulb in the villa entrance.

"By the way, did you end up finding the right person? You know, for the letter?"

The guard is struggling to screw the bulb into the socket. He gestures to the guard to come down and climbs onto the stool himself.

"Nope. It's still sitting there on top of my desk. But another letter arrived two days ago. I was sorting the mail and put it aside. Let's see. That letter should be right—"

He rummages through all the pockets in his uniform.

Even after the man comes down from the stool, the old guard is still searching his pockets. The man flicks the switch and the light comes on. The guard finally hands him an envelope and spits in the direction of the flowerbed.

"Since you've already read the first one, I guess it's okay if you read this."

The second letter is written on a different kind of paper that crackles like a rice cracker. When he spreads it open, characters with small bottom consonants seem to be teetering and tottering.

"Today, I bought a dress with lots of buttons. After I'd done them all up and was about to button the last one, I discovered there was no hole to put it through. I looked in the mirror and saw the back of my dress was wrinkled around the neck. I'd put the third button in the fourth hole. So I had to undo them all and start over. As I was doing them up, I had a thought: When did the button of my life go in the wrong hole? I thought long and hard, but I have to say it was after that time. I don't doubt it was difficult for you, too, Mr. Park. I want to go back to the very beginning, but I've come too far. I sound like a sappy song, don't I? But there's nothing moving about this. I'm sure you don't even remember anymore. You probably chalked it up to inexperience and moved on. No one will recognize me now. I've changed too much. Actually, I hope no one recognizes me. There was a time I wished someone would. But that's all in the past."

Whoever wrote this letter blames a person by the name of Park Seongcheol.

"What does it say this time?"

The old guard looks over the man's shoulder. The smell of mint stings his nostrils.

"Here. Why don't you see for yourself?"

The guard fishes out a pair of reading glasses from his front pocket. With them hanging off the end of his nose, he holds the letter at a distance and mumbles out loud. The man sits on the ledge of the flowerbed and puts a cigarette in his mouth. He finds himself thinking about Choi Myeong-ae. It's probably because of the dress she'd been wearing.

"Well, from my experience," the guard says, crouching beside him. "You know the old saying, how a stone you throw without a thought will end up killing a frog?"

The man offers the guard a cigarette, but shaking his hand, he takes out another mint candy from his pocket and unwraps it.

"I quit three years ago. The doctor said my lungs were black, like they were covered with coal dust. You want one?"

The guard gets to his feet awkwardly and searches his pocket for another mint.

"No thanks. To be honest, I've had enough of mint."

Though the deadline is a week away, the man's thoughts have not progressed beyond "the kiss." As soon as he thinks about toothpaste, Choi Myeong-ae with her black dress crosses his mind.

He had seen her again in the lunchroom that day. She'd been with Mr. Kim, eating by the far window. The lunchroom was self-service, so the rice and side dishes were set out in large pans on the buffet table. He wasn't craving anything, so he simply moved down the line, and ended up scooping only a bit of rice and soup for himself. With the tray in his hands, he glanced toward the windows. There were no empty seats that looked out onto the plaza garden. He had a habit of seeking window seats, since he couldn't bear enclosed spaces. That's when he saw Choi Myeong-ae and Mr. Kim sitting near the spot where the dirty trays were returned. The clatter of stainless steel trays and utensils rang throughout the lunchroom. The only empty seat by the window was beside her, so the man took the seat next to her. She had been smiling brightly, but her face stiffened instantly.

"Look at this! Tofu soybean-paste soup with braised tofu and stir-fried tofu?" he prattled on. "Are we doing a tofu commercial next?"

Choi Myeong-ae, who had been nibbling on the braised tofu, backed her chair away a little, and then said to Mr. Kim, "It seems a little salty. What do you think?"

The man picked at his rice. Because of all the toothpaste he'd been using, he could hardly taste the seasoning. He stared at her profile, chewing on the ends of his chopsticks. She spooned up some soup, but feeling his gaze on her, she dripped a little on her skirt.

"Miss Choi, we've met before, haven't we?"

She nodded.

"When?" he said, facing her. "Where? It's driving me crazy."

She stared directly into his eyes. "About ten days ago. In the screening room when you were late and ended up tripping and falling."

Mr. Kim laughed, his mouth full of food.

"—so that's why I'm always sucking on candy now, just like a little kid," the old security guard said, as he finished his story.

So lost in his thoughts about Choi Myeong-ae, the man had missed everything the guard had said.

The guard gets to his feet and brushes dirt off his rear end. "Don't take everything I've said too seriously. Just consider it as the rambling of an old man."

Rolling the mint in his mouth, he steps into his aluminum booth. The man will never learn why the guard is always sucking on candy. The faint strains of a pop song drift over from the amusement park.

•

The man is looking through a scrapbook containing all the advertisements he'd worked on over the years, both domestic and international. He's used up four tubes of toothpaste so far. He's tasted it, he's even squeezed some onto his fingers and felt its texture, but still nothing. All he can think of is something that has to do with kissing. *The breath that invites a kiss.* Toothpaste isn't the only reason he keeps dwelling on kissing; at this thought his face heats up.

He has no appetite. Even soybean-paste stew smells minty to him. There were at least a dozen brands of toothpaste on the market. The key was to make theirs stand out.

Acacia, bamboo salt, salt, anti-plaque, close-up . . . Thinking, he flips through each page of the scrapbook. Right then an old newspaper insert flutters to the floor. The second he bends to pick it up, he recalls the two letters that had been addressed to a man named Park Seongcheol. He had run into the security guard a few times after, but there hadn't been a third letter. He peers down at the newspaper ad that's on the floor until the blood rushes to his head. The insert had yellowed with age. A white insect as tiny as a dot is crawling across the top of the page.

It's time to rest.

There's a familiar picture printed on the page. It's a painting called *The Angelus* by Jean-François Millet. He often saw its reproduction in barbershops or coffee shops out in the country. In a field where the sun is setting, a young farmer and his wife, who have finished their day's work, listen to the ringing of the church bell and bow their heads in prayer. Because of cheap printing, the colors didn't turn out, and the peace that's conveyed in the original couldn't be felt here.

After all, we were both spring chickens back then. He recalls the phrase from the first letter. This advertisement had been his first project. Between the headline "It's time to rest" and the size and price of the apartment listed at the bottom, lines from many different poems had been borrowed to compose an elegant description. When he had first come to Seoul as a senior high-school student, he had moved thirteen times, from one rental unit to the next, until he started working. Each time he packed and unpacked his things, he longed for a place where he could put down roots, a room where he could rest.

All he knew about the apartment complex was the name of the construction company. When his ad had been chosen, he had even received a bonus. Then two years later, he'd learned through the news that the entire complex had been shoddily constructed. The residents stood in disorganized lines, staging a protest in front of the construction company building. The one leading the protest by shouting slogans kept stammering in front of the news camera. The camera captured the image of an old woman who had collapsed from exhaustion. The old woman with dark, thick skin like a turtle's shell wailed it had been her life's dream to own an apartment in Seoul, that everything had gone up in smoke, and burst into tears.

Saeho Construction, shame on you for your houses of cards! We will fight until we get our money back! The camera swept over the crude signs. It was then that he saw it: *Give us a place to rest!* Two years had passed, but people still remembered the line from the brochure.

Five years went by. No one blamed him, the one who had created the advertisement. The incident fizzled out.

Mr. Kim, who had been a junior manager back then, said to him, "It's not your fault. Those people would have first researched the apartment's price per square foot and the investment value. They would have inspected every inch of the showroom, and for those who care about their kids' education, they would have checked out the schools nearby. Only after all that would they have even considered your ad."

Gradually the man forgot all about it.

When he's brushing his teeth for the fifth time, the phone rings. He picks up, his mouth full of toothpaste. All he hears is a fast dance track in the background. The caller hangs up without a word. In order to spit, he runs toward the sink and ends up stepping on a tube of toothpaste that had fallen on the floor. The foam he spits out is pink. He looks in the mirror and discovers his gums are raw and bleeding.

•

By the time he gets to Seoul, he's already ten minutes late. Everything had been the same today. The Hawaiian maiden on the billboard had been smiling her smile, and the roads had been heavily congested. The man races down the steps of Seoul Station and across the underpass, and emerges from underground on the other side. His dress shirt is clinging to his back from perspiration. Someone is running behind him. Light steps catch up to him.

"You're late again."

It's Choi Myeong-ae. With a small bow, she hurries ahead, leaping into the revolving door.

The lobby of the building where he works was selected as the shoot location. Crew members are busy moving potted plants to one side, dragging a payphone to the middle of the lobby, and setting up the revolving door. It's the first time a toothpaste commercial won't show anyone brushing their teeth. In fact, there is no bathroom, no female model with her hair wrapped in a towel.

"How can you have a toothpaste commercial without showing any toothpaste?" asks Chae with a cigarette in his mouth, as he flips through the script.

Choi Myeong-ae and a male model are getting their hair and makeup done in one corner of the lobby. With her hair twisted up, she's wearing a tailored jacket and pencil skirt that hugs her hips and thighs. The male model has on a tie. This commercial doesn't feature a green apple or kiss. In the end, Mr. Kim's own idea had been chosen from the many scripts. In a busy lobby where many people are coming and going, a man enters the revolving door. He sees a beautiful woman heading toward him. She gives him a radiant smile and exits through the revolving door. He goes back in the door and chases after her. Then the words: *It takes a star to know a star. For only the very brightest—Supernova.*

It is late afternoon when they wrap. The crew surround the two actors.

"Wow, these new models are even better than the pros out there! Miss Choi, you sure you haven't done this before?" the director says in a loud voice.

"Hold on!" cries Choi Myeong-ae, breaking away from the crowd. "Mr. Park Seongcheol!" she calls to the man.

He glances around, but there is no one standing next to him. She smiles, walking toward him.

"Or should I say Mr. Tão Bom? Thank you for everything. Let me treat you to dinner next time."

She joins the crew and steps into the elevator. There's only one person who thinks his name is Park Seongcheol.

The shelf is filled with hundreds of videotapes, arranged by year. He removes one from the top shelf. In the screening room, he sticks it into the VCR. He sits close to the large screen.

On a Brazilian orange farm, golden oranges roll forward. An inspector picks one up and gives a thumbs up, declaring, "Tão bom!" A celebration breaks out. The indigenous people shout "Tão bom!" and dance and laugh under the orange trees. One in a straw hat, sporting a handlebar mustache, raises his thumb and drawls, "Tão bom!" Beside him, a maiden with long hair takes a sip of orange juice from a glass and flashes a bright smile. And then subtitles appear at the bottom: "So good." The man quickly presses pause. That smiling maiden was Choi Myeong-ae. At the time, she had been a high-school senior, her eyes large and clear and face still plump with baby fat. The rounded tip of her nose made her look like an indigenous maiden.

This commercial was a sensation. The whole nation came to know the Portuguese phrase "tão bom." If you walked into a bar, you were bound to hear "tão bom!" all over the room. Even a new expression— "tão tão bom"—was coined. Still, the commercial was considered a failure. People went to the supermarket and looked for Tão Bom orange juice, but there was no juice by that name. No one remembered the actual product name. Belatedly, the manufacturer released Tão Bom juice, but the product wasn't the only thing that was passed over. It was Choi Myeong-ae. No one remembered the pretty girl with the bright smile. No agency recruited her to be their model. And so she disappeared from view.

Just as she'd said in the letter, they were both spring chickens back then. Though she had managed to book a major part in a commercial, she wasn't able to catch the spotlight. For a young girl whose future seemed full of promise, being completely overlooked was too much to bear. He has no idea what she has done for the past five years. He has no idea how she met Mr. Kim, how she managed to become the face of a new brand of toothpaste. He can only guess how far she must have wandered to get to this point.

•

There are painters dangling from scaffolding on both sides of the billboard. The bus doesn't budge. At the end of this road is the West Sea. Once apartment buildings started to go up on this reclamation ground, the road wasn't able to handle the sudden increase in traffic volume. Today's high tide was at 3:15 A.M. As he slept, the tide came in and went out. The painters whitewash the billboard with long-handled paint rollers. They pull on ropes passing over pulleys to go up and down, and kick off the billboard to maneuver slowly to the side. With each move, the whiteness spreads. What will go on the billboard now? Gripping the hand strap, he stares up at the roof.

As the road became a high-traffic area, the cost to rent this advertising space increased dramatically. When the bus tilts, his face presses against the window. With one eye, he sees the large rearview mirror on the side. Inside the convex mirror is a familiar face. He squeezes past people to move closer to Choi Myeong-ae.

"I'm an Incheonite," she says with a laugh. "I got on at Yonghyeon-dong. But aren't you going to ask me the same thing you always ask? Aren't you going to ask how we first met?"

She is no longer the plump-faced teenager from five years ago, but every time she smiles, the face of a high-school senior flickers like a second image in a hologram. Her nose was the reason he hadn't recognized her. The tip, which had been somewhat bulbous, is now sharp and pointed.

"Actually, I finally remembered how we first met," he says. He notices a slight tremor in her cheek.

"H-how?" she stammers.

"Was it a month ago? In the screening room at work. I was late that day and I tripped coming in."

She flashes a bright, dazzling smile. He hasn't seen her smile this way except in the juice commercial. The bus enters the freeway and starts to speed.

"When the commercial comes out and people start recognizing you, you might not be able to take the bus like this. You might miss taking the bus then. But hey, you know those billboards on the roof of a building? I bet you'll never guess what's actually behind them."

Frowning a little, Choi Myeong-ae looks up at him. He finds himself glancing again at her teeth, which are as straight and white as porcelain. No matter what anyone says, he can't think of a more perfect girl for Supernova toothpaste.

Early Beans

The foul stench came from the dumpsters. Uncollected garbage was piled like pyramids around the apartment complex. At night, rats came out to gnaw at the trash. Liquid leaked from the bags and flowed down the asphalt and hardened in chunks. To avoid getting his dress shoes dirty, the man leapt over the stains like an athlete competing in the triple jump event. Dressed in pointy shoes and a white dress shirt with the top two buttons undone and tucked into snug jeans, he looked like an amateur cowboy who had just stepped out of a Western movie. He shaded his face with one hand, and with the other, clutched a cell phone instead of a pistol. He didn't run into a single person as he walked to the parking lot. Even the playground was deserted. The stench and the unbearable heat were to blame.

He stopped in front of a car parked neatly in its spot. The car was like a pan on high heat. He flung open the door, started the engine, and blasted on the air-conditioning. He sought some shade while he waited for the car to cool down. Heaped up on one side of the lot was all kinds of junk—everything from an old refrigerator, stereo, and mattress to even an electric rice cooker. A full-length mirror also stood among the garbage. As if it had been left out in the rain for some time, the varnish was peeling off the frame like scabs. The man went up to the mirror and gazed at his reflection. He puffed out his cheeks, stroked his chin, and opened his mouth wide to check between his teeth. He then curled back his lips and bared his teeth, braying silently like a donkey.

Fifteen minutes later, his car slipped smoothly out of the complex's gates. The old security guard sat dozing in his booth, unable to fight off the after-lunch drowsiness. No one saw the man leave.

To get onto the main road, he had to pass through a 400-meter school zone. Children dismissed for the day began to pour out of the school gates. Street vendors who had come in time for dismissal sat on the ground, leaning against the stone wall in front of the school. The children ran across the street and swarmed around stalls filled with helium balloons, baby chicks, and sweets. They stood in the middle of the road, not bothering to move out of the way. The man's car inched forward, only to lurch repeatedly to a stop. Suddenly, a soccer ball sailed over the stone wall, bounced off his windshield, and rolled under the car. It was followed by a tanned boy in a track suit who crawled under the car to retrieve it. Another child cut across the street to go after a chick that had escaped from his grasp and a herd of children ran toward the ice cream store. The man honked his horn again and again. The kids didn't budge. He stuck his head out the window and yelled. The children slowly squirmed out of the way, but as soon as his car moved forward into the small opening, other kids blocked the way, playing a game of slap-match cards in the middle of the road. They were so absorbed in their cards that they didn't hear him shout.

Each child was like a lightning strike. With lightning, there are no warnings. There are only two ways to avoid getting electrocuted: you have to lie flat on the ground or put up a lightning rod. He drove with his foot resting on the brake pedal to ward against this human lightning, which could strike any time from the alleyways, their openings like the entrance to a maze.

By the time he finally came onto the main road, twenty minutes had passed. The man glanced in the rearview mirror. His curly hair, freshly washed and straightened with a blow dryer for half an hour, was still up the way he'd styled it, and every time he shifted gears, he caught a whiff of cologne from his underarms. A large shopping center was located three blocks away. Should he get her perfume or earrings? The rest of the afternoon would fly by as he sauntered around the mall, peering into glittering display cases that looked like jewelry boxes. It would then take half an hour to get to Athens, the cafe where they were supposed to meet. He still had enough time to think up a funny joke while he decided on her gift.

Every time they met, the woman demanded a joke. In the six months they'd been seeing each other, his stock of jokes had run dry. In the "Sparrow Series," even the last sparrow had met its end from a hunter's bullet and in the "Big Mouth Frog Series," the curtain had lowered when the big mouth frog arrived at the bathhouse that was closed for the holidays. But not once had the woman laughed. She didn't even crack a smile, just like the comedy judge on *Make Me Laugh*.

The man stepped on the gas. It was her birthday that day, and he needed to come up with an unforgettable joke. Just as he finally gained some speed, lightning struck again. He slammed on his brakes and watched a motorcycle weave in and out between cars and disappear up ahead. He caught the white letters stamped on the rear luggage compartment the size of a ramen box: MAN ON A BULLET.

He couldn't let down his guard for a second. With the rise of these new "quick delivery" businesses, the road was filled with countless dangers. These motorcycles, which could pop out any second, were able to race from downtown Seoul to Incheon in a mere fifty minutes. For this reason, he could no longer speed.

The sun beat down. Heat rose from the asphalt. He needed to turn right in order to get to the shopping center. But as he turned on his blinker and sped up to change lanes, something leapt in front of his car. He wrenched the steering wheel, but he felt a thud. An instant later, a man landed on the windshield with outstretched arms. The car veered onto the sidewalk and crashed into the stone wall of a barbecue restaurant. The steering wheel slammed into his chest, causing his head to snap back. Struck by lightning at last.

The windshield was streaked with blood, saliva, and greasy prints from the man's gloves. The door didn't open easily because the hood had buckled in when the car crashed into the wall. After he kicked open his door, the first thing he saw was the crushed motorcycle, which had been tossed all the way to the median. Gasoline gushed from the cracked fuel tank. He noticed the writing on the luggage compartment: LIGHTNING DELIVERY. 675-1234.

The restaurant customers came running outside. They gawked at the car and the motorcycle while still chewing their food. Some had rushed out in such a hurry they didn't even have their shoes on. He was lucky there hadn't been anyone on the sidewalk. The cars behind had to screech to a stop to avoid running over the motorcyclist who had been thrown into the middle of the road. Drivers stepped out of their cars and stared. The rider was lying on his back. His red helmet was also emblazoned with the words LIGHTNING DELIVERY and a phone number. Someone from the crowd flipped up the plastic face shield of the rider's helmet, revealing a youthful face. He looked to be a high school senior at most. Facial hair grew unevenly on his chin and cheeks. As soon as the sunlight hit his face, his closed eyelids flinched.

"Do you think you can move?"

Lightning nodded slowly. Blood was oozing from a deep gash on his elbow. He must have scraped it along the asphalt. The man helped the boy sit up, taking care not to move his neck. A bystander ran over and draped the boy's other arm around his shoulders. He stood up with their help, but as soon as he tried to take a step, he moaned and sank back down to the ground. His thighs felt rigid; they were swelling rapidly under his jeans. He looked around for his motorcycle. It had been dragged from the road and was now leaning against a tree guard on the sidewalk. It was crushed so badly that its front wheel was suspended in the air.

"My bike!"

His face turned pale. An ambulance arrived. The restaurant must have made the call.

Lightning broke his left shinbone and fractured his right ankle. His arms were covered with scratches. Because of his swollen leg, the nurses were forced to cut off his jeans. His skin swelled like an inflatable tube, practically splitting open the fabric the instant it was cut. After getting an X-ray, he waited to go into surgery. He and the man were the only ones left in the hallway.

"Do you have a smoke?"

Lightning didn't care, even though they were in a non-smoking area. He smoked the cigarette right down to the filter.

"What would have happened if I hadn't been wearing a helmet?" he mumbled. He snickered. "Me break a leg? Imagine that. I never thought this would happen to me. I believed this kind of thing only happened to other people. But it's been a real interesting experience. Have you ever broken your leg?"

Instead of waiting for the man to respond, he went on mumbling. "It's strange. I can't feel anything below my knees. My brain tells my toes to wiggle, but they don't listen. It's really frustrating. So how do you think my mother felt when she told me to study, but I didn't

listen?" He started to sniffle. "I miss her. I think it'd be good for everyone to go through this. Everyone should break their leg at least once."

The man listened with one ear, glancing at the clock in the hallway.

"Don't worry." Lightning continued to talk while gazing blankly at
a spot on the wall. "It's not your fault. I might be stupid, but at least
I'm honest." Lightning thumped his chest and laughed again. "Let's
face it. Today's just not our day."

When the man went back to the scene, his car was still sitting in
the middle of the sidewalk, smashed into the stone wall of Pyongyang
BBQ House. Pedestrians glanced at the wreck as they stepped off the
sidewalk onto the road to get around. The restaurant owner hadn't
allowed the car to be taken away until the man returned. The bumper
and headlights were broken and the hood was badly dented. He tried
to close the car door that had been left open, but it no longer closed.
The motorcycle was still propped up against the tree guard. Just as
Lightning had said, there was a thick manila envelope in the luggage
compartment.

"Can I ask you for a favor? There's a package in the back. You
think you could deliver it for me? Our company's motto is 'Speed
and reliability you can trust.' If that package isn't delivered today—"
Lightning had drawn his thumb across his neck, as if cutting off his
head. Then as he was wheeled into the operating room, he sat up and
motioned the man over. "There's a space below the recipient's name
on the package release form. He needs to sign there. Don't forget!"

A truck towed away the car and motorcycle. There was a deep
gouge in the wall where the car had rammed into it. The restaurant
valet who had been standing outside led the man into the restaurant.
Behind the counter, a woman in her mid-fifties was counting out
some change.

"It's true what they say—lightning strikes on a clear day. I thought
we were having an earthquake!" she jabbered. "Our frightened

customers tripped and fell as they rushed outside." She covered her mouth with its half-faded lipstick and laughed.

She made him look closely at the wall. It was a cement façade with stones embedded in the surface. The impact, however, had cracked the cement and loosened the stones. She had roamed the riverbanks to gather these stones; everyone knew the trouble she had gone through to find the perfect pieces. She said she would calculate the cost of repair and call him the next day. As he was leaving, she called out, "You're lucky money can take care of this, but what about my poor nerves?"

To get to Incheon, he first went to Sindorim Station. He hadn't once used public transit since he'd gotten a car. Although he'd learned every one-way street and alley in Seoul in the seven years he'd been driving, he was completely lost underground. The station was like a maze and the subway map looked as intricate as a tangled ball of yarn. He followed the arrows to the transfer gate but soon lost track of them and had to stop. In the midst of those who seemed sure of where they were going, he noticed elderly people who were equally lost as him, or women from the countryside, looking as if it was their first time in Seoul. He would follow the orange arrows but would soon lose them and start to follow the green ones instead, winding up back at the platform where he had first gotten off the train. He found himself going in circles. There were things that weren't marked by arrows. Sometimes, the arrows pointed straight ahead, and then changed directions abruptly. When he came across an arrow that pointed up to the ceiling, he stopped in his tracks. He had no choice but to ask someone.

He still had about two hours left. If everything had gone according to plan, he would be strolling around the air-conditioned shopping mall by now, looking for her gift. But because of a motorcycle called Lightning, his plan was slowly unraveling.

The Incheon-bound train was practically empty. The man sat alone in a three-seater, away from other people. He glanced at the few passengers scattered throughout the car. Most were dozing with books open on their laps or looking through the window at the passing scenery outside. The man studied the package in his lap. It seemed like a book or manuscript of some sort. The recipient's address had been written with a permanent marker on a large envelope from Dolmen Publishing: *Professor Byeon Yeongseok, 435 Dohwadong, Incheon.* Below the name and address were the words *Urgent Mail* in red and in parentheses.

He had never been to Incheon. He had blindly stepped onto an Incheon-bound train, but had no idea where to go next. It might have been somewhat easier to find an apartment, but instead, he had to find a house with just the street address. He didn't know the station closest to the house, so he had no choice but to go all the way to Incheon Station, which was the last stop. A piece of paper was stuck on the other side of the package. It was probably the release form that Lightning had told him to get signed. Scrawled in the margins were some notes, plus a rough sketch of a map and a series of seven digits, which he assumed was the professor's phone number. At a glance, the map looked like an anchor or the male gender symbol, and the writing was barely legible: *Nasan Shopping Center, Dohwadong three-way street, Civil Defense Educational Center, Donghwa Fish and Tackle, three-forked road, right turn, Prosperity Pharmacy, magnolia tree.*

Finding the house by consulting the map and notes wasn't going to be easy. The notes mentioned a three-way street near the fish and tackle shop, but the map omitted the three-way street. And a magnolia tree? A magnolia tree blooms in early spring and loses its blossoms so quickly that thin, bare branches would be all that would be left right now. The man tried to remember what a magnolia tree looked like without its blossoms, but he couldn't. If he wanted to get to Athens on time, he couldn't afford to wander aimlessly. Why hadn't he said no to the boy's request? He began to grow annoyed with himself.

Outside, the same boring scenery paraded by and ringtones sounded throughout the train. They passed motels with unlit neon signs that faced the tracks. The signs were old and dusty.

"Mommy, why does that house have so many windows?"

A young woman and her little girl were sitting diagonally across from him. The little girl had been looking out the window the entire time. It seemed she was just learning to talk; she asked her mother question after question. The motels obviously looked different even to the child's eyes.

"Oh, that? It's called a motel," the mother whispered.

"What? I can't hear you," the girl said, rubbing her cheek against her mother's.

The mother raised her head and cast a furtive glance at the other passengers. Perhaps she, like him, was picturing that intimate act.

"You don't need to know."

The child moved away from her mother, and once again glued her face to the window.

The train rattled along, beating out a regular rhythm. The man's head was resting against the window, vibrating along in time. He tried to think up some funny jokes.

The woman knew all kinds of jokes. There wasn't one she hadn't heard before. When they first met, he'd thought she was collecting jokes the way some collect folktales. To come up with the latest, he looked through the five most popular daily papers every morning and went into the jokes chat room on the PC Communication website. He even flipped through women's magazines at the bank. But before he could go any further, she'd already known the punch line. *Make me laugh. If you make me laugh, I'll give myself to you.* When she propped her chin in her hand and watched his moving lips, a feeling of frustration came over him. Out of habit, he felt for his phone in his back pocket every time a cell phone rang.

Whenever the train went around a bend, the connecting doors slid open and he got a clear view of the other cars. Three high-school girls in uniform were walking in single file through the cars, heading toward him. They flicked the grab handles as they walked, making them swing in semicircles behind them. They chattered non-stop. The passengers stared after them. The girls were tall, and though they were dressed in the same school uniform, each girl looked a bit different in it. Their shirts were wrinkled and sweat-stained, and the skirts looked as if they had been shortened, stopping well above their knees and clinging to their hips and thighs, ending in pleats like fish fins. Each step exposed their thighs through the side slits. All three carried large identical shopping bags.

They passed him, joking and poking one another in the side. They smelled of sweat and perfume, and wore foreign brand-name backpacks that were popular among students, with character keychains dangling from the zippers. First a stuffed Donald Duck went by, and then Hoppangman, the moon-faced Japanese cartoon superhero with a red-bean bun for a head. The man, who had been trying to think of a funny joke, glanced up at that moment and made eye contact with the third girl. She had dark, round eyes like black beans and smooth, milky skin. What dangled from her bag caught his attention. It was a keychain with a clear plastic cube containing three dice, each one a different color. Every step sent the dice bouncing off one another.

He couldn't think of anything funny. It was 4:35. At the bank where the woman worked, the automatic shutters near the entrance would be coming down now. She was three years older than him and it was her twenty-ninth birthday that day. Until he'd met her, he'd always been surrounded by women with large mouths. Once in kindergarten, he had drawn a picture titled "My Mom." Whenever he gazed up at his tall mother, who constantly nagged him, all he could see was her large mouth moving ceaselessly. In the picture, his mother's mouth took up two-thirds of her face. "My Mom" had even received an honorable mention in a nationwide children's art competition. But when he had first seen the woman counting money through the bank window, he hadn't known anyone could have such a small mouth. Her lips had been pursed so tightly she'd had only a trace of a mouth, like that of a Japanese geisha. He loved her small mouth.

He caught the cloying whiff of perspiration and perfume again. The girls who had gone on to the next car were coming back. Though the entire car was nearly empty, the girls chose to sit directly across from him. The three shopping bags went onto the overhead shelf. The thin one sat squeezed between the two larger girls. He looked down, keeping his gaze fixed on the floor. One of the reasons he avoided taking the subway was because he didn't know where to look. Once he'd found himself in a bit of a fix because he'd kept making eye contact with a stranger who was sitting across from him.

As soon as he lowered his gaze to the floor, he saw the girls' legs. Now that they were sitting down, their short plaid skirts rode up their thighs and became even shorter. Their six bare legs were as fresh as turnips just pulled up from the field, and their calves were round and firm. The girls hugged their backpacks and started to whisper back and forth. The key chains that dangled from their bags each resembled its owner. Like ordinary teenage girls, Donald Duck, Dice, and Hoppangman laughed for no particular reason. Donald Duck couldn't close her knees because of her chubby thighs. He glimpsed them glued together past her open knees. As for Dice, though her knees were clamped shut, her thin thighs formed a triangular gap under her crotch. His gaze kept being drawn to that spot. It was quiet inside the train, and he could hear every word they were saying. Maybe he'd get lucky and pick up a funny joke.

Below their dusky knees were scratches, scabs, bruises, and even insect bites. He learned they were juniors at an arts high school. Seventeen. It was an age when scrapes and falls were still common. They laughed hysterically at things that weren't funny, things he already knew. Maybe the woman, too, had laughed just as easily when she was seventeen.

"Seriously. I think I only got half right."

At Dice's words, the other girls' faces stiffened. For a moment, they said nothing. Then the girl whose face was as round as Hoppangman's nudged Dice with her shoulder. "Not this again."

Donald Duck ate a Pepero cookie stick, breaking off the end little by little with her front teeth. Pursing her thick lips, she said, "That's what you said last time and you ended up getting the highest mark."

Dice let out a big sigh. "I'm serious this time. I guessed on half."

They took out their exams from their backpacks and started going over the answers. They groaned each time they learned they had gotten the answer wrong. The man kept glancing at their legs. All of a sudden, Dice's knees, clamped shut until now, relaxed and spread open. He didn't miss the triangular gap widen. He coughed and turned toward the fire extinguisher, but then Donald Duck's pudgy thighs came into view. Unless he moved to another seat or closed his eyes, he wouldn't be able to escape their legs.

The girls seemed completely oblivious to his growing discomfort. In fact, they didn't even seem to see him. Donald Duck twisted her body to the left and crossed her right leg over her left. Her skirt hung down the seat, exposing her thigh, which resembled a boiled potato. The elastic bands of her stockings cut deep into her flesh. Scooting her butt forward, she switched legs and crossed them again. The man caught a flash of her white panties. She now spread her thighs in the man's direction. It seemed she had suddenly put on weight; white stretch marks crawled all the way down to her calves.

"At this rate, I won't get into a Seoul university."

Dice stretched her arms above her head, and her knees relaxed even more. Just then sunlight shone into the gap. Deep inside the crevice was a mole as large as a coat button. He was a young, healthy man of twenty-six. His thoughts immediately rushed to that secret spot where the two legs met. His white shirt grew damp and clung to his back. Sweat dripped from his forehead. He swiped his forehead repeatedly with his sleeve. Her thighs made him picture her round, firm buttocks and the dimples above.

The girls' reckless behavior continued. So engrossed were they in their conversation about university entrance exams and how they'd bombed their finals that they didn't seem to notice anything else. They were the ones to blame for wearing such short skirts with slits on the side. If an older woman had been present, she most certainly would have had a word for them, but the entire car was now empty. The girls twisted and fidgeted endlessly in their seats. They crossed their legs and even spread them apart several times. Then it was the man who closed his legs in alarm. His curly hair, which he had spent half an hour straightening with a blow-dryer, grew damp and began to curl again. He seemed completely invisible to them. Bupyeong Station was announced. The girls lazily got to their feet and retrieved their shopping bags from the overhead compartment, standing with their backs to him. As they bent to put on their backpacks, their short skirts flipped up and they flashed their rear ends at him, as if they were doing the can-can. Then they stood by the doors next to him. The smell of sweat wafted over.

The subway approached the platform. The girls burst into laughter. "I won, didn't I?" Dice said.

Donald Duck and Hoppangman each took out a 5,000-won bill

and placed them on Dice's palm. Dice rolled up the bills and stuck them in the front pocket of her shirt.

"Men," Donald Duck muttered, munching on her cookie stick.

Hoppangman kicked the train doors. "They're worse than Pavlov's dogs. They start drooling as soon as the bell rings. How can there be no decent men out there?" She slammed her fist into the doors. "Jesus died a long time ago."

Dice snatched away Donald Duck's cookie stick and popped the rest into her own mouth. "You don't think Jesus was a man?"

The girls spoke loudly on purpose. They were no longer the same girls who had been comparing test answers and worrying about university admissions. The doors slid open and they stepped off, cackling.

His face was flushed with all the fantasies still ringing in his head. He wiped his face with his sleeve. Dark smudges appeared. Just as the train started to move again, there was a tap on the window. He turned around to find the three girls peering at him, their faces right up against the glass. They laughed maliciously. Dice brought her hand up to his face and then slowly raised her middle finger. Her lips moved deliberately. He couldn't hear what she was saying, but he read her lips. *Fuck you.*

There was a long line of taxis in front of Incheon Station. The drivers stood outside their vehicles, smoking, while waiting to pick up fares. Someone ran by, bumping into the man's arm. He blindly got into a taxi.

"Where to, mister?" the driver asked, hurriedly grinding out his cigarette and climbing inside.

He had no idea where to go. The driver looked at the man in the rearview mirror.

"The Civil Defense Educational Center. No, I mean Nasan Shopping Center."

When he couldn't decide on the destination, the driver said in a burst of annoyance, "Hurry up and pick a place."

The taxi driver let him off at the wrong spot and drove away. When he had walked over two blocks, a building with the sign *Nasan Shopping Center* appeared. His sweat-soaked jeans were plastered to his legs, and his skin chafed with each step. He wanted to take a shower. His cologne had long since faded away and there were now yellowish half-moon stains under his arms.

Lightning's notes were all mixed up. After he passed the shopping center, he turned right and saw a Chinese restaurant instead of a fishing store. The woman would have changed out of her bank uniform by now and was probably catching a taxi to go to Athens. He hadn't been able to think of a funny joke, let alone buy her a gift. Right then, the phone number on the package caught his eye.

Professor Byeon Yeongseok politely gave him the directions to his house. It was an awkward distance, too far to walk, yet too short to take a cab. He started out blindly in the direction the professor had said. It was a sweltering day. The man scuffed the tips of his leather dress shoes on the cracked, uneven pavement. Far ahead, he saw the fish and tackle store. When he turned right after passing the store, he spotted a long alleyway lined with similar-looking houses.

He had to slow down to spot the magnolia tree amid the other trees that rose past stone walls. A schoolgirl was plodding along about fifty meters ahead. She dragged her feet, weighed down by her backpack, which seemed full of books. An electrical pole came into view. The professor had said to watch for an electrical pole, that if he came to one, he was almost there. The girl stopped and unrolled the waistband of her skirt. The skirt, which had been much too short, now hit below her knees. In that time, the man caught up to her. She glanced back and in that second, he noticed the keychain that dangled from her backpack. Inside a clear plastic cube were three dice of different colors.

Dice's sleepy-looking eyes, dark as black beans, glinted. Her gaze darted around the alley to make sure there was no one nearby. She spat on the ground, and then came closer. They were nearly the same height. He could smell sweat, soap, and perfume on her. The large shopping bag she had been carrying was gone and her green nametag flashed from her shirt front pocket: Byeon Myeongju. Right then, everything clicked. Byeon was not a common last name.

Dice whispered quickly, as if to herself. "So you actually managed to follow me here."

People have more courage when they're in a group. But now, she was alone.

"All I did was follow the ringing of your bell," he sneered.

"What do you want—a slap or a date?"

"Please, don't flatter yourself. I'm not here because of you. I'm here to meet Professor Byeon Yeongseok."

He didn't miss the slight tremor in her pupils.

She spat again. This time, the wad of saliva hit his dress shoe. "You asshole, wasn't that enough of a show for you? How much more do you want?"

When he tried to resume walking, she spread out her arms and stood in his way. "You actually plan to tattle on me? You obviously don't know, but I've been at the top of my class for eleven years straight. Why would my father, who's never even met you, believe anything you have to say?"

"Let me worry about that. That dark mole on your thigh will be proof enough." He strode forward and started examining the house numbers on the front gates. Dice ran up to him and tugged at his sleeve.

"Come on, what do you want?"

Her voice was composed once more. He smiled as she tried to strike a bargain with him.

"If you get back on the main road and keep going, you'll see Nasan Shopping Center. Wait for me there. I'll be going to the library soon."

She then walked up to a gate and pressed the doorbell.

"Who is it?" said a dignified voice from the speakerphone.

"Dad, it's me."

Her voice, shrill until a second ago, now became the tired voice of a high-school student.

The man added quickly, "Lightning Delivery!"

Having figured out the situation just then, she glared at him. "Jesus, what shitty luck."

The automatic gate opened to reveal the house hidden behind the stone wall. Flagstones dotted the grass that stretched all the way to the front door. Dice, who led the way, tripped on one of the stones. The magnolia tree, which had lost its blossoms, couldn't even be seen from where it was, hidden behind a large chestnut tree. A middle-aged man came to the front door and took Dice's backpack from her.

"Dad, I'm so tired I'm going to collapse," she said, her voice now that of a spoiled child.

"That certainly was a lightning-fast delivery," the professor laughed as he signed the release form. Dice stood glowering behind her father.

The man sauntered out of the gate. The voices of father and daughter drifted over the wall. "How did you do on your exam?" the professor asked. Her peevish voice soon followed.

He stood in front of the pole and smoked a cigarette. The number of cars had multiplied noticeably as it got closer to rush hour. All of a sudden, the man remembered that he was supposed to meet the woman. He glanced at his watch and realized it was ten to six. There was no way he could get to Seoul in ten minutes. Plus, he was so hot and tired that his brain felt like a squeezed-out tube of toothpaste. No matter how hard he tried to wring out a funny joke, he couldn't think of one. He took out the cell phone that had been pressed against his rear end all day in his back pocket. He turned it off.

When he had lit his fifth cigarette, Dice finally appeared. Her wispy bangs were wet as if she had just washed her face. She was now wearing a T-shirt and a pair of short shorts with flip-flops. She shuffled her feet as she walked and hissed under her breath, "Don't talk to me and you'd better keep far back."

He followed her, maintaining a wide gap between them. Her calves were tanned and covered with scratches.

Not once did she look back. She glanced at the best-seller list on the window of a book rental shop, and then she disappeared inside a supermarket for a long time. She eventually stopped at the steps of a worn-down building. A sign that read "Quiet Study Hall, Air-Conditioned" was stuck in the window of the second floor, and names of students who had been admitted to prestigious universities were listed on the grimy banner that hung across the top of the building. Dice skipped up the steps, dropped off her bag, and came back down.

"I was born and raised here, so everyone knows me. On top of that, I'm a model student, so I'm pretty much the talk of the town. Next year, my name will be going up on that banner." She ran ahead and hailed a taxi.

The taxi driver glanced at her and then at him in the rearview mirror. "Sir, you're a lucky man."

Every time the driver made a joke, Dice responded with a witty comment. She gave a small shout as they were passing a movie theater. An enormous Godzilla was pictured on the big poster, the product of a failed nuclear experiment. People formed a long queue in front of the box office. Dice craned her neck, watching until the theater grew small. She mumbled to the man, "Have you seen that movie?"

The taxi driver chimed in. "You like movies? I like watching them on my days off. You know how many movies a person can watch in a day? I watched five once, but by the end the storylines got all mixed up."

She told the driver to stop in front of the brightly lit New York Bakery. As soon as they climbed out, Dice spat on the back of a token stand. "Pervert. He was ogling my legs in the rearview mirror the whole time."

In front of the bakery, he followed Dice into the underground passage that was connected to Bupyeong Station. He was anxious about losing her in the crowd that surged out of the exit. Dice stood before one of the blue storage lockers that covered an entire wall. She fished out an identification card from her pocket and shook it in his face. "My older sister's. It comes in very handy sometimes. She thought she lost it and got herself a new one."

People continued to insert coins, open locker doors, store or remove objects, and then quickly disappear. What could be inside all those lockers? Dice turned her key in the lock, and the door swung open. As she was pulling out the shopping bag from the locker, it caught on the hinge and a corner ripped. It was the same shopping bag that each girl had been carrying on the train. Clothes showed through the tear.

"Wait here."

She left the man standing outside the women's bathroom and disappeared inside.

She didn't come out for a long time. Women glanced at him as they went in and out of the bathroom. The smell of urine drifted out. As he waited for her, he pictured the large dark mole on her inner thigh. His face grew hot. He kept his head lowered just in case other people would guess what he was thinking. Just then, a tall woman walked out of the bathroom and stepped on his foot. She had on light blue high heels that matched her light blue halter dress. The heels were pointy like ice picks. "Oh, I'm sorry," she said with a polite nod and walked quickly past him. Her hair came down to her waist. He glimpsed light blue eye shadow on her lids as well. The clacking of her heels on the tiled floor sounded cheerful. Even after the sound of her footsteps had faded away, he could still smell the tropical scent she'd left behind.

The man waited in front of the bathroom for an hour. Now that the evening rush hour was over, there were fewer and fewer people using the bathroom on their way home. The janitor came out of the bathroom, dragging a wet mop behind her. When she crouched in the corridor to remove some gum from the tiles, he said to her, "Excuse me, but did you see a high-school student inside?"

The janitor's eyes drooped drowsily. She disappeared inside and then stuck out her head a moment later, rubbing the sleep from her eyes. "There's no one here. I checked the stalls too, but they're all empty."

His big toe started to throb. It was then he recalled the woman who had quickly disappeared after stepping on his foot. He vaguely recalled seeing cuts and scrapes on her legs.

Inside Dice's shopping bag would have been clothes, makeup, and a wig. She would have changed in the bathroom and made herself up. He hadn't been able to recognize her, even when she had walked right past him. This girl could be hiding anywhere right now, watching and laughing.

He rushed up the steps into the station square. The neon signs of pizza parlors, along with cosmetics and clothing stores, lit up the streets like broad daylight. He ran after several tall girls, but they weren't her. Women with similar clothes, similar hair styles, and similar perfumes strode endlessly down the streets.

The man ran all the way to the movie theater they had passed earlier in the taxi. There was a long lineup in front of the ticket booth. He tried to buy a ticket, but the two remaining showtimes were both sold out. He hadn't been able to recognize her when she'd been right in front of him. So how would he ever recognize her in the dark with her face made up, even if she was staring him in the face?

The security guard had dozed off with the television on and his feet propped up on his desk. No one saw the man return. As soon as he stepped into the apartment complex, the stench assaulted him. The garbage bags seemed to have multiplied. As he walked under the security light, he saw someone out of the corner of his eye. But it was just his reflection in the full-length mirror. Someone had hurled a rock at it and cracks ran like a spider web from its center, causing his reflection to splinter into pieces like a mosaic. His curls, which had come alive from perspiration, were matted like a steel wool pad, and his shirt hung pitifully over his thighs. He looked as if he'd been struck by lightning. It was only then that he remembered the courier in the hospital, his own totaled car in the shop, and the barbecue restaurant with the caved-in stone wall. Tomorrow was going to be a busy day. The man took out his cell phone from his back pocket. As soon as he turned it on, a clamorous tune rang out. He had chosen a folk melody so that it would be easier to distinguish his own amid countless similar ringtones, but the digitalized song sounded only obnoxious. It was the woman. She said that in all of her twenty-nine years, she had never been so insulted. She told him never to call her again, and then after yelling at him non-stop, she hung up.

He had to stop often as he walked, since garbage kept sticking to the bottom of his shoes. Across the way, on the roof of a darkened apartment building, there was a pointy object he hadn't noticed until now. It was a lightning rod.

Onion

1

The tow truck driver lowers the chain from the boom to the middle of the cornfield. A man standing among the stalks jumps up and grabs the hook dangling in the air. The windows of the flipped-over car are shattered. He passes the hook through the rear window and windshield, and loops it securely around the frame as if he's wrapping a bundle. As the winch drum turns, the car slowly rises above the three-meter-high stalks. The hood is crumpled like an accordion and the seats, wrenched loose from the floor, jiggle each time the chain shakes, as if they will plummet to the ground any second.

The two policemen watch, their foreheads wrinkled and Adam's apples protruding from tilting their heads so far back. One officer is tall and skinny as a pole, and the other has thick folds hanging over his belt. The tall one looks at the cornfield and then toward the hill where the ambulance carrying the two victims had gone. Back at the station, the lunch they had just been about to eat is sitting on their desks untouched; the black bean noodles would be thick and rubbery by now.

The tall one stamps out his cigarette beneath his heel, and the fat one stares at the road, his cigarette still clamped between his lips. If the driver had slammed on the brakes, there would be distinct skid marks on the road. He looks everywhere, but there's not a single mark. The sweat from his face and neck falls onto the asphalt. He flicks away the cigarette, which he'd smoked to the filter. The truck drops the car onto the road with a clunk.

The seats, visible through the hole the Jaws of Life had cut to remove the driver and passenger, are stained with blood. The tall officer spreads open a bundle of accident report forms and jots down the plate number and car model. On top of the rubber floor mat is a sandal, flipped upside down. It's a plastic shower sandal, neon pink, with drainage holes and grips on the bottom. The fat officer finds a booklet in the gap beside the seat. The words on the cover are difficult to make out because of the blood. He rubs the booklet against the seat, and the words inside a red box show up. It's a department store catalogue. Every blank space is covered with vehicle plate numbers. This game had probably started before coming here, while they were stopped at intersections, waiting for the green light. It was game where you would pick a car at random and add up all the numbers in the license plate, and whoever ended up with the highest final tally would win. They couldn't have been playing the game on this winding road where there was barely any traffic. They would have needed binoculars to see the license plate of the car in front.

The driver had been speeding along at over hundred kilometers an hour on this bend. But negligence didn't seem to be the cause of the accident.

"Hey, you know what centrifugal force is?" the tall officer says, as he's lighting the fat one another cigarette.

The fat one wipes his forehead and shakes his head. "I can't even think in this heat."

The tall one crosses the lanes to the other side. Spread below the cliff are potato fields like the terraced fields in the Philippines. If the car had flown off the road at high speed, it would have landed not in the cornfield, but in the middle of the potato fields below the cliff.

When the fat officer yanks off the loose glove-box door, the junk inside comes cascading out. An empty disposable lighter, two pairs of cotton gloves still in their packages, cheap facial tissue, a cassette tape of old pop music, its ribbon loose and tangled. He puts each item in a plastic bag. Something glints from deep under the seat. He sticks his hand under the seat, his face pressed against the rubber mat, and pulls out the object. It's a sashimi knife about thirty centimeters long, wrapped in something like a long strip of cotton gauze.

The tall officer holds up the knife to the sun. The tip shines. He brings his thumb to the edge of the blade, testing its sharpness. Blood springs instantly to the cut. "Jeez," he mumbles, hastily sticking his thumb in his mouth.

Dozens of stalks of corn have been uprooted in the spot where the car landed. Pulled by the tow truck, the car rattles slowly along the road, only its rear wheels touching the ground. The officers climb into their car.

"What time is it?"

"Two forty."

"There goes our lunch again."

"What do you want to eat?"

"Nothing sticky or spicy. Damn, today's a scorcher!"

The tall one, who has gotten behind the wheel, hesitates for a second when he comes to a blank space in the accident report form. The other officer is examining the sashimi knife in the plastic bag. This was no accident. The driver was taking the woman to see the ocean one last time, but he'd had a change of heart and stepped on the gas, charging toward the cornfield. He scrawls hastily into the blank space: *alleged double suicide.*

He steps on the accelerator. They pass a gigantic billboard. It's a new sign, the paint still drying. In the center of the billboard is a road that's been rendered with accurate perspective. *One World. One Path.* It's an advertisement for a mobile network called 020 One Communications. In no time, the police car speeds down the hill past the tow truck.

2

He stops putting the chairs on the tables and pats the front pocket of his shirt for his cigarettes. The paper pack looks full, but there's nothing inside. He tears off the top and checks again. Empty. He can't even gauge cigarette packs anymore. There are times he crumples up a pack, only to find a cigarette, now broken, inside. He crushes the empty pack, tosses it into the dustpan, and goes back to putting the chairs on the tables. For the past week, he hasn't picked up his knife once. Not since the news reported three cases of Vibrio infections in Ganghwa Island. He puts the last chair on the table and turns around, his back pressed against the glass tank. There are five flatfish, three rockfish, and some sea eels, which, together, would make about one and a half kilograms of food. The flatfish cover every inch of the tank floor, and the rockfish swim leisurely above them. Everything appears larger under the water. The tank is set up against the restaurant window, so that those passing on the street can see. Sometimes when he's having a cigarette in the kitchen, he sees their broad, distorted faces between the swimming fish. Mothers often drag away their children, who refuse to leave the tank.

He opens the back door and heads to the bathroom. Midori, the restaurant where he works, is situated between a restaurant that specializes in a popular sausage stew and one that specializes in hot stone bibimbap. These shops are arranged in a square, facing out, and in the center courtyard is a shared bathroom. If he stands at the back of the restaurant, he can see into all the other businesses through their back doors. The raucous voices of drunk customers ring out. He hears the strains of a pop song sung off beat from the stew restaurant. He fills a rubber bucket with water and rinses the mop. Each time the mop moves up and down, dirty water splatters onto his feet. The man is wearing neon pink shower sandals. When he's in the kitchen all day, his feet swell, just like a bar of soap that becomes bloated from sitting in water. But shower sandals are the most comfortable; they don't slip on the tile floor and water drains through the holes. Plus he doesn't have to distinguish the right side from the left, and can put them on any which way he pleases.

He starts mopping from the back of the restaurant, finishing at the entrance. Sensing a presence, he turns around to find a face close to the glass of the tank, peering into the restaurant. Since only one rockfish is swimming, he can easily see out. The person stays pressed up against the tank, blinking two eyes that bulge like those of a rockfish, but instead of watching the fish like the other passersby, the eyes peer into the restaurant. Every time he stops mopping and looks back, he cannot help meeting those eyes.

The bathroom entrance is splattered with vomit. He even spots bloated strands of udon noodles in the orange-colored slurry. It is definitely the work of a customer from the stew restaurant. There's nothing more telling than vomit. Through the open door of the stall, he sees a middle-aged man on his knees, his hands gripping the toilet and his pants wrinkled and stained. He puts the bucket and mop back in their proper place. As he steps back into Midori, he stops in his tracks. There is a woman sitting at the bar.

"Sorry, we're closed."

Instead of getting up, she buries her head in her arms and slumps over the bar.

The man starts to take the chairs off the tables. She doesn't budge, even when he places the last chair back onto the floor. Her legs, which dangle halfway down the bar stool, are marked by varicose veins, and her calves bulge out like a blowfish. She sits atop the stool like a twenty-kilogram sack of rice. The man is used to customers like these. Customers who would come in drunk and order more drinks, only to fall asleep. Several times he has even hailed a taxi for them and sent them home. But when he goes to shake her awake, he smells wet newspaper instead of liquor. He ducks under the counter and stands before her. He sees the neat part in her tangled, frizzy hair. She raises her face and moves her lips, but no sound comes out. She licks her lips and tries again.

"Give me anything . . . Too late, isn't it . . . Sorry . . ." she mutters, trailing off at the end of her sentence.

He stirs the bottom of the tank with the net to scoop up the smallest flatfish. Because he has to reach all the way down to bring it up, he has to dunk his whole arm into the briny water, even up to his armpit. The water in the tank is from the East Sea; he'd gotten it with the live squid. He has never been to the East Sea, but if he puts his hand in the tank and closes his eyes, the sea spreads before him. Inside the net, the flatfish arches its body like a bow and flaps around. He presses down on its head and picks up his sashimi knife to cut around the gills. The way to fillet a flatfish is logged into his mind like a flowchart, and so he can fillet even while watching the television screen that hangs on the opposite wall. He quickly scrapes off the scales and glances at the woman. A scale flicks off and sticks to his glasses. He cuts close to the backbone, leaving the tail and back fin, and slices the fish into triangles. He sweeps the air bladders and other organs off the cutting board. On the floor to his right is an empty lard can that holds everything he discards, but the entrails fall on his shower sandal instead and get trapped between his toes. He realizes he forgot to put the can back in its place after he had finished mopping the floor. From this point everything starts to go wrong. The knife keeps slipping, so the fillet pieces turn out uneven. He even drops the knife, and so has to pick it up again. In his fluster, he ends up knocking over the can a few times.

The cutting board is a little higher than the counter, so that the customers sitting at the bar are able to watch him fillet fish. Though she's slumped over, the woman, too, is watching his hands out of the corner of her eye. On the julienned radish he places the fish bones, still attached to the head, spine, tail, and fins, and on top of these he arranges the fillet pieces. He pushes the plate toward her. As the final flourish, in order to prove the freshness of the fish, he pokes the head with the tip of his knife, making its mouth open slowly to show its sharp teeth. It is usually at this point that the customers clap. But right then, the fish's limp tongue pops out like a piece of gum, and the woman jumps to her feet. Her heel catches on the stool footrest, and as her body pitches forward onto the cutting board, her hand comes down on the handle of the sashimi knife resting on the board, sending it flying in the air. It glances off his cheek and impales his shower sandal, penetrating his foot. The knife vibrates, making a strange noise. It's similar to a musical saw performance he once saw on television. The woman shrieks, covering her face, and collapses back on to her stool. He grips the handle with two hands and pulls out the knife. With each pulse, blood beads from his cheek.

3

She is about to climb the stairs to Ocean Palace Day Care, but goes back outside and heads to the pharmacy across the street. She pays for a health tonic, and as she sips it, looks up at the windows on the second floor. The colored letters have already faded. She and Miss Hong, her classmate from college, had spent all night sticking them on the windows when they had opened a year ago. Someone forgot to close the window yesterday, making the letters on the panes overlap, so that the sign reads *day are*. She slings her bag over her shoulder and climbs up the steps. Colorful footprints lead all the way to the door.

From the moment the van brings the children to the center, chaos breaks out. She stumbles on the toy blocks, now strewn across the floor. Two of the older boys pretend to be Superman, dashing about the room with one fist at their hip and the other stretched out in front, hopping over crawling babies like they're hurdles. One boy's outstretched fist hits a girl in the chest and she begins to cry. When an older child cries, the little ones who had been content until then start to cry as well. She changes the newborns' diapers and is giving them their milk when Miss Hong opens the refrigerator and laughs. The water bottle cap has disappeared again. Bottle caps are always going missing.

Two children playing on the slide vomit everything they ate for lunch. She puts shoes on the little one and is pulling out the other child's shoes from the shelf when a plastic bottle cap rolls out. She finds a fistful of caps stuffed deep inside the shelf. The child, with his eyes shining, hides his hands behind his back, and says, "Whoa, look at all those caps! I wonder who put them there?"

Gazing at the lying child, she recalls that human nature is fundamentally evil. She loads the sick children into the van and drives to the pediatric clinic. She parks in the lot and even before she can set foot in the clinic, her ears are assaulted by screaming and wailing. There isn't a single empty seat in the waiting room. Her feet mash the crackers children have dropped on the floor and candy sticks to the bottom of her shoes. The two children scamper off to the play area. Her hair, which had been neatly pulled back this morning, has come loose, and stray strands cling to her sweaty face. All through the night in her sleep, she had heard children's songs and their bawling. Looking after more than thirty children was a difficult task for just her and Miss Hong.

She sees an empty corner seat with a jacket tossed on it. She pushes it aside and sits. She feels something soft and hard under her bottom, like a purse. She closes her eyes. She hears endless whining, intermittent howls from the injection room, and soda cans falling in the vending machine. The younger child, who is coming down the slide, crashes into the older one, who has climbed up the wrong way. "Teacher!" the smaller child screams, bursting into tears.

She awkwardly gets to her feet, and glimpses something like a reddish lump out of the corner of her eye. What she had been sitting on wasn't a purse at all, but a newborn baby. Smothered by her rear end, the area around the baby's eyes and nose has already turned blue. She makes eye contact with a young woman coming back from the pharmacy counter with a prescription in hand. The woman walks in her direction, her body still showing signs of postpartum swelling.

She pulls the children off the slide and drags them toward the clinic entrance. Another baby, who is cruising along the front edge of the sofa, trips over her feet and falls, but she can't afford to help. The younger child cannot keep up and trips on the outside steps. She hears a woman's animal cry ring out from within the closed doors. She picks up a child in each arm and runs all the way to the parking lot.

A black sedan is blocking the lot exit. All the windows are tinted dark, so she can't see the driver's face. She starts the van and waits for the car to pull into a stall. She is sweating, and her blouse is glued to her back. An ambulance, with its siren blaring, pulls up before the clinic entrance. People rush down the steps. The ambulance turns its siren back on and speeds away. The black car is still blocking the exit. She finally leans on her horn.

Even after she sends the children up to the day care center, she remains inside the van. The nurses and the other mothers who had brought their children to the clinic will remember her strange behavior. One of them will be sure to recall the child who had called her *teacher*, and the police would begin a search of all the childcare facilities in the vicinity. The apartment she is renting is located two bus stops away. She wonders if she has enough time to fetch some personal items and clothes before the police descend, but she knows it's too late. They would already be staked out at her apartment, waiting for her. She clutches her hair and lowers her head onto the steering wheel. She sounds the horn by accident. She jumps out of the van and heads for the main road. She steps off the sidewalk, waving her arms to hail a taxi.

She calls the day care from the station. When the phone has rung more than ten times, the distraught voice of Miss Hong comes on the line. She hears the same children's songs and their crying in the background.

"Miss Kim?" Miss Hong shouts. "What happened? Where are you?"

She hangs up. It seems the police have already been there. She puts her hand in her pocket and crumples up the bus ticket. Even her parents' home is no longer safe. She boards a subway train and rides a line that loops around Seoul. The people sitting next to her change many times. She buys a newspaper and holds it close to her face, but nothing registers. Because she's staring at a single spot for too long, the middle-aged man sitting next to her starts to read from her paper. She gets off at Jamsil Station. She doesn't realize she has gone through

Jamsil three times already. She crosses over to the opposite platform and lines up with the crowds heading home from work. A man in his late twenties smiles at her. He's wearing snug-fitting black jeans. Wasn't this the same person who'd been climbing the steps in front of her on the other side? Why was he following her? Right then the train arrives and she quickly boards, standing close to the door. When everyone has gotten on and the doors are closing, she leaps back onto the platform.

Her heels are so worn she keeps stumbling. She hasn't eaten all day. The streets are turning dark, and the streetlights begin to come on. Only a few frizzy locks are still caught up in her yellow hair tie. There is a run in her stockings, stretching like a spider's web from a hole in the heel, all the way up to her thigh. She leans against an embankment wall of an apartment complex. Under the end of the gutter pipe is a rust stain. Her back grows damp from the trickling water. A drunk man stumbles along and whistles at her. She starts walking again, but her legs are like the limbs of a chopped-up octopus, moving on their own accord. She sees a lighted store sign up ahead. Midori Japanese Restaurant. Along the entire front window is a large water tank, where fish swim leisurely in the dim lighting. She puts her face up to the glass and peers between the fish. Inside the empty restaurant, a man is mopping the floor. He's wearing neon pink sandals and his pant-legs are rolled up. She pushes open the bamboo door. Since all the chairs are turned over on the tables, there is no place to sit. She walks toward the bar and pulls herself onto a bar stool.

4

He puts the chairs on the tables and starts mopping from the back of the restaurant. Because of the cast on his left leg, the cleaning takes twice as long. Every time the mop bangs against the table, water splatters. He wedges the mop into his armpit and smokes a cigarette. The feeling still hasn't returned to his left cheek. The sashimi knife had cut his cheek in the shape of a boomerang, and then penetrated his foot, leaving a three-centimeter crack in his bone. The orthopedic surgeon, paged out of her sleep, kept yawning while performing surgery.

"It almost hit your eye. You need to thank your glasses."

She stitched up his cheek as if she were hemming a skirt. When they had finished applying a plaster cast on his foot up to his ankle, it was past two in the morning. He checked the waiting room, but the woman who had followed him to the hospital door was gone.

The heat is oppressive. Inside the cast, his foot is getting itchy. The itch keeps moving, from his foot to his thigh, and then to the inside of his ear, until he can't find it anymore. He feels as if he's being electrocuted. He flings down his mop and scratches at his whole body. Welts and scrapes emerge on his skin, and scars, hidden until now, begin to stand out.

At Myeongdong Sushi, the last place he worked before coming here, he had gotten the ellipsis-like scar that dotted around the knuckle of his left thumb. It had gotten wet before it was fully healed, and so he'd ended up with an infection. He touches the scar like a wounded soldier feeling his chest for a bullet wound. That time, too, he had been filleting fish while two young men drank at the bar. As they got drunk, they started to argue. One started to talk about the deplorable state of the world, how everything was heading to ruin, while the other blamed it on the failures of their generation. They grew angry over their different opinions, but the real provocation was when one man whacked the other in the head, which caused him to fall head-first into his soy sauce dish. Soy sauce spilled all over his white shirt. He brushed off his shirt, and then shoved the other man in the chest. The chair was knocked over and the man tumbled to the floor. He jumped to his feet right away. His gaze landed on the

man's sashimi knife. He snatched it up and slashed at the air. The
man had been using the same knife since he first started filleting fish.
The silicone handle was slip proof and the blade, stamped with the
Zwilling J. A. Henckels mark, had a non-reflective matte finish. He
rushed toward the two men and grabbed the knife by the blade. The
blade went around his thumb.

He had almost lost his thumb then. His thumb needed to be ban-
daged until the stitches were removed. Though it was his right hand
that did the filleting, he wasn't able to work quickly. To avoid getting
water on his thumb, he had to constantly keep his thumb upright,
like a hitchhiker. Having an extra finger was just as uncomfortable as
missing one altogether. The man turns over his hand and peers at his
scars. He'd gained scars both big and small every time he moved to
a new place, starting from twelve years ago when he'd been snagged
by a hook at the Noryangjin Fish Market, where he'd worked as a
handyman. Busan and Company, Island Seafood, Sushi, One Sea,
Midang, Myeongdong Sushi, Midori . . . His scars are his resume.

He empties the bucket in the bathroom. He steps into the restaurant and stumbles. It's her again, sitting at the bar. This time, she's
the first to speak.

"Sorry, I don't know what to say," she mumbles. "I didn't mean to
get so startled . . ."

"You know, fish don't have pain receptors." Every time he moves
his mouth, the ends of his boomerang-shaped scar nearly meet. "They
don't feel pain."

The woman is wearing the same clothes from the other night. "I
was just surprised at the tongue . . . Never thought fish would have
them . . ." she says, as if she's sighing.

Her heels are so worn that the metal edges are showing. Her heels
ring out on the deserted sidewalk. She follows him at a fixed distance.
If he starts to take big strides, she follows quickly with small steps.

If he stops and glances back, she stops, too. Every time her heel gets stuck in the crack of the pavement, her foot comes out of the shoe and lands on the bare ground. She then goes back, flops down on the ground, and yanks out her shoe, as if pulling out a nail. She puts it back on her foot and practically runs after him. The clacking of her heels sounds like tap dancing.

5

They are driving to the port on the east coast. Inside the glove box is his sashimi knife, which has gone everywhere with him for the past five years. The owner, who was concerned about restaurant sales not improving even after fifteen days, didn't try to stop him from leaving. His knife and neon shower sandals were all he took from Midori, where he had been working for the past twenty months. The sandal was the only thing that fit his foot cast. At the port, he plans to meet Mr. Kim, who had been a supplier for Midori. Mr. Kim had driven through the night from the East Sea to Seoul, and filled the restaurant tank with live squid, fish, and water from the ocean. The man planned to buy a truck with a water tank like Mr. Kim's. If he could get leftover squid from Mr. Kim at a discounted price and sell them to the sushi restaurants in Seoul, he could double his profits. He was going to open up a small sushi restaurant where the East Sea lay outside his window, instead of only in his imagination.

"That's him. He's been following us from back there," she says. Her protruding eyes shift anxiously.

He glances at the side mirror on her side, but the driver of the red sports car in the next lane is only doing neck circles to relieve stress.

The freeway leading to the East Sea is packed with countless cars. His car begins to heat up like an oven. A news helicopter hovers in the sky, taking footage of the summer holiday traffic. Whenever it comes into view, he glimpses through the open door a camera operator with a video camera on his shoulder. The helicopter roars above, its shadow wavering over the cars. He leans halfway out the window to look up, his toes resting on the edge of the brakes. In the end he opens the car door and sticks out his foot, but he can't feel any air on it because of the cast. His right foot chafes against the shower sandal and the skin starts to peel. His car model was discontinued a while back, so there aren't many left in Seoul. Every time he switches gears, he hears the cogs mesh. Rust is showing where the paint has chipped.

The woman is chewing on her thumbnail, with her bare feet on the dashboard. Every fingernail is bitten down, and her shoes have left red marks that look like shackles on the tops of her swollen feet. Every fingernail is bitten down. On top of her crossed knees is a department store catalogue. Tiny writing fills all the white space that's not taken up by advertisements.

The woman is on the run. But he doesn't ask why she's running. Right now, her eyes, like those of a rockfish, are as shiny as marbles. As he looks at her, he recalls a word he hasn't thought about for a long time. *Family.* It triggers many other words for him. *Soybean paste stew. Light bulb. Cutlery set. Children. Tricycle . . .*

Right then the car behind him honks. He sees the tank truck, which had been stalled in front of him, speeding away. The man hurriedly pulls his leg back in the car, closes the door, and steps on the accelerator. He realizes only later that he has left the shower sandal that had been on his foot on the road. The red sports car in the next lane cuts in front of him with a roar. The woman stops chewing her fingernails and flips through the catalogue again. In the blank space above pictures of a stone bed and a running machine, she writes down the numbers in a license plate. Because so many plate numbers crowd the blank space, it's hard to read them. They start to see more and more Gangwon plates as they cross into Gangwon Province.

At the gas station, while the man fills up and buys some kimbap for their lunch, she looks for a payphone. She fishes out a slip of paper from her pocket and dials. The phone rings. A tired voice answers.

"About July 12 . . ." she says.

The receptionist raises her voice. "Pardon me?"

"July 12 . . ." she says.

"Ma'am, you'll have to speak up. Hold on." The voice moves away from the receiver. "Excuse me, could you tell your children to keep it down? I can't hear a thing with all the noise."

The receptionist comes back on the line. "Could you repeat your child's birthday?"

"July 12 was a Wednesday . . . Was a newborn smothered to death that day?" she asks, her voice trembling.

There's silence on the other end of the line. The receptionist says coldly, "You think you're being funny? If you've got nothing to do, just go to sleep."

The line goes dead.

6

The pitted field looks like a hammer-throw field. Under the scorching sun, the humpbacked woman pulls out weeds by their roots, thrusting her rear end in the air. She tosses them out of the field without a backward glance. Not one falls inside the field. She leaves crooked holes in her wake. All summer she pulls weeds, but after a rain shower, the weeds are thick again. Then she has no choice but to pull them again.

From the highway, it's easy to miss the old house in the woods. There isn't even a shabby sign for those passing on the highway. The house is hidden behind a chestnut tree. The woman barely catches sight of its red roof tiles between the branches. When they drive across a bridge and up a hill, along a road just wide enough for a single car to pass, the backfield of the house appears. The humpbacked woman, who had been sitting on the ground pulling weeds, gets to her feet. They glimpse a mongrel behind her thin, bowed legs. It rubs its chin on the ground and growls at the two strangers.

Their room is at the end of the hall. The front window looks out to the backfield, and the side window looks out to a kitchen built from a shipping container. The motor of the old refrigerator makes loud noises all day. A corner of the kitchen has been refloored and turned into a small store. On the dusty wooden shelf are a box of Mon Amie pens, envelopes, toothpaste and disposable toothbrushes, soap, candy, chips, and instant noodle bowls. The woman is grumbling as she returns to the room, holding a bag of candy covered with a thick film of dust. There are four rooms along the narrow hallway, two rooms on each side. If the man stood in the middle of the hall and stretched his arms out, his fingers would touch the walls. They sometimes run into the other guests. Then they have to turn their bodies and flatten themselves against the wall so that the other person can pass.

The old woman, who had weeded her way to the end of the field, is now heading back this way. The man's car is parked along the edge of the field, its wheels hidden by tall weeds. The disposable razor scrapes along his cheek, moving over his thick scar. He's shaving, using the woman's mirror. When he had first seen the old woman, he had assumed she was scattering seed. But even after weeding the whole field, all she does is simply wait for the weeds to grow back. Summer is almost over. It's too late to sow corn.

The woman is sitting in a plastic chair, squinting at the sun. Crumpled candy wrappers fill a bag. Each fruit candy is wrapped in a different-colored cellophane according to its flavor. She holds up the wrapper to her eye and gazes at the sun. The children had done the same, glued to the window like beetles. The man sees her and laughs.

"You look like a squid," she says.

One side of his face is still unshaven. "It's like I can see underneath your skin."

The bathroom is much too big for their room. She stands at the dim sink, washing her face, and gazes into the mirror. Her face is covered with soap foam. Everything from the past month feels like something that had happened a hundred years ago. The moment she leaves this house in the woods, her hair will turn white, and her face will grow wrinkled, and her fingernails and toenails will become long, like strands of thread.

Yesterday she had called the day care. After the phone had rung over ten times, an unfamiliar voice had answered. She was about to ask if she'd gotten the right number, but there was no need, because she heard the all-too-familiar voices of the children and the songs she'd heard countless times. So she replaced the receiver gently in the cradle. Her place at the day care was gone. The paper hats she had made and glued, the letters, the mobiles—slowly they will become someone else's creations and all traces of her will disappear. It all seemed like a game she used to play as a child, where she would flick her stone across the sand and draw a line wherever it fell, claiming those areas as hers. But each time, her piece had ended up in some ridiculous spot, completely different from what she'd intended. Her eyes sting from the soap. She turns on the cold water tap. All of a sudden, hot water gushes onto her hands. She shrieks and backs away. She had forgotten that the hot and cold taps were reversed.

The mongrel follows the man around constantly. If he's putting on his shoes, the dog comes bounding and puts his front paws on the man's shoulders and licks his glasses. The man picks up a baseball and puts it in the dog's mouth.

She uses the living room phone to call the pediatric clinic. All day, he trains the dog in the yard. If he throws the ball, the dog stands in place, blinking its big eyes. The annoyed voice of a receptionist comes on the line.

"On July 12th . . ."

"It's her," the receptionist whispers to someone.

"Please, it's important," the woman cries urgently. "What happened to the baby who was smothered to death that day? I saw an ambulance taking someone away. I saw it with my own eyes, so how can you pretend you don't know what I'm talking about?"

"Oh, that?" the receptionist says with a laugh. "You're mistaken. A pregnant woman who came with her child went into labor. She started crowning right here, and so they even decided to name the baby after this clinic."

Even after she hangs up, the woman sits before the phone for a long time. Outside, the man limps along in his cast. He picks up the ball and throws it at the dog once more.

"Go on, get it! Get it, boy!"

The dog picks up the ball in his mouth and runs back to the man.

"That's it. Good boy!"

He hugs the dog and they both fall to the ground. In the dog's mouth is a ball wet with saliva.

He looks through the business listings in the phone book and underlines all the sushi and seafood restaurants. There are over ten restaurants by the name of East Sea Sushi. On the first day they had arrived at the house, he had called Mr. Kim, but the fishing boat was docked at port because of a storm moving north through Japan. Even if the boat were able to go out, the man needed to wait until the price of squid fell. In the meantime he needed a job. His sashimi knife is in his car.

Gangneung Seafood, Gyeongsang-do Seafood, Gyeongchun Seafood.

"Excuse me, are you looking for a cook by any chance?"

He makes many calls, but no one is hiring. From the first letter of the alphabet to the last, he calls over forty places, but even before he can finish talking, the line goes dead. The port is located about forty minutes away. *Family, soybean paste stew, light bulb, children, tricycle,* and *dog.* He wants a dog and a yard. He moves down to the last restaurant. Haedong Seafood.

A middle-aged man picks up the phone. Brass bowls crash together in the background.

"Young people, they just want something easy. They quit the moment things get hard. We weren't like that when we were young. Kids these days . . ."

The owner talks non-stop. It seems he's sitting at the counter, tallying up bills and handing out change.

"I mean, I gave him one little lecture yesterday, and he's a no-show today? Can you believe it? Jeez," he says. He hacks and spits.

"Well, I can fillet anything that swims. Heck, I can even make anything swim in water," he says, desperate.

"What? I don't need all that fancy stuff. All I want is someone who's hard-working. We start a bit early, but I'm sure it's the same everywhere. Let's see, come by around ten tonight. It'll be less busy then. By the way, people who are always late . . ." he stops speaking for a moment, searching for the perfect word. "I can't stand them. See you soon."

With that, the owner hangs up. It's only when the man is copying down the number on a different slip of paper that he realizes he had called Haerang Hangover Soup, not Haedong Seafood.

"We're experiencing significantly higher volumes heading into the city due to the summer holiday traffic. We've been having a long, hot summer this year—"

The man listens to the traffic report and spreads open a map to find detours into the city. He has about an hour to get to the restaurant. The woman hesitates. She is planning to ask him to drop her off at a bus terminal as soon as they enter the city. The dangerously narrow road ends and they finally come out to the highway. The dog, who had followed them all the way to the bridge, falls behind. The house in the woods cannot be seen anymore, hidden by the chestnut tree. The sparsely placed streetlights cast weak light onto the road. Up ahead, he sees a newly paved road. He steps on the gas pedal.

The man's car smashes into a steel beam. The impact sends the car flying. It skims the stalks of corn and lands upside down in the cornfield. The car had crashed into one of the two beams supporting a colossal billboard, which depicts a road marked with reflective paint. This billboard road, which had sprung to life in the car's headlights, is buried in darkness once more. The small dent the car made in the steel beam is barely noticeable. The woman's hair is hanging upside down. It squirms like the limbs of a swimming squid. He calls out to her, but his mouth doesn't move. He tries to lift his arm to check the time, but his arm doesn't move either. Nor can he move his legs, head, or his other arm. But there's no pain. The thought crosses his mind that he's become a fish. His mind is so clear that he even starts to think up an excuse to tell the restaurant owner for being late.

7

A helicopter hovers in the sky. The midday sun beats down. The camera operator peers into his viewfinder and searches for a focal point. Cars that look like miniature toys are lined up along the highway. What he shoots will air on the nine o'clock news for about twenty seconds. He has put up with the scorching sun for two hours now, all for these twenty seconds. He's thirsty. He imagines gulping down a glass of cold water and takes a sweeping shot of the endless line of traffic. Those who see the helicopter stick their hands out of their cars and wave. A sandal appears in his viewfinder. It's a neon pink sandal. He zooms in. Even from where he is, he can tell it's a shower sandal. He dreams of making a movie one day. He captures the pink sandal left behind by someone going on vacation, but it doesn't make it on the nine o'clock news. The report of a world leader's visit to Korea runs long, and so most of what the camera operator captures is cut in editing. Only a far shot of the traffic at a standstill is aired for a mere five seconds.

Ha Seong-nan was born in Seoul in 1967 and made her literary debut in 1996, after her graduation from the Seoul Institute of the Arts. Ha is the author of five short story collections and three novels. Over her career, she's received a number of prestigious awards, such as the Dong-in Literary Award in 1999, Hankook Ilbo Literary Prize in 2000, the Isu Literature Prize in 2004, the Oh Yeong-su Literary Award in 2008, and the Contemporary Literature (Hyundae Munhak) Award in 2009.

Janet Hong is a writer and translator based in Vancouver, Canada. Her work has appeared in *Brick: A Literary Journal*, *Lit Hub*, *Asia Literary Review*, *Words Without Borders*, and the *Korea Times*. She has received PEN American Center's PEN/Heim Translation Fund grant, the Modern Korean Literature Translation Award, and grants from English PEN, LTI Korea, and the Daesan Foundation. Her other translations include Han Yujoo's *The Impossible Fairy Tale* and Ancco's *Bad Friends*.

**OPEN
LETTER**

**OPEN
LETTER**